My Beard
is
White Now

To Kevin and Judy,

Cathleen C. Robinson

Enjoy!

Cathleen C. Robinson

2022

Hadley, Massachusetts

Printed in the United States of America
by Collective Copies, Amherst & Florence MA

ISBN 978-1-951928-54-4

Library of Congress Control Number: 2022914173

Copies may be ordered from
www.levellerspress.com/off-the-common-books/

Table of Contents

Prologue

My beard is white now, but I remember. They're all gone. Momma, long time now. Sophie, my sister, she died of cancer, oh, must be 'bout twenty years back. All gone. 'Cept me. Dad was the first to go. In fact that's what started all the leaving.

My beard is white now, but I remember. I can still see that old guy in his World War I uniform dusted off special for the occasion. Other days, he was just a drunkard down at the American Legion over there on West Street. Yantik, or however the hell you spell it, that was his name. People used to say he was "shell shocked" from the war, but that day there was no stink of drink on him. I'll give him that. He did it straight sober.

I saw him come up the path to our front door and I knew it was trouble because in Hadley, Massachusetts nobody ever came to the front door. You always went around to the back door, the door that would open up to where you stacked all the wood for the fireplace, and you'd leave your boots in there if'n it was winter. Then you'd keep on walking right into the kitchen where you could have yourself a warm cup of coffee or tea. Momma, she sure loved her tea. And most days you could help yourself to something tasty just out of the oven. Or if'n it wasn't winter, which it wasn't when Yantik came that day in Spring of '44, you could come up the steps, wooden ones then, right to the porch which Daddy put in before he went to the war so's Momma could get some air and some light into her kitchen. You open that door, you was already into the kitchen.

Well, that day like most days, I was up in Sophie's room with the binoculars my Daddy gave me when he went off to the war and I was looking out the window. You could see clear across the fields to the Connecticut River and even beyond that to the Meadows where a lot of us still plant our crops. Or you

1

could turn the binoculars the other way and you could see all the way down to the Congregational Church in the center of town.

Only that day I watched Yantik coming down the street and I wondered where he was going. And then I knew. Yessir, he came straight up the path to our front door. He had that blue uniform on with some medals clinking over his heart. They glinted in the spears of sunlight hitting against his chest. He knocked. Then he knocked again. I dropped the binoculars on Sophie's bed and ran down the steps into the kitchen. "Momma," I yelled at her. She looked so pretty with her roses apron on and she was peeling some potatoes and listening to some music on the radio. It was staticky, that radio, but how Momma did love her music! "Something not Polish," she used to say. "I gotta have something besides a Polka." "Momma," I yelled again. "Yantik is at the door. Knocking on our door!"

She looked over at me and smiled. Momma had a beautiful smile back then. It reminded me of butterflies, happy and dancing about in the warm sunshine. She started over towards the side door, and I pulled on her arm. "No, Momma, the front door. Yantik is at the front door."

Well, that smile of hers just dropped off her face like it was an old rag and it hit the floor. She got all white and trembly-like. I pulled her across the kitchen floor and through the hall and past the stairs and into the front room where she could hear it for herself. Yantik knocking. Still knocking. "Well, aren't you going to open it, Momma?" I asked her but she stood stock still with a white ghost face on.

I went over to the door and pushed up the lever that was keeping the door locked shut. That lever wouldn't have kept anybody out who would have had a mind to break in. Not that anybody ever broke into houses in Hadley back in those days. I pulled on the handle. Hard. The door wouldn't budge. It was mud season in New England. You know, the middle of spring when all the wooden things around were swollen with wet. Well, that door wouldn't budge. Also I was little back then, just five years old and not strong yet like a man. Way back then, yessir, way back before my face even thought about growing a beard, let alone a white one, which mine has turned into over the years.

Yantik kept knocking. I looked at Momma and she was shaking her head and saying, "No, no, no." I pulled on the door some more. "Yantik! Stop knocking," I shouted. "Our door is stuck." I pulled some more and then looked back to get Momma to help me pull but all I saw was the back of her body, her straight shoulders, and her white legs walking. She was walking away, back down the hall. I yelled at him again. "Stop knocking! We hear you. The door is swelled up shut. Go 'round back to the kitchen door."

Yantik stopped knocking. I could hear his boots scrape against the stone step. You didn't have concrete steps back then. You'd find a big old stone, rubbed more or less flat by the glaciers a thousand years or so before, and you'd put that right up there in front of the front door.

Anyways, that day I ran down the hall. "He's coming, Momma! Yantik is coming 'round to the porch."

I ran into the kitchen and there was Momma sitting at the table. She was staring across the table to the side door which was already open because it was a hot day, hot for spring, and really hot right there in that kitchen because Momma had been baking bread that morning. She watched Yantik step up to the porch and even though he could see Momma plain as day sittin' there, he knocked at the door and the screen part of it sort of shivered when he put his fist up against the wood part.

"Ma'am?" he said.

"Don't tell me," she said. "Just don't tell me and then it won't be true."

"I'm sorry, Ma'am. Truly, truly sorry. But whether I tell you or not, it'll still be true. Your husband is dead. Shot dead in France. I'm truly, truly sorry for your loss."

Yantik stood himself up real straight, straighter than I ever seen him before, and he saluted. He made one of 'em military turns and marched across the porch, down the steps and out to our driveway. I watched him go. First there was all of him, still marching, then half of him, then a sliver of him. Then none of him.

It was 1944. I was five almos' six, and my soldiering Daddy was gone.

Chapter One

It was not the time for sitting at the kitchen table, hands lying in her lap, one fist gripping the other, eyes staring unseeing at the old soldier peering in from the porch screen, ears not hearing the words she never wanted to hear. It was the time for getting up and flying into action. The time for answering the boy child in front of her, Seamus, the one those cruel Polish boys down the street called "Shame on you." His father, it was, who had died, her husband. Her dead husband. And Sophie would be home soon, back from cheerleading tryouts, and she too would be standing in front of her, waiting for words, waiting for action.

The soldier left. Actually not a soldier, just poor old Yantik, made useless by the World War. "Sorry, Ma'am," he'd said. "So very sorry." Then he turned, clicked his heels against each other, placed the white envelope on the small table at the side of the door, and marched across the porch, down the steps and out the dirt path Stan had promised to turn into stones when he was back from the war.

Now, who would make the stone path?

Siobhan MacKenna Norowoski sat at the kitchen table and stared out through the screen. Seamus tugged on her arm. "Momma? Momma?"

With a suddenness that startled the boy, Siobhan reached out and grabbed for her son. She pulled him close, wrapped her arms around him, and let her tears fall into her son's hair. He let her hold him. Somehow he knew to let her hold him, hold him tight, which usually he didn't like; he'd squirm and squirm until he could wiggle free. It was a game they played, mother and son, but little Seamus knew they weren't playing that game that day.

"Momma? Momma?"

The smell of bread burning in the oven brought Siobhan to life. She sprang up from the chair and rushed to the stove, grabbing a thick towel before opening the oven door. She held the charred loaf in her hand and stared at it. Then with unaccustomed fury she threw it into the sink where it made a sizzling sound when it landed on the drops of water lining the sink bottom.

"I told him not to go! I told him he didn't have to go!" she yelled at the burnt bread. Then she whirled around and yelled at Seamus. "He didn't! He didn't have to go! He could have got the farmer's permission to stay. He was needed here. Here!" She pointed to the floor.

Seamus looked at the floor, puzzled. Then he ran to his mother. "Momma? Momma?" He wrapped his arms around her skirt and hugged her tight.

Siobhan bent over her son and once again muffled her tears in the golden flax of her son's hair. Stan's hair had been like that when he was a boy, all golden sunlight. That's what the old women said at their wedding. All the Polish women who shook her hand stiffly after the ceremony and then went to sit on one side of the American Legion hall, the side opposite of where her father sat with the few buddies of his who could afford the trip from Boston.

Siobhan knelt and looked into her son's eyes. "My good little boy. You are the man of the house now."

"But Mommy, what did Yantik mean? Why did he come here?"

Siobhan didn't answer her son but once again pulled him to her and held onto him. She began to rock back and forth and a kind of a moan-song came from her.

They heard footsteps, light, bouncy footsteps, and mother and son jumped apart from one another. They turned to watch Sophie come across the porch. She had on her cheerleading uniform and it waved back and forth as she stopped to pull open the latch on the screen door. The skirt brushed against her legs which were white and glistened. Her eyes opened wide when she saw her mother and little brother kneeling on the kitchen floor.

"It wasn't me!" she shouted. "I didn't do anything." Sophie turned to glare at her brother.

Siobhan let go of her son and sat back against her heels. She shook her head. "No, no you didn't." And then she began to cry again. It was a little cry at first and then it got louder until she was wailing.

"Mom, what--" The color drained from Sophie's face. She turned to her brother. "What did you do?"

Seamus stood small and quiet. "They shot Daddy. In France. Yantik told us."

"What?" Sophie slumped into the chair, the very one her mother had been sitting in when Yantik came and delivered the news that would change their lives.

Seamus nodded solemnly.

"That's a lie!"

Seamus shook his head. Brother and sister stared at each other in quiet. Then they looked over at their mother. Siobhan had her arms wrapped around herself, hugging tight as if something might break and fall out if she didn't hold it in. She was swaying back and forth, the moan-song humming out from her mouth.

Sophie glanced back at her brother, fury in her eyes. "Why did you tell her that? You know that Yantik is a drunkard. You can't trust anything that old man says."

Seamus's little body stiffened with pride. "It's the truth. Yantik was wearing his uniform. The one that has all the medals on it." He went over to screen door and let himself out onto the porch. He took the white envelope and then handed it to his sister. She held it as if she had never seen an envelope before.

"Mom?"

Siobhan looked up at her daughter, her dazed eyes shiny wet. She nodded. "It's true. Your father died. In battle."

Seamus nodded and he went over to reach his thin white arm around to hug his mother's shoulders. He looked back at Sophie. "In France."

"Mom? Is it true?"

Siobhan stood and went to embrace her daughter. Seamus wiggled his way in between the two of them. The envelope fell to the floor and not one of them stooped to pick it up.

Soon after that, they began arriving, ladies with casseroles and galumpkis and pierogies, cabbage dishes and bread. They didn't stay. They marched in with their bowls and their pans, names scribbled on strips of adhesive taped on the undersides. They put them on the counter and then they hugged Sophie and Seamus saying how sorry they were. They didn't hug Siobhan; they just patted her hands and avoided her eyes. Then they left, their long skirts made of the cloth from bags of flour brushing the tops of their sturdy black shoes. Farmers' wives. One had even received a visit from the uniformed Yantik the year before and she was the only one who looked up at Siobhan, looked into her eyes and said, "I know. I know."

Siobhan didn't say anything. She just sat in the chair next to the kitchen table, still and stony.

It was Sophie, the one who always complained when told to help out, who stood and received the dishes from the worn calloused hands of their Polish visitors. It was Sophie who said, "Thank you. You are so kind." It was Sophie who organized the dishes on the counter, who took the charred bread from the sink and threw it into the garbage. It was Sophie who set the table for dinner and told Seamus to put the silverware out. "And don't forget the napkins."

Seamus dutifully followed his sister's orders, stealing a glance every so often at his mother. And it was Seamus who went to pat his mother's back whenever Siobhan's eyes filled again with tears.

Sophie sent Seamus to the shed room next to the kitchen to get a few onions and then she skinned and sliced them, thin, like her father always liked them. She put some butter into the frying pan and waited till it spit with the heat. She threw in the onions and then some pierogi to warm them up. Seamus poured water into glasses for his sister and his mother and milk into his own.

They sat to eat dinner. "Bless us, Oh Lord," Seamus began the grace before meals. When it came to the prayer they always said before eating, "And watch over our Daddy," they fell silent.

It was Siobhan who changed the prayer. "And Daddy, watch over us."

Sophie and Seamus cleared the table. Seamus watched his sister take the knife and scrape some shavings off the bar of soap into the dish pan.

"I can do that."

It was automatic. Seamus said that every night. And every night Sophie said, "Not 'til you're six. Dad said I couldn't until I was six. And you can't either." But that evening, the evening after the afternoon when Yantik came to the porch door, Sophie turned and looked down at her little brother. "You know what? Yes, you can. You're the man of the family now. You can shave the soap. Go get the stool from the shed." And for the first time since Yantik walked up to the front door, Seamus smiled. In seconds he retrieved the stool from the shed and climbed up to stand beside his sister. He reached for the knife.

"Not so fast, Pip Squeak."

Seamus narrowed his eyes. "I'm not Pip Squeak no more. I'm the man of the house."

"Any more."

"What?"

"You're not a Pip Squeak *any* more. Not *no* more."

Seamus shrugged his shoulders and reached to take the knife from Sophie. She drew her arm away from him. "You have to learn to do it right."

"Sophie, I can do it! I see you do it every night."

"Nevertheless. Watch me how I do it. You could hurt yourself real bad. You take the knife like so in your right hand.

You hold the soap in your left. Keep your fingers on the underside of the soap so you don't slice them off. Now, always cut away from yourself. Very important. Never cut towards yourself. Or you could accidentally stab yourself. Okay. You try now. And don't you dare cut yourself or Mom will kill me." At the word "kill" Sophie stood up straight and still; her fist tightened around the knife.

Seamus watched the gulp in his sister's throat. It was fighting to get out. He reached over and patted her back as if he were petting a puppy. Standing on top of the stool, he was nearly as tall as his sister. His eyes were big and solemn. "Don't cry, Sophie. Don't cry."

She shook her head and reached across in front of Seamus for the towel lying on the countertop. She blotted her tears dry.

"Sophie?"

"What, Pip Squeak?" She put the knife down on the counter and lifted Seamus off of the stool to the floor. "Stop fooling around. We gotta get these dishes done. I got homework, you know."

Seamus took the dish from his sister's hand and began to dry it. He rubbed the towel in circles around the plate. "I wish I had homework. I wish I could go to school."

"You'll get there soon enough. And then you'll wish you could stay home and play."

Sophie's arms moved mechanically through the chore of washing the supper dishes, rinsing the soap off, and then handing them to her brother.

"Sophie?"

"What now?"

"Sophie, I don't remember Daddy."

Sophie gave her brother a sad smile, then flicked the dish rag in his face. "Of course you don't, you were just a little Pip Squeak when he went away."

"But it's bad."

"What's bad?"

"That I don't remember Daddy. So I can't be sad. I want to be sad. Like you and like Momma."

Sophie handed her brother the skillet. "Use both hands. It's heavy. No, it's not bad. How could you remember Dad? You were only three when he left. A really little Pip Squeak." She smiled. "A very annoying Pip Squeak."

"But I'm sad for Momma. I don't like it when she cries."

"Ummm."

"And I don't like it when you cry neither."

"Either."

"What?"

"You don't like it when I cry *either*. Not *neither*." Sophie leaned over and kissed the top of her little brother's head.

They both jumped, startled at the knock on the side door. They turned to see who was there. "Uncle Tony!" Seamus cried. He dropped the towel and ran to throw open the screen door and launch himself into his uncle's arms.

"Hey, hey! Watch it, Little Man!" Caught off guard, Tony reached out to the wall to steady himself as one of his crutches clattered against the porch floor. "Grab my other leg, willya?"

Seamus bent to retrieve the crutch. He handed it to his uncle who hopped across the door sill into the kitchen. Sophie went to kiss Tony on the cheek. "Hi, Unk."

"Hello, Beautiful."

"You should shave, Unk. You look like a bum." Sophie's voice had a playful reproach in it.

"It's not Sunday."

Seamus suddenly remembered. He drew his head back. His pale blue eyes were big and solemn. "My Daddy died, Uncle Tony. Kilt. Kilt in the war in France."

Sophie came to stand behind her brother and she reached down to ruffle her hand through her brother's hair. "I bet Uncle Tony already knows."

Tony nodded.

"Did Yantik come to your front door?" Seamus asked.

Tony nodded again and then looked beyond his niece and his nephew to some point and place far away. His jaw quivered and then he bit down on his lower lip. "Shoulda been me.

Shoulda been me that went off to war. Not Stanislaus. Me." He slumped down onto one of the chairs at the kitchen table.

Sophie looked over at her uncle's left leg, useless since that day he'd been drunk, soaking wet drunk, that day long ago when he and his younger brother were teens and out in the fields spearing tobacco. If he hadn't accidentally driven the spear through his left leg. If he hadn't then tried to hide the wound from his parents, from his father who, in another of his famous rages, would have beaten his son till the lad was yellow and blue with bruises. If the leg hadn't bled and bled until his mother discovered the blood-soaked sheets the next morning and screamed. If it hadn't then gotten infected with the gangrene. And if he hadn't lost the use of the leg and never again electrified the town's basketball fans in the Hopkins gym with his sensational shooting.

If.

Sophie reached over and threaded her fingers through her uncle's hair. "They didn't realize, Unk, that you with one good leg could do more than most with two." She lifted her hand and her uncle's hair sifted through her fingers. Her voice was dreamy. "Your hair is like Daddy's. Was, I mean. I mean that Daddy's hair was--"

Tony patted his good leg and Sophie sat on it.

She leaned against her Uncle's broad chest so like her father's. Tony pulled Seamus in and rested his head on top of the boy's. The only sound was the drip, drip from the faucet. Sophie stood, went over to the sink, gripped the faucet and turned it, daring it to leak again. She grabbed the towel off the counter and blotted her face dry.

"Your mother?"

"She went to bed." Sophie looked up at the ceiling. Her parents' bedroom was above the kitchen.

"No." Seamus pulled away from his uncle. "No. She isn't sleeping. She's looking at pictures. Up in her bed."

Tony shook his head. "Wedding pictures, no doubt."

"Why was everybody so mean to Mom when she and Dad got married?"

Tony eyed Sophie. "That's what she told ya?" His voice had a defensive edge to it.

Sophie blushed. "Sorta. Actually she doesn't talk about it much. She just says it wasn't as happy a day as it should have been."

"Yeah, well, she's right about that. Ma dying just days before."

Sophie nodded. "I'm named for her."

Tony looked across the kitchen to his niece. "She'da liked that. She'da liked you."

Sophie blushed again. "Maybe not. Mom doesn't like me."

Tony gave a light laugh. "She mighta liked you just for that reason."

"What are you doing here?"

Startled, Tony reached for his crutches and struggled to stand. Sophie and Seamus turned to stare at their mother standing in the doorway. Siobhan's dark hair, tear-wet, hung in straggly clumps against the sides of her chalk-white face.

"I came to say how sorry I am. To help, if I can."

Siobhan eyed her brother-in-law stonily. "Will ye be sayin' this is my fault as well?"

Tony shook his head in disgust. "'Course not. Where do you get these ideas?"

Siobhan trembled with fury. "Where do I get these ideas? Where!? Your mother takes ill days before the wedding, our wedding, me and Stan's, and she drops dead? Your father, crazy in the head, shakes his fist at me? Blamin' me. And now, Stan, Stan is gone."

Tony dropped his gaze, unable to face the fury in Siobhan's eyes. "Nobody is blamin' you, Siobhan. Nobody ever blamed you."

Siobhan stepped forward shaking with rage. "Everybody blames me! Everybody in this whole damn town blames me."

Anger lit up Sophie's eyes. "Mom! Stop yelling. We lost Dad. And Uncle Tony lost his brother. He's hurting too!"

Siobhan crossed her arms over her chest and glared at her brother-in-law. "Really? Really? How much are you hurting? I can smell the stink of drink on you from here. I smell you."

Tony sighed and shook his head. "You're a hard woman, Siobhan. A hard woman. I came here to help. You don't give us a chance. Any of us."

Fire flashed again in Siobhan's eyes. "Well, I don't need your help! I don't need the help of anybody in this damn town." She threw the words in Tony's face.

"Then I guess I'll be leavin'."

Seamus pushed the chair out of his uncle's way.

The three of them watched as Tony hobbled to the door. He stumbled, nearly losing his balance when he reached for the latch on the screen door. Seamus ran to hold the door open for his uncle. Tony took a few steps across the porch and then turned to look at Sophie who hadn't moved from her sanctuary at the sink.

"Your mother doesn't need help. Or so she says. Well, okay, so be it, but if you or," he glanced down at Seamus by his side, "this little guy need help, any kind of help, you come to me. Ya hear?"

"I know, Unk. Thanks. Bye for now."

"Bye, Uncle Tony." Seamus waved to the man's broad back, a farmer's broad back, as his uncle hopped down the path and disappeared around the side of the house.

Sophie turned and yelled at her mother. "What is wrong with you?"

"You'll not be raising your voice to me!"

"That's the only way you ever hear me, Mom. The only way." The shock of realization electrified her face. "I know why! You don't love me! It's because of Dad's family, right? Because I'm named after Dad's mother. I'm right, aren't I? And you--" She glanced down at her brother.

"I didn't do anything!"

"You're named after Mom's Dad. The one we never met. Who died before we were even born." She whirled around to face her mother again. "That's it, isn't it? That's why you love Seamus so much."

The boy began to cry. "I didn't do anything. Sophie, don't be mad at me." He ran and wrapped his arms around his sister's waist.

Siobhan watched her children from across the kitchen. She raised her chin at Sophie. "That's a lie, Sophie, and you know it. I love you more than you can ever know. I don't know why you look for reasons to fight with me. Honestly, I don't. I love you, Sophie, but you just exhaust me."

Siobhan turned and left the kitchen. Her children listened as their mother's soft footsteps climbed the stairway back up to her bedroom.

Hers alone, now.

Siobhan heard her children come up the steps soon after the clatter of dishes down below her bedroom had stopped. "Shhh," she heard Sophie whisper to Seamus. "Mom's sleeping."

But Siobhan was not sleeping. In spite of the shock of her sadness, she smiled as she saw her son's exaggerated tip-toe past her door. It was open just a crack, just enough to see Seamus. Just enough for Sophie to stop and stare in at her mother lying fully dressed across the bed. Sophie gave her mother a tentative smile. Siobhan closed her eyes as if she had fallen asleep at that very moment and couldn't see her daughter. If she had smiled back, then Sophie would have to come in. They'd have to talk, and Siobhan couldn't, she just couldn't. Not that night.

Moments later when Siobhan opened her eyes, the children were gone and she heard the animation in Sophie's voice as she read to her brother. Siobhan would have sworn that all her emotion was gone, spent in the hours since Yantik had stood at the screen door in that ridiculous uniform that hung so loose on the scarecrow of the old man's body. But the soft sound of Sophie's voice brought fresh tears and she felt a wave of overpowering love for her daughter wash over her and toss her once again back into the turbulent waters of her emotions. That was her job, Siobhan's, the mother's job to read to Seamus before he went to sleep. He'd curl his head into the space her body made as she wrapped her left arm around his head and over his shoulder. She could imagine her daughter in that rare posture of motherly tenderness and that made the tears flow faster.

Siobhan sat up on the bed. The room whirled around her and she put a hand to her forehead. Her head felt heavy, waterlogged. She moved slowly as she got to her feet and walked over to the nightstand on the other side of the bed. She picked up the photo album she had brought up earlier that evening from the desk in the front parlor. She sank back down onto the bed and slowly turned the pages of the album. The pictures of her wedding, hers and Stan's.

She was remembering.

They were opening even earlier that crisp morning in Boston. It was still dark, although the gray light in the east hinted that morning was hugging mother earth and climbing up on her higher and higher, fighting to bring day to yet another part of the world. Seamus MacKenna pulled on the rope to draw up the heavy canvas curtain that covered the front of his stall in the market. They were still there, those old men who hadn't had his luck in making a new life miles across the ocean from Ireland. Where they got the wherewithal was beyond him, but on the other side of the narrow path separating him from them, the old men sat huddled around the rusted steel drum in which they'd built another fire to warm them through yet another night. They looked like miniature mountains, black shadows, worn and torn woolen blankets tossed around them and hiked up high to cover their heads and shoulders.

The smell of coffee, hot and strong, brought a smile to Seamus's face and he rubbed his rough reddened hands together in anticipation. His only child, daughter Siobhan, rounded the corner at the far end of the row of stands. He could just make out her shadow--a little darker against the gray--as she came down the path that divided the stalls of the market. He glanced back over his shoulder and watched while the black huddled forms shrugged the blankets off their shoulders and, clumsily, painfully, struggled to their feet.

It was a ritual. Siobhan made a big pitcher of black coffee every morning and toasted some slices of soda bread. Breakfast, it was, for her father and herself and for the three men who spent each night huddled around the barrel. They would wait, respectfully, watching as Siobhan and her father drank the coffee and ate the bread. Then they'd make their hesitant way over to MacKenna's stand.

"There be a little coffee left?" the oldest would ask.

And Siobhan would always lift the lid, peer in, and say the same thing every morning. "Just a spot. Would ye be wanting some?"

"If it's no trouble, Miss." The three old men would hobble towards her extending their broken, chipped and coffee-stained mugs.

"Thank ye, thank ye. God bless," the oldest would say and the other two would nod their thanks and the yellow white of the few teeth they had left would flash in the open wounds of their mouths.

"A mite early today?" one of them asked.

Seamus grunted as he pulled at the display stand. The three hustled as best they could to help him drag the display cases from the back of the stand to the front.

"Asparagus due today. First of the season. From Hadley. That's at the far end of this great state."

"Ah," the three nodded solemnly.

Siobhan pulled her shawl in tighter and hugged herself. She was shivering. It might be the end of May, but the chill of winter hung on and that, combined with the wind blowing in off the ocean, made for a blustery morning. She peered out from under the roof of their stand. The others in the market had arrived and were busy setting up their stands.

Asparagus, first of the season. From Hadley.

Siobhan sat in the corner of their stand and pulled out her sewing from the bag she'd left there the night before. She was darning over a hole in one of her father's socks. She was sixteen years old and as far back as she could remember, it had always been this way, just she and her father, her mother dying three days after giving birth to her one and only child.

Less than half an hour later, Siobhan accompanied her father down the path to where the trucks would pull in just after dawn. That's when she saw him, the man her heart would tell her that she wanted.

He was standing up in the bed of the truck, the back of it flipped down, and he was haggling a price with Kevin O'Hare. Despite the chill of the morning, he wore only a tee shirt and the muscles of his arms bulged tight against the sleeves of it. "You're killing me, O'Hare," the man-boy said, grinning as he stuffed money into the front pockets of his worn jeans. "Who's next? Fresh and tender grass, folks. Hadley grass. The best," he shouted out. Siobhan practically pushed her father towards the man's truck. Once there, she stepped to the side to read the lettering painted on the cab. "Norowoski Farms."

"Norowoski," she said, getting the feel of the name against her lips. She caught her father's eye watching her and blushed. She marveled at that, the blush. Lots of men, "little boys," she called them, had whistled at her, threw her their best blarney and nothing, they got nothing in return from the dark-eyed Irish beauty.

Her father reached up a hand. "Seamus MacKenna."

"Stan Norowoski. How many bunches, Sir?"

So his name was Stan, Siobhan thought, Stanislaus, more likely, that "ski" in his last name being Polish.

"And what about you, Pretty Miss?"

Siobhan was startled to realize that he was looking down at her. "Oh, I'm with him." 'Oh, Lord!' she thought. 'What if he thinks that I'm here with my husband? That my father is my husband?' "I mean," Siobhan stammered, pointing to Seamus, "with him. That's my father."

Stan glanced down at Seamus who was loading bunches of asparagus into the large box he'd brought with him down to the trucks for that very purpose. "Your father, eh?" He noted Seamus's thinning hair, most of the red gone now, replaced with gray, and then back at Siobhan. "So where'd you get all that black hair?"

Seamus grinned. Something in that sly grin of her father's as he eyed his daughter irritated her. "She got that from her mother, God rest her soul."

Stan jumped down from the bed of the truck. He stuck his hand out to Siobhan after brushing it first against the sides of his faded jeans. "Stan, Stan Norowoski."

The touch of his hand sent a little thrill rippling up Siobhan's arm. It was a big, warm hand and, though bigger than hers by a lot, it was a hand her own felt right at home in.

"And you are--?" Stan leaned in close, his face inches from hers. His eyes were a light blue, a pale, washed out blue. His hair, the color of straw, was rumpled as if he had climbed out of bed and then went straight out to board the truck and drive the hundred plus miles into Boston.

"Siobhan," her father said. "Her name's Siobhan."

"Shove on? What kind of name is that?"

Siobhan burst into giggles which thoroughly embarrassed her. There was an awkward moment while she struggled to compose herself. Stan glanced back and forth between father and daughter. Seamus just grinned at Siobhan. He was not going to bail her out.

"Siobhan," she said finally, getting a grip on her young adulthood. "It's Irish. It means 'Joan.' The feminine for 'John' who was an Apostle, and Jesus's closest friend." She watched as Stan's eyes lit up in amusement and she wanted to smack herself. What was she, a catechism teacher?

Stan turned to her father. "And I suppose Seamus means something?"

Siobhan couldn't stop herself. "It means 'James.'"

Stan glanced back at her, grinning. "Another apostle?"

Siobhan felt faint under the direct gaze of those pale blue eyes. "Well yes," Siobhan stammered.

"And what's your last name? Peter? Or some Irish version of another apostle?"

Seamus burst into laughter and Siobhan wanted to kick her father. She didn't enjoy being made fun of but the more she said, the worse things seemed to get. She blurted out, "It's MacKenna. It means 'sprung from fire.'"

At that Stan doubled over in laughter.

Siobhan's face reddened with anger. "So what's Stan stand for?"

The young farmer from Hadley straightened. He tried unsuccessfully to wipe the mirth off of his face, but the attempt left him with a sort of smirk. "Stan stands for Stan. Hell if I know."

At that, Siobhan turned and stomped her way back up the path to her father's stand. She heard Stan call after her. "Hey, hey! Don't go away mad. Hey!" But she kept on going and it gave her a sweet feeling of revenge to hear the apology in the young man's voice. And there was something else--the hope that she would see him again.

Chapter Two

Seamus had his left elbow propped up on the kitchen table and he rested his head over his hand. With his right hand, he listlessly stirred the oatmeal his sister had prepared for him. It was lumpy. Sophie brushed past him and sat down at the other side of the table. "Eat your breakfast," she commanded. She opened her math textbook and slid it over towards her own bowl of oatmeal. Algebra threatened to be her nemesis, but she was very proud of being one of only two girls in the class, all the other girls opting for Home Economics. Sophie was determined to be as good as the boys in that class; the news of her father's death the day before, however, had made it impossible to concentrate on homework.

"I don't want it. It's sticky. Momma makes it better." Seamus shoved the bowl away from him.

Sophie, annoyed, looked up from the textbook. "Well, do you see Momma in the kitchen? Who got up early to get your breakfast before she went off to school? Who, Pip Squeak, who?"

"Don't call me that. I hate it. I hate this oatmeal." He jumped out of his chair, crossed his small white arms over his chest and stood glaring at his sister.

Sophie studied her brother. Seamus was seconds away from crying and it wasn't about the oatmeal. It was about her mother who sent Seamus away from her door a half hour earlier saying she was sick. Sophie felt her heart soften. "Come here."

Seamus went over to his sister and climbed up on her lap. "Is Momma really sick?"

Sophie put her arm around her brother and pulled him in close. "No, Pip Squeak. I don't think she's sick. She's just sad about Daddy dying. We're all sad about that."

Seamus drew his head back and looked into Sophie's eyes. "But what if Momma gets sick for real? Does being sad make you sick? What if Momma gets really, really, really sick and dies? Then we won't have a Momma or a--" Seamus's voice cracked as fear overpowered him.

"Not going to happen." Brother and sister turned to face their mother standing in the doorway. Seamus jumped off his sister's lap and ran to throw his arms around his mother's legs. Siobhan reached down for her son and patted his shoulders. She glanced up at her daughter. "Aren't you going to be late for school? Don't you have that math test today?"

Sophie closed the textbook. "I was thinking maybe you could write a note saying that--"

"No."

"But Dad--"

"No. We're not going to make excuses. We're going to be as strong as your father was. He did what he was supposed to do. You'd best be getting off to school." She went over to the table and picked up Seamus's untouched bowl of cereal. "Thank you for this." She nodded at the cereal and then looked at her daughter. "That's exactly what we're going to do. We're going to go on living our lives. That's what your father would want us to do. And so that's what we're going to do."

Sophie stood and slapped her hand hard over the algebra text. "You're unbelievable, Mom! I don't think Dad would mind a bit if we took a minute to stop our lives and remember him." She scooped up her schoolbooks in her arms and snatched her sweater off the back of the chair. It was her cheerleading sweater, the one with a big gold H on the back. "I have practice after school. We're getting the new kids ready for tryouts." Sophie was halfway across the side porch when she turned, whirled back into the kitchen, bent over and kissed the top of her brother's head. "Bye, Pip Squeak. Be good." Then she spun around again and was gone down the path off to school.

Siobhan watched her go. "My very own pet tornado," she said softly.

It was later that morning while Siobhan sat in front of the sewing machine stitching a hem in a new skirt for Sophie that the dump truck backed into their yard. Siobhan looked up and watched dumbfounded through the window on the other side of the sewing machine. The truck clanked and groaned and then the back end of it squealed like a scared pig as it rose high into the air. Seconds later dust spun upwards as a load of rocks rumbled noisily out of the truck onto the ground in front of the porch. Then the bed of the truck lowered back down, squealing again. Siobhan heard the shifting of gears and the truck lurched forward and disappeared from her view. She couldn't see the driver.

"Tony," Siobhan muttered.

"Momma! Momma!"

Seamus came running up the porch steps, into the kitchen and down the hall to where his mother sat, her hands resting on top of the sewing machine. He was holding a puppy which was squirming to get out of the boy's tight grasp. "Did you see? Did you see?"

"Don't let that dog pee in here!"

Seamus looked down as if he were surprised to see the puppy in his arms. "She won't, Momma. But did you see, Momma? Did you see the rocks that Uncle Tony dumped here? He's going to make us a stone path, Momma!"

Siobhan leaned back from the sewing machine. "Oh, so that's what he's up to."

"Since Daddy can't make it, Uncle Tony is going to. And I am going to help--" The boy stopped suddenly. "Uh-oh." He held the puppy away from him.

"Take that dog outside. She's peeing all over you."

Seamus turned and ran back down the hall. Siobhan could hear the puppy whine. She stood and followed her son

down the hall and out onto the side porch. She watched as
Seamus put the puppy down and then rubbed his hand against
the grass. "You peed on me again!" he admonished the puppy
who was busy trying to lick the boy's hand. "You have to stop
peeing or Momma will never let me have you."

Siobhan crossed her arms over her chest and leaned
against the door frame. She didn't have an excuse anymore. It
was as if her son read her mind. He suddenly turned and,
stricken, looked back at his mother. "But Momma, Daddy isn't
coming home now. Does this mean I can't never have a puppy?"

To her son's constant and insistent begging for a dog,
Siobhan had always said, "When Daddy comes back from the
war." She sighed and smiled down at her son. "What are you
going to name your puppy?"

Seamus's eyes opened wide. "You mean it, Momma? You
mean it? I can keep her?"

"Well, not right now. She can't leave her mother yet.
She's not weaned. You have to take her back to her momma. But
when she gets a little older," Siobhan sighed, "you can bring her
over here for good. But you have to teach her not to pee in the
house."

Seamus leapt up from the ground, raced across the stairs
and threw his arms around his mother's skirt. "Thank you,
Momma. I love you. Thank you, thank you, thank you!" Then just
as suddenly he ran back down the stairs and over to the puppy
who had started to climb up the pile of rocks. He snatched the
dog and held her up to eye level. Her little legs furiously pedaled
in the open air beneath her. "You can stay here when you're
growed up!"

"You'd best be taking her back to the mother dog. She'll
be getting hungry."

Siobhan watched as her son ran across their yard to the
farm next door. She stared at the spot where Seamus
disappeared into the Tudryns' barn. Then she shook her head
and dropped her gaze to study the pile of rocks dumped in front
of the porch. An ugly frown marred the porcelain beauty of her
face.

This is the way it was that afternoon: Siobhan would shake her head, shake away the memories and the shock and the sadness. Other women had lost their men and found the strength to go on living, the strength to raise their children into adulthood. She would set her jaw in the firmness she'd often seen on her own father's face, and she would start to sew the hem on Sophie's skirt.

And then something would seize her mind and take it away, and she'd be remembering again. Remembering how she looked forward to that Norowoski truck from Hadley, arriving early in the breathless morning, and she'd hope that it was Stan bringing in the asparagus, then the beans, then the corn as the season summered on, ripening each crop in turn. Siobhan would hope that it was not the other one, that older brother Tony with his bad leg, or worse, that father of theirs, unkempt and smelly and foul-tempered. But the days that Stan came, her heart would stutter in a way that it never had before. She'd look up at him standing high in the bed of the truck, and, if she were lucky, the sun would be shining and it would glint gold through the young man's hair. It seemed like interfering when her father Seamus took a liking to Stan and made a point of butting into their conversation.

Yes, her mind would be back in those early years of knowing Stan, and Siobhan's cheeks would be wet. She'd flick away the tears, set her jaw again, and refocus on the hem of Sophie's skirt. Once, she discovered that she'd caught some of the skirt material in the underside of the hem and she set to ripping out the mistake with a vengeance.

So it was late afternoon when she heard the screen door slam and realized she had sleep-walked through making her son his lunch several hours earlier. She heard Seamus punch his footsteps down the hallway to then stand in front of her, his face flushed red with anger and humiliation.

"I want you to change my name!" he yelled at her.

"Why? What happened?"

"I don't want Grandpa's name anymore. I want a Polish name. Like all the other kids."

Siobhan reached over and tried to brush her son's hair from his eyes with her fingertips. It was matted and wet, maybe from sweat, maybe from tears. At the gentle gesture, Seamus's blue eyes filled with tears. He jerked his head out from under Siobhan's hand, the anger a mask over his wanting to hurl himself into his mother's arms and sob against her chest.

Just then, there was another slam of the screen door and Sophie appeared before them. Siobhan's eyes widened at the rip in the hem of her daughter's cheerleading skirt. The white blouse was pulled out from under the waistband and hung in ragged edges over Sophie's hips. Her pony tail was dragging at her neck--that is, the few strands of it that remained in the rubber band. The rest of her hair formed a disheveled mess around her head. Her cheeks were flushed and her eyes flashed fury.

"What in heaven's name, Sophie?"

The girl bent over and hugged her little brother. "I taught them, Seamus! I taught that stupid Iggy and that dumb Leon good. Just see if they dare call you 'Shame on You' again."

Siobhan bit her smile and tilted her head in mild reproach. "Sophie, you were fighting? Am I ever going to see you act like a young lady?"

"Mom!" Sophie's temper flared. "Those rotten kids are bigger than Seamus! They are twice as old as he is! And they pick on him. Well," she crossed her arms over her chest, "they are *not* going to do that anymore."

"What did you do, Sophie?" Siobhan wondered if she should just pick up the phone and listen to the party line. But even though it would all be Polish gibberish, she knew what they would be saying. The women of Hadley would again have reason to fault Siobhan. What a hellion of a daughter she was raising.

But nevertheless one Siobhan was very proud of. She listened as her children ran up the stairs. "Well done, Sophie, well done," she whispered. She folded up her daughter's skirt and the mending she had so unsuccessfully tried to do that day, put it in the basket on the floor next to her feet, and draped an old towel over the sewing machine.

It was time to think of supper.

Once again Sophie was uncharacteristically docile, picking up the dishes and setting to washing them after they finished eating. Seamus only mildly complained that he didn't know a single boy that had to help with dishes. "It's women's work. I'll bet Iggy and Leon don't have to dry dishes!" His sister didn't need much encouragement as her brother begged her to tell him again and again how she punched the lights out of those stupid bullies.

"Yeah, stupid bullies! When I get bigger, I'm going to punch their lights out, too."

Siobhan lingered at the supper table, her back to her children, as she sipped her tea. She felt that she should scold them, tell them fighting wasn't the way to solve problems, but then their father had been in a war fighting, and...well, she just couldn't say anything.

Siobhan heard a car door slam and then through the screen door and across the porch she saw them. Tony and two old Polish women in their flour sack dresses and worn Oxfords. They walked around the pile of rocks and stepped up onto the porch, the women lifting their skirts. Siobhan felt her body stiffen. "Holy crap!" she heard Sophie whisper.

"Uncle Tony!" Seamus dropped the dish towel onto the floor and ran to open the screen door. Tony leaned against his crutch to hold the door open and respectfully gestured for the elderly women to pass into the kitchen. Siobhan stood, her shoulders squared and rigid. Tony hopped around the table pulling out the kitchen chairs and ushering each of the women into place. He turned to Sophie. "You think you can make these fine ladies some tea?"

Sophie glanced at her mother. Since Siobhan's stony expression hadn't changed, Sophie shrugged her shoulders and set to making another pot of tea. It wasn't real tea. Since the war, real tea was scarce. The German U boats made sure of that. Siobhan had dried some plant leaves last summer and that's what she used for tea. But she still had a few porcelain cups from her mother's set which she and her father had brought from Ireland. Siobhan would pour that brew into her cup and call it tea.

Tony looked to Siobhan, pulled out another chair, and, with the sweep of his free arm, seemed to beg her to sit also.

"It's my house. I'll stand."

Tony shrugged. He remained standing as well, leaning on his crutches. Then one of the women began to speak. She was the smaller and the older of the two, the skin of her face carved with hundreds of wrinkles, some small and feathery fine, some deeply gouged into the folds around her eyes and into the sacks of her cheeks. Her hair was thin, wispy white; her scalp tanned and spotted underneath. She spoke in Polish. Tony raised a hand and the woman stopped. Tony turned to Siobhan.

"You remember my great aunt? Amelia Norowoski? You met her at the wedding."

At the mention of the woman's name, Sophie came to life. "Oh, we washed her dish last night." She went to the end of the counter where a number of clean casserole dishes were stacked. She began to look at the names taped to the bottoms of the plates. Sophie smiled when she read the third dish and she took it over to the old woman. "Thank you," she said. "It was delicious."

Amelia Norowoski reached a gnarled and veined hand across the table and took the dish. She did not smile. She did not say anything.

Siobhan watched, her own pale face smooth and expressionless.

Tony turned to his aunt and nodded. Amelia resumed speaking. It was a low, aged voice with cracks and crevices in it, and as she talked she lifted her gnarled hands every so often to garnish her story. Siobhan noticed the rosary beads threaded through the fingers of the woman's left hand. It was a long story, made longer by the pauses so that Tony could translate for

Siobhan. Sophie went to the table and sat down, motioning for Seamus to sit on her lap.

Seamus's clear blue eyes, his father's eyes, went from Amelia Norowoski to Tony, back and forth as the woman talked and his uncle translated. Amelia Norowoski told about the day Stanislaus was born and how his mother suffered in labor for three days and then, what a miracle! a perfect baby boy. How he had a sweet, sweet way about him, "much as his own beautiful son," and she looked to Seamus, her lips curled in what must have been a smile. She went on. How everyone loved him, that little Stanislaus. Everyone in the whole town of Hadley. How he made his First Communion in their own Polish church. You should have seen his angel face and his hands so white and pure folded in prayer. How smart he was in school! How much he helped his parents on the farm! How good he was at the basketball. And then so much he loved this country that his parents had adopted that he went to fight for its freedom! A brave, brave son of Hadley.

Siobhan stood still, her arms crossed over her chest. Except for the rapid blinking of her eyes, one would have thought she hadn't heard a word that was told to her.

And then, Amelia Norowoski spoke her final sentence. Tony hesitated before translating, but when the old woman glared at him, he spoke dutifully. "And that is why my nephew will have his funeral Mass in his own church and in his own cemetery. I have already spoken to the priest." Tony avoided Siobhan's eyes.

He had barely got the words out when the fire of anger lit life into Siobhan. Her jaw trembled. She leaned over the table, her face a foot away from Amelia Norowoski's, her hands balled into fists around the top rung of the empty chair. "No! He will be buried in *our* church. The church that accepted the both of us. The church that does not look down on people because they are not Polish. Not in your church which did not accept me!"

The old woman did not flinch from Siobhan's fury. When she spoke, it was in the same emotionless drone with which she had recapped her nephew's life story. Tony translated. "He will have his funeral in his Polish church. His real church. Stanislaus belongs to all the town of Hadley." The old woman stood, pushing up from her chair by placing her hands hard against the top of the table. "Anna," she motioned to the younger woman at her side. Siobhan remembered then who she was. Stan's cousin. So much older than Stan that she could have been his mother. Tony leaned over his crutches and extended his arm to guide the women to the door. Amelia Norowoski brushed his hand away. She said something to him in Polish.

As the little procession made its way across the kitchen floor and out on to the porch, Tony looked back at Siobhan. "You have to understand--"

"No, *you* have to understand. His Mass will be at St. John's."

"There could be two funeral Masses," Tony suggested. His voice had a conciliatory tone uncharacteristic of him.

Siobhan, Sophie and Seamus stood watching the old woman and her daughter make their cautious way down the steps and around the rock pile. Sophie put her arm around her mother and rested her head on her mother's shoulder. The cups of tea, untouched, grew cold on the table.

Seamus suddenly broke free and ran out the door after his uncle. "But Uncle Tony! When do we make the stone path?"

Chapter Three

Sophie hadn't left for school yet the next morning when Siobhan heard the rumble of the tractor in the fields behind her barn, the fields that had lain fallow since Stan went to war. 'Maybe he's plowing his own fields,' she thought. Stan's father's farm was next to theirs on the north side. He had carved off half of it as a wedding gift for his son. The older son Tony was to inherit the family house and the remaining lands.

But the grinding roar seemed so close. Siobhan dried her hands on her apron and ran out the door, crossed the porch in a few quick strides, tumbled down the steps, skirted the pile of rocks, and sprinted across the back yard and around the barn. She watched as Tony came down the length of her fields on the John Deere, his right hand busy shifting gears while his good leg pumped the brake on the turns. Attached to the tractor was a plow which busily chewed up the weeds and scruffy growth that had survived the winter. The freshly turned earth smelled clean and Siobhan swallowed hard against the lump growing in her throat. The sound, the smell, the look of the land freshly turned for planting--it felt like yesterday that her Stan had sat on the tractor in late spring and they had planned for bountiful crops. It was a hopeful time of beginnings, spring on a farm. There was no thought given to drought, or powdery mildew, or fungus or ravenous bugs that might plague the crops during the summer ahead.

Siobhan shook her head. "Why won't that man leave me alone?" she asked out loud. She jumped when she felt her daughter's hand on her shoulder. She looked down and saw Seamus standing next to her. Sophie gave her mother a mischievous grin. "He's not afraid of you, Mom. You can't scare him off."

When Tony stopped the tractor just in front of them, Seamus ran to him. "Can I drive the tractor with you, Uncle Tony? Can I? Can I?"

Tony motioned for the boy to climb up onto the tractor and onto his lap.

Terror gripped Siobhan. "No!" she screamed.

Tony put the tractor in gear. He had one arm wrapped snug around Seamus who sat in front of him. Over the roar of the tractor, he yelled at Siobhan. "Do you think I'd let anything happen to him?" He then drove off down the field laying open another row of freshly plowed earth. Siobhan listened as Seamus squealed with delight.

Sophie patted her mother on the shoulder. "Mom, you have to learn to relax." Then she turned to head back around the barn to the house. She yelled over her shoulder. "Can you fix my cheerleading skirt? I need it for after school."

Reluctantly, Siobhan turned and headed back to the house. As she climbed up the steps, she met Sophie flying across the porch towards her. "I'm late," she shouted to her mother.

Siobhan grabbed for Sophie's shoulder which slid out from under her reach. "Why do you need your cheerleading uniform? There's no cheering in the spring."

Sophie gave her mother an exaggerated roll of the eyes. "Mom! It's tryout time. We're training the new kids."

"And you need your uniform for that?"

But Sophie was already down the driveway dashing off to school. "What is she up to?" Siobhan muttered.

Siobhan hid a smile when she saw Seamus climb up the porch steps. His tee shirt and jeans were covered with powdery dust and his face was streaked with dirt. But the smile beaming through all of it was beatific. He was happy. He wasn't thinking about a father shot dead in a continent an ocean away. Tony was right behind her son, hopping up the steps, the crutch making alternate punches against the wood.

"We're thirsty, Mom! We been working hard."

"And I suppose only lemonade can quench your thirst, eh?"

"Yup, and for Uncle Tony, too."

"Hey, Little Man!" Tony said to Seamus. "You wipe your feet when you go into the house after working. Women work hard, too, and you don't want to be tracking dirt into their clean house." Tony hopped up and down on his good leg to shake the dirt from his boot. A little cloud of dust sprang up and settled on the floor around the rug.

Seamus imitated Tony.

"No, you don't have to hop. You got two legs. Just rub your shoes back and forth on the rug. Like my horse does, pawing at the ground. That's it. That's the way. If'n your shoes are really dirty, then you take them off. It's the polite thing to do."

Siobhan opened the ice box and took out the pitcher of lemonade. "I suppose you're hungry too?" She nodded at Tony who was leaning on his crutches.

"Yup, we're hungry, Mom. We need us some sandwiches. Uncle Tony likes peanut butter and jelly, too."

Siobhan pulled out a chair for Tony and took his crutches from him. "You're not going to make a habit of this, are you?"

"God forbid." Tony collapsed on to the chair. He took a napkin and wiped the dirty sweat from his brow. He glanced down at the cloth napkin. "Oh, sorry."

Siobhan swiped the soiled napkin off the table and slapped down a clean one. "I imagine you bachelors over there don't pay much mind to manners."

"No, ma'am. You're right about that."

Siobhan slapped together a couple of sandwiches and plunked them down on the table. She regretted treating her son so roughly, so she paused and brushed Seamus's hair off his forehead with her hand. It was a caress. Then she leaned her back against the kitchen counter and folded her arms over her chest as she watched the "men" eat their lunch.

"We done with the plowing, Mom. We're going to do the wheelbarrow next."

"Wheel harrow," Tony corrected. He reached for the lemonade and slurped noisily.

"Tony," Siobhan said at last. "Why are you doing this?"

"Well, that's what I need to talk to you about." He patted the table next to him. "Please, Siobhan, come. Sit down."

Siobhan didn't move. She dropped her arms to her sides and her whole body stiffened.

Tony looked across to Seamus. "Hey, Little Man, didn't you tell me you had to go visit your puppy? Why don't you go and do that right now?"

"But, Uncle Tony, we--"

"Yes, yes, we goin' to do the wheel harrowing. But Uncle Tony needs a little rest first. I'll just sit right here and talk with your mother. Go on now. Go see about that puppy."

"But you won't--"

"No, don't worry, I won't start without you."

Uncle and mother watched as the little boy sprang up from the table and ran out the door, down the steps and across the lawn. They watched as the boy disappeared into the yawning black hole that was the open doors of the Tudryn barn.

"You can't be a father to that boy."

Tony turned to stare at his sister-in-law, her back still against the kitchen counter.

"No one is taking my brother's place. No one can--" Tony's voice cracked and he stared down at the table.

It was then that Siobhan realized Tony's pain. She felt a spot inside of her go soft.

"Anyway," Tony lifted his head and looked across the kitchen to his sister-in-law. "That's not what I've come to talk to you about. Please--" he patted the table again. "Come, sit."

Siobhan hesitated then warily crossed the kitchen floor and pulled out a chair opposite Tony and sat down. She needed that table, that something hard and solid between them.

"You need to plant your fields."

"I plant my field."

"Not just that little garden of yours. Not just for you. You need to plant the fields and sell the crops."

"I can take care of my own family. We are doing fine."

"You need to plant your fields, Siobhan. I don't know what the army is going to give you for--." Tony looked out the window. His eyes focused on something far, far away. Then he shrugged and turned back to face Siobhan. "But whatever it is, it's not going to be enough. You have Sophie and Seamus to think about. Kids nowadays have to go to college to make something of their lives. That's going to cost."

Siobhan opened her mouth to speak but Tony held a hand up. "Hear me out. You have to plant *all* of your fields. I know you think you can do it all. And I'm sure you can. But you saw my aunt last night. You saw what doing it all does to a woman. To anybody. It rubs them raw and rough and pounds them down. You need some help."

"Sophie--"

"Yes, Sophie can help. But she's a young kid. Her summer days shouldn't all be spent in the fields, getting old before her time. She should have some fun, too."

Siobhan hadn't thought about the future. She'd been thinking about the past, about what was gone, and now fear of the future began to take hold of her. She struggled to keep from trembling.

Tony leaned towards her. "I can help. You know I will. But I can't do it all. I have my own fields too."

"I can--"

Tony held up his hand again. An expectant silence fell between them.

"There's a way out of this, Siobhan. There's a new program outta Westover. You know, the Air Force base. Maybe you don't know, but there's some German prisoners of war bein' kept over there, and there's a new program where we can get some of them prisoners to work our lands."

Siobhan stood so quickly the table shook. Fear and rage fought for control over her body.

Tony raised his hand again. "Now, listen. Listen, Siobhan. Don't you think it's fair that them that took our Stanislaus should give something back to us? The way it works is this. I go over in the truck and I pick up some of them

35

prisoners and a guard. I bring them over here and the guard watches them while they do the work on our lands that we can't do because all our young men are over at the war."

"I don't want *any* Krauts working our lands!" Siobhan's jaw trembled as she struggled for control. "I don't know what I'd do if I saw any of them, let alone invite them to work the very fields my Stan loved so much. It'd be like they were defiling his very name. I won't have it!"

"Siobhan. Please sit. Please sit down. Think about this. Think about Sophie and Seamus. Think about their future. You have to plant your fields and harvest them, sell your crops, and earn the money for your family's future. "

Siobhan's jaw was set.

"You don't have to have anything to do with them prisoners. I can oversee them."

"I don't want them on our lands."

Tony sighed. "Ok, look Siobhan. In a week or so, you have to plant. I'd plant for you, you gotta know I would. But I have to be realistic, here. I can't do mine and Dad's. I need help. Mickey, the kid that helped me last summer? Well he got drafted and he's going off to the war. I'm putting in for some of them prisoners to help me."

"I don't want them."

Tony held her gaze. Then he reached for his crutches and stood. "Thank you for the lunch."

Just then they heard footsteps on the porch and turned to see Seamus, the puppy squirming under his firm grasp.

"See! Uncle Tony, see! This is the one I'm going to keep when her mama's done feeding her."

Siobhan was surprised to see the tears in Tony's eyes. Her brother-in-law reached out to scratch the puppy behind its ears. "A worthy pup, Seamus. You've picked a worthy pup. Whatcha going to name it?"

Seamus's face went blank. "I just call her Puppy. I don't know, Uncle Tony? What do you think we should name her?"

"We'll have to think on that one, young man. Listen, you going to help me hook up the wheel harrow, or not?"

"Oh yes! I forgot! I'll be right back." Seamus ran back out of the house and headed across the yard to the Tudryn barn.

Tony stood staring after the boy. "He's so like Stan," he muttered. He shook his shoulders. He did not look back at Siobhan behind him. "You think about it, Siobhan. You think about it long and hard. Don't let your anger get in the way of your good sense. You need them prisoners here."

Siobhan watched as Tony crossed the porch, the thrust of the crutches making hard punching sounds, hard and definitive, like blows of a hammer nailing something shut.

Chapter Four

In the end it was Father Murphy who settled the fight. Two Masses, one right after the other. A morning of Masses to honor one of Hadley's own. One at Holy Rosary for all the Polish people of Hadley, and one at St. John's, the so called "Irish" church, the parish home of Stan, Siobhan and their children. The latter had become the parish home of the increasing number of Hadley residents not lucky enough to boast a Polish ancestry. They hammered out the treaty over the kitchen table--Tony, his aunt and his cousin, Father Murphy, and Siobhan. The Polish priest did not attend. In his mind there was nothing to be settled: Stanislaus Norowoski had been baptized at Holy Rosary, the only true Catholic church in town. Made his First Communion there. Confirmation, too. Had he married a nice Polish girl, he would have been married there as well, but God is forgiving. Stanislaus Norowoski would have his funeral Mass at Holy Rosary. There was nothing to discuss.

"So, we have two Masses," Father Murphy had said, his eyes gentle and pleading.

In the end Sophie's argument convinced her mother. "Two Masses, Mom. Think about it! Who gets two Masses for their funeral? Only Dad."

Then they had to decide which Mass would be first. They called the Polish priest who informed them Stanislaus Norowoski would have his funeral Mass at eleven o'clock that coming Saturday.

"We can have the Mass at St. John's at nine," Father Murphy said.

Siobhan, numb, nodded. She felt the will to fight ebb from her. She was exhausted when they then turned to the matter of which cemetery her husband would be buried in. Not buried there now, of course, maybe not buried there ever, his body currently resting in some plot in some spot in the north of France. It was just a formality, putting Stan's name on the Norowoski family tombstone. A symbolic sprinkling of water and prayers of farewell. Tony pointed out that the Norowoski family plot had many open spots already paid for. "My crazy father! When my mother died, he bought so many plots and that big gravestone." Tony rolled his eyes. "For me, for my supposed wife and children. For Stan, for you--" He stopped when Siobhan turned to him and glared.

"What do you say?" Father Murphy said. There was another call to the Polish priest who said it would be okay for the Irish priest to attend the burial rite at St. Brigid's cemetery.

Siobhan nodded again. She just wanted it to be over. She just wanted everyone to stand up from the table, leave her house and give her back her own home again.

"And we can get that young man from the band at Hopkins to play taps. The one who plays the trumpet so well." Father Murphy turned to Sophie. "What's his name? His family goes to the Congregational Church in town."

"Oh, you mean Buddy Brown? He's not Catholic."

Father Murphy nodded. "That's the one. It doesn't matter. Playing taps is not Catholic or Protestant. God is pleased that the young man uses the talents He gave him. I'll ask that Brown boy to play. And I'm sure the local veterans will attend the ceremony, to honor Stan with a military tribute." The priest turned to Siobhan. "The town also wishes to honor Stan with a reception after the funerals at the Polish American Club."

Siobhan hated the feeling that her life was no longer under her own control. She felt like a puppet, as if everyone in the town was pulling the strings and she was forced to do their dance. And that of course would have to be a Polish polka.

Later Siobhan would remember that the Mass in her parish church was sparsely attended, just she, her children, Tony, and a few townspeople, some Protestants even from the

Congregational Church. She would remember that that funeral Mass seemed warm and intimate, comforting, even. She cried and her tears felt cleansing.

In contrast, Holy Rosary Church was packed well before eleven o'clock and the Mass seemed to go on forever in a language of which Siobhan and her children could only recognize a few words. Old-timers in their WWI uniforms lined the sidewalk leading up to the church doors. They saluted as Siobhan and her children walked between them. Even Yantik was there.

Seamus stood on the kneeler and looked all around the church.

"Get down," Sophie hissed, embarrassed that people might turn to stare at them.

"But where's Daddy?" His little voice was clear and innocent and caused the old women around them to smile, their eyes glistening bright with tears. "I want to know!"

Siobhan pulled her son to her and sat him on her lap. "He's in heaven, Sweetheart. Remember? He left us to be with God. He's telling God all about us right now and he's watching over us." She brushed the hair on her son's forehead. 'You need a haircut,' she thought.

"He's watching me right now?"

"Yes, Sweetheart. This very minute and always from now on."

"He's taking care of me up in heaven?"

"Yes, my Sweet." Siobhan kissed her son on the forehead and slid him off her lap onto the seat of the pew.

"But I want to see Daddy!"

Sophie glared at her mother. "Everyone's looking at us," she hissed.

Siobhan glanced up at her daughter. "This is more important than worrying about people looking at us." She turned back to her son. "You can see Daddy any time you want. Just look in your heart because he'll always be with you. His soul will always be with you. And when you go to heaven, a long, long time from now, you'll see his body too. Daddy'll be standing next to Jesus and waiting for all of us."

"Is Daddy an angel?"

Siobhan could sense the sad smiles on the faces of the old Polish women sitting in the pews near them.

"No, Daddy is Daddy, like he always was, but he's standing right there with the angels next to Jesus."

"But doesn't he miss us?"

Siobhan hugged her son. "I'm sure he does, but this way, he can watch over us and protect us. He'll always be with us. Always. Forever and ever."

Seamus rested his head against his mother's shoulder. It had been a long morning of church for a five year old and his head bobbed as he fought to stay awake.

Siobhan felt absent from her body, her mind floating off to some place vacant, empty. It would be years before Siobhan would admit that, looking back on it all, the Polish Mass was a celebration worthy of the sacrifice her beloved Stan had made for his country.

It seemed the entire town turned out at the Polish American Club after the burial. An old woman, a friend of Tony's aunt, patted Seamus on his head, smiled and said something in Polish. A younger woman translated. "You have your Daddy's eyes."

Seamus's face took on a troubled look. It wasn't long before his lower lip began to bob up and down and his face went white. Soon he was crying. Sophie rescued her brother from the line of sympathy and well-wishing. Behind her back, Siobhan heard her daughter ask Seamus what was the matter.

"I kilt Daddy."

Siobhan felt a cold shiver zip up through her heart. She was standing at the head of an unending line of those wanting to express their sympathies. At that moment Siobhan was accepting the condolences of someone she didn't know, but someone who remembered the outstanding athlete Stan had been.

"He could shoot from anywhere on the court." The old man rocked back on his heels, his mind watching the memories. "You know..."

Siobhan barely heard the man's words as she listened hungrily for what Sophie might say to Seamus.

"No way, Seamus. What makes you think you killed Daddy?"

The boy spoke in broken sobs. "That lady said I had Daddy's eyes. That's why he couldn't see, Sophie, and, and, and he couldn't see the enemy soldier coming up, 'cuz I took his eyes. He couldn't hide and that's why he got shot."

"Oh silly." Sophie wrapped her arms around her brother. "That's just an expression. It just means your eyes *look* like Daddy's. It doesn't actually mean you took his eyes."

"So Daddy had his very own eyes? He could see?"

"Yes. It wasn't your fault. Lots of people die in a war. It really isn't anybody's fault. Except maybe the stupid people who start the wars."

"But if Daddy could see, how did he get shot? Couldn't he run away and hide?"

"Hmm," Sophie pulled her head back from her little brother and put on a thinking face. "Well, I don't think anybody knows for sure, but I'll bet it's because the German soldier was hiding and sneaking up on Daddy. That's why he didn't see him."

Seamus nodded solemnly. "Yes. That's what happened."

Siobhan left a man's hand dangling in the air in her direction as she turned around and knelt beside her son and daughter. She hugged them both. She felt the touch of a hand on her shoulder and looked up to see the flushed face of her brother-in-law. His breath was heavy with the sweet smell of alcohol. Siobhan wrinkled her nose in distaste.

"Uncle Tony!" Seamus wrapped his arms around his Uncle's leg.

"Why don't I take this young one? Why don't we go get some food? You must be really hungry."

"I could eat a horse!"

Tony laughed. Siobhan stood and drew back from his breath.

"And your father? I haven't seen him. He can't honor his son?"

42

Tony shook his head. "We all have our own ways of grieving, Siobhan. He's an old crumpled up memory of what used to be a man."

"Still--" Siobhan began.

Sophie, sensing trouble, looped her arm under her uncle's. "I'm hungry, too. Can I go with them, Mom? Unless you need--"

"Okay," Siobhan gave in. "But we're not staying. After this line is through, I want to go home."

Sophie eyed the line of well-wishers that stretched out the door onto the sidewalk and she patted her mother's arm. "I think we'll be here a while. It's actually kinda nice. All these people proud of Dad. All--" Suddenly Sophie was overcome with emotion.

Tony put his arm around his niece's shoulders. "Let's go. I suggest we start at the pie table."

Chapter Five

Siobhan flung the hoe against the earth, packed hard after a winter of snow and ice. She was angry that she had waited so long to plant her vegetable garden. She turned when she heard the rumble of Tony's truck as it rolled over the gravel of her driveway. "Now what," she muttered angrily.

She picked up the hoe and swung around brandishing it as if it were a weapon. Then she propped it against the freshly turned soil and held it out at arm's length like a rifle at the ready. Cold hands grabbed at her heart when she saw the prisoners jump down off the truck. Their backs faced her and she saw the large PW painted on their gray uniforms. "M for Murderers is more like it," she said, under her breath. Tony hopped down from the driver's seat of the truck and pointed to the rock pile in front of the porch. The prisoners turned to follow him.

"Oh!" Siobhan gasped out loud. They were boys! All of them, except for one older prisoner who looked like he could be their father. Boys! Blond, fair-haired boys! She couldn't tell from where she was standing, feet on the hard clumps of overturned soil, but she doubted they were even shaving yet. Could a boy-soldier like one of them have shot her Stan? Then she noticed the US army soldier standing up in the bed of the truck supposedly guarding the prisoners. The sun was behind him and he stood like a black cardboard cutout. His right shoulder was considerably higher than his left. His feet were spread apart for balance and he had a rifle slung over his shoulder. His right hand moved up and down as he took drags on a cigarette. A cap shaded his eyes.

Tony waved his hands about explaining how he wanted a path carved out in the earth from the bottom step of the porch

44

to the driveway and then the stones fitted into it. She could hear him yelling in Polish.

Suddenly her thoughts screamed, 'Seamus! No!' She remembered the boy saying how he was going to help Uncle Tony build the stone path for his mother. She dropped the hoe and began to run towards the house. 'Where is he?' Then, just as suddenly, she pulled up short, her heart thumping. Her son was in the Tudryn barn. She remembered then. He had asked to go over and play with his puppy. Seamus would be heart-broken that he wasn't helping Tony build the path, but no way--no goddam way!--was her son to be working with those German murderers.

Tony pulled a sledgehammer off the bed of the truck and handed it to one of the prisoners, telling him to break apart the larger stones. The soldier jumped down off the truck and it was then that Siobhan saw that his left leg was shorter than his right and twisted in such a way that the foot was turned outward, even when he walked. He went to stand near the prisoner wielding the sledgehammer. He slid the rifle strap off of his shoulder and griped the gun in his hand. The prisoner looked up at the soldier and nodded. He got the message.

There were ten of them in all plus the guard. Tony beckoned to one of the prisoners to follow him and they walked past Siobhan on the way to the barn. Siobhan studied the face of the German POW who kept his eyes averted, not daring to stare at the pretty woman standing in the field next to the driveway. He was even younger than she thought. Fifteen, sixteen, maybe, with the faintest of blond stubble on his chin. The boy came back out of the barn carrying several shovels and a garden rake. Three of the prisoners set to digging the path while the other two began sorting through the pile of rocks. They picked out the smaller ones, placing them close to the porch, and they carried the larger ones over to the prisoner wielding the sledge hammer. As the hammer hit the stones, the sound sang out into the air, a staccato of high-pitched pings. The American soldier limped away and slid his back down against the trunk of the crab apple just beyond the porch, coming to rest his buttocks on the ground at the base of the tree. His legs stretched out in front of him and the rifle rested over his knees. Smoke curls came out from below his cap which was pulled low over his eyes.

Siobhan turned and headed over to the Tudryn barn. She was determined to keep Seamus as far away from those German assassins as she could. Just then, the boy appeared in the doorway of the barn, the puppy held tight in his arms. He stopped suddenly and stared at the prisoners hard at work to make his stone path. Tears sprang to his eyes and Siobhan put her arms around her son as soon as she reached him.

"But he promised! Uncle Tony promised--" Instinctively Seamus held the puppy tighter in his arms and it yelped in discomfort.

"Here," Siobhan reached for the puppy. "Let's take him back to his mother and we can talk about this."

Seamus followed his mother into the barn. He fought against his tears. "But I was supposed to make the path! Me and Uncle Tony."

"I know, Sweetheart, I know, but they're making Uncle Tony take the prisoners and have them do the work. He didn't have a choice." In her heart she cursed her brother-in-law for not talking to Seamus first. For not talking to *her* first. "I'm sure Tony needs you for another job." She brushed the hair out of her son's eyes. "A job the prisoners can't do." 'And he damn well better,' she said to herself.

Siobhan was doing it again. It was getting to be a habit. Sometime after lunch, she would slip away up the stairs to her bedroom. She would ease the door shut as if she were doing the reverse of a child sneaking out of the house. She held her breath until the latch of the door clicked shut; then she tugged off her shoes and picked up the photo album from the nightstand next to her bed. She would lie down across the top of the bed, the bed that had been hers and Stan's, and she would clutch the album close to her chest.

Siobhan would promise herself that this would be the last time. It was time to move on. To get on with her life. But even though she said those words to herself, she couldn't figure out what they meant, "Get on with your life." And so the next afternoon, despite the intentions of the day before, she would climb the stairs to her bedroom. About one o'clock. After lunch. Even though Seamus didn't take naps anymore, it was a quiet time when the little boy would go over to the Tudryn barn and lie down with the puppies. She followed him over there once and watched as her son petted the mother dog and all her other pups, before lying down next to her in the bed of crushed straw, his chosen puppy curled against his tiny body.

So even though she had promised herself the day before that she would stop doing it, Siobhan left the lunch dishes on the table, went up to the bedroom, pressed that photo album of hers and Stan's life together against her chest, and stared up at the white ceiling, ignoring the spots where the paint had started to peel and the flakes of white aimed down at her. She focused on one spot only, and stared at it until she no longer saw it, but saw something in the past instead. She smiled, remembering.

Siobhan was living her life backwards.

She was a practical person, Siobhan had told herself. It was not practical to find your heart excited on the days that truck came out to Boston to their market, the truck that the one special Polish farmer drove, the tanned, blond-haired Stanislaus. She didn't like the way her father looked at her on those mornings, a silly grin on his face like he knew a secret she didn't. She didn't like the way her legs seemed to race her body down past all the other stalls in the open-air market to where the trucks would pull in from all over Massachusetts, some even from Rhode Island and New Hampshire. She didn't like it the way her eyes would scan the parking lot, looking just for that one special truck, and that one special driver. Stan, Stanislaus. The next week, the time after she had made a fool of herself explaining what her name meant, he'd looked down from his perch up on the truck and said, "'Steadfast in character.'"

Siobhan had pretended confusion as if she didn't know what he meant. "What the devil would ye be talking about?" she'd shouted up at him. The rays of sunlight sifted through the pale yellow of his hair, and she found herself breathless.

"'Steadfast in character.' That's what Stanislaus means." Then he just sort of smirked and Siobhan found herself wanting to smack those smirking lips and then kiss them ferociously. The feeling made her dizzy and she wanted to shake herself silly.

And then it was Saturday again and Siobhan leapt out of bed. Stan would be coming in the truck from Hadley. She just knew it. It wouldn't be that older brother of his, the one with the bad leg; Tony, that was his name. He had a rough way of barking out at the customers and hurling the produce down at them from the bed of the truck. Today, it just had to be Stan's turn. She was ready for him. He'd not be getting her all flustered that Saturday.

But when the truck pulled in down at the end of the path between all the stalls of the open-air market, Siobhan wasn't the first to run down to meet it. She was still in her father's stall, trapped. One of the women in a neighboring stall had come with a letter for Siobhan to read to her. It was from back home, back in Ireland, a letter the woman's aunt had persuaded a priest to write for her. Margaret O'Herlihy, the woman waving the letter in Siobhan's face, was desperate for the news of her beloved Ireland. Siobhan often read for the men and the women in the market. Sometimes she even wrote the letters back to Ireland for them as well. Siobhan was one of the few who could read and write. Her father had made sure she knew how, paying one of the nuns at St. Matthew's to tutor her in the evenings, paying for the luxury out of the precious and scarce funds he managed to earn at the market.

And so Margaret O'Herlihy listened with watering eyes as Siobhan read. The woman's aunt told of the continuing hard luck in farming the rocky soil back in Ireland. How dear everything was and how few men were left to do the work.

Margaret picked up the hem of the apron she wore and blotted her eyes. "I'll send her some money, I will."

Siobhan stood on her toes and peered over the woman's gray head. She saw that indeed her Stan had come. She could never mistake that tall, broad-shouldered figure of him silhouetted by the sun behind. But Margaret was tugging on Siobhan's sleeve. "You'll go with me, won't ye?" she was asking.

Siobhan shook her head but the image of Stan's silhouette stayed in her mind. "I'm sorry, what?"

"You'll go with me, won't ye? To the bank, to see about sending me poor aunt some money?"

"Yes, yes, of course." Siobhan handed the letter back to the old woman who held it as though it were treasure. Siobhan stifled the impatience tugging at her body. "So, we'll talk about it later, okay?"

"You're a dear sweet girl, you are," Margaret said, caressing Siobhan's hand.

It was all Siobhan could do to keep from snatching her hand away, turning her back on the woman, and sprinting off down the path to meet up with her Stan. She wasn't sure when she started thinking of him that way, her Stan, but it felt right.

"Thank you, Margaret. Thank you, but really, I must go now. I've got to help my father with the buying."

"Yes, of course," but Margaret clung onto Siobhan's hand and in the end Siobhan had to snatch it from her, smiling a quick apology. Her legs wanted to run but she forced them to walk.

She heard Stan's booming voice shout down to her father. "I've got the best green beans in all of Hadley. Hell, in all of New England."

When Siobhan got to the farmers' wagons, she saw that Stan had jumped down from the bed of the truck and was talking in earnest with her father. He had his arm around her father's shoulders. He was taller than her father, but then again, maybe not, if her father could ever again get his youth back, unfold his body, throw back his shoulders, and stand up straight until that hump in his back that seemed to grow more each day was gone. Yes, if Seamus could unfurl his body, perhaps he'd even be taller than Stanislaus, never mind that the lad was "steadfast in character."

Out of the corner of her eye, she saw the two men huddled in earnest talk about something. Her father nodded; Stan nodded. Then the young farmer grinned a big broad smile and clapped Siobhan's father on the back.

Siobhan feigned lack of interest and walked by the pair of them as if to do some bargaining with the farmer whose truck was parked alongside Stan's. But she paused first at Stan's truck and lifted up a handful of beans. Then she let them sift through her fingers and fall back into the basket on the bed of the truck. They were indeed the best in all the world, her heart concluded. But she walked on.

"Siobhan, Siobhan!" She heard him call for her. She pretended not to hear him, forcing Stan to run up alongside her and reach for her elbow.

"Oh, it's you."

Stan's closeness embraced her space and her body was torn between flinging herself against his broad chest and running for her very life.

"Yes, it's me. Listen," he said, breathless. "I was talking to your father and well, he said it would be okay with him."

"What would be okay with him? The price of your beans?"

Stan looked puzzled for a moment and then laughed. "No, no. I'm saying this all wrong. But back in Hadley next Saturday night, there's going to be a dance, and your father said it would be okay for you to go--"

"What?" Siobhan forced a stern look of disapproval on her face while inside she wanted to laugh and dance an Irish jig. "You're invitin' me father to a dance?"

"No, no!" Stan laughed again. He had one of those big booming laughs that made Siobhan want to crawl inside of it and be happy forever. "Your father said it would be okay for you to come back to Hadley with me next Saturday and go to the dance. A fourth of July Polish style. You can stay overnight at our house. You'll love my mother. And I'll bring you back the next day. Sunday. After church, of course."

Siobhan whirled to face him so suddenly that Stan was caught off guard and ended up his face just inches from hers. She felt the heat of his body. And something else. She felt something else, like the pull of a powerful magnet. "Let me see if I understand this. You asked my father if I could go to a dance with you as if I were some small child incapable of making me own decisions?"

Stan stepped back and Siobhan felt as though there was just enough air now between them that she could breathe again. But, her father's permission!? The very idea!

For the first time in their brief acquaintance, Stan's confidence waivered, and Siobhan thrilled to see an apology struggle across his face. "Well, I just thought--"

"Oh, you were thinking, were ye? I think not. If you were thinking, you'd have known to be talking to me directly. I'm a grown woman, you know. I make me own decisions. And you--" she spun around to face her father who had come up behind them. "You'll not be havin' any say in the matter."

Her father's face flushed as he struggled to keep from laughing.

Stan sputtered, "Well, I just meant that, I mean I thought it would be out of place to--"

"If'n it's me you want to invite to a dance, then it's me you ask. Not me father. But since you've asked him, you go right ahead and take him back with you. You'll make a fine pair dancing, you will. I can manage everything here. Have yourselves a fine time."

Stan wore a look of disbelief, shock even, and, oddly for him, humility. "No, no, I just thought I should ask--"

"You call that thinking, do you?" Siobhan felt she would break out in laughter at any moment, so she turned abruptly and forced herself to stalk away from him.

It was electrifying, that touch of Stan's hand on her shoulder. She made herself wrench her shoulder out from under what her body suddenly wanted more than anything, his touch.

"I think I'll be seeing what the others have for beans." Siobhan began to walk away to the other trucks parked nearby.

"So, you're saying 'No'?"

She was several feet away from him when she turned and shouted back. "No to what? I haven't been properly asked anything I could be saying No or Yes to, now, have I?" She fought to keep annoyance on her face when all she wanted to do was dance about and say "Yes, yes, yes!"

Stan threw his arms up in the air and headed back to his truck.

Siobhan's eyes were closed as she lay on her bed, the photo album wrapped in her arms over her chest, but she was smiling. Remembering how the next Saturday, he asked her directly, "proper like," to ride back with him to Hadley, God's country, for the dance that evening. Part of the Independence Day celebrations. His mother was inviting her to stay overnight at their home. He'd bring her back to Boston safe and sound on Sunday. "After Mass, yes, of course."

It took a while for her to say 'yes.' First she had to set him straight that the only God's country in this wide, wide world was across the sea in Dingle, Ireland. "That's in County Kerry as any educated person knows." When Stan seemed to make fun of the name of her hometown, Siobhan faked fury and accused him of poor breeding and ignorance. After a proper apology was given, she went on to say that her father needed her for the Saturday market day. When Stan was quick to say, "But Seamus said--" she glared at him. "I'll be doing me own talking to me father."

But finally Siobhan said, "I suppose it'd be all right. Accepting your mother's invitation, I mean. It's the polite thing to do."

"So the answer is 'yes'?"

Siobhan was so excited she didn't trust herself to say anything. She nodded, and turned her back to hide from him the joy that lit up her face. "But you'll have to wait. I need to go home and get meself some change of clothing. Something fitting for Mass on Sunday, and for the dance, of course."

Stan nodded, not knowing that all the while she had a suitcase packed and ready back at her father's stall in the market.

Siobhan smiled even then, seventeen years later as she stared unseeing at the ceiling above her bed. Remembering.

"Momma?" Siobhan was startled to feel her son's small hand patting her hair. She sat up suddenly, surprised at the wetness of her face. The photo album slid to the floor. Siobhan flicked away the tears on her cheeks with both hands.

"Are you sad, Momma?" Seamus's voice was small and scared.

"Oh no, Sweetheart." She turned from him and fumbled for the handkerchief lying on the nightstand next to the bed. "Momma was just sleeping. Taking a nap. And you know how the Sandman comes and puts some sand in your eyes so you can fall asleep? Well, that's what it is. Just some sand left over that Momma has to wipe off."

Siobhan blew her nose loudly.

Seamus looked unconvinced. He stood defenseless in front of the bed.

"Sweetheart, what's wrong?"

"Those men came back. Those men who shot Daddy. Uncle Tony made them work hard to finish the stone path. I was going to make the stone path, but now--" The boy's small shoulders shivered as if a cold wind had just sliced through his tiny body. Siobhan reached over to her son and pulled him up onto her lap. She held him close and rocked him back and forth.

Suddenly the boy brightened. "But Momma, a good thing is going to happen!"

"What's that, my sweet?"

"You know Iggy and Leon? Those boys who made fun of my name and Sophie beat them up?"

"Yes, I remember. Although," Siobhan wiped the hair off her son's sweated brow, "fighting isn't really the way to settle things."

Seamus pulled back from his mother and jumped off the bed. "But Daddy was fighting! He was fighting for a good thing. He was fighting to save Hadley from Hitler!"

Siobhan sighed. "Yes, I know. Well, what were you going to tell me about those boys? They aren't still calling you names, are they?"

Seamus's cheeks puffed round and red with anger. "Yes, and it's worse'n ever."

Siobhan's back stiffened. "What do you mean?"

"Now they are calling me See-A-Moose, and they say that if I send Sophie after them, they'll be ready for her and they'll get their big brothers to beat *her* up."

"I think I should have a talk with those boys' mothers."

"No." Seamus's shoulders relaxed. "You don't have to. It's all gonna be fixed."

"Fixed? How so?"

"I told Uncle Tony about it and *he* is going to have a talk with those guys. He's even tougher 'n stronger than Sophie."

In spite of herself, Siobhan smiled. She wouldn't want to be on the end of Tony's anger.

"But Momma?"

"Yes, Sweetheart." Seamus dodged his mother's attempt to brush his hair off his forehead again.

"I'm hungry. And all the prisoners left a long time ago."

Siobhan glanced at the clock on the nightstand. Her eyes grew big. It was past six o'clock. She jumped up off the bed. "Oh goodness. Of course you're hungry. Momma's got to get supper going. Did Sophie--?"

"Sophie's still at school. Nobody's here, Momma. It's really, really, really quiet. And sad. The house is quiet and sad."

Where was Sophie?

Siobhan was alarmed. And ashamed. She flew out of the bedroom and tumbled down the steps, Seamus right behind her.

"But Momma? What's wrong? What's wrong?"

"That's the last time! The very last!" Siobhan scolded herself for not being an adult, for not remembering that she had responsibilities, children, children to feed, to lead, to teach the right path. "No more!" she shouted aloud as she hit the bottom step.

"But Momma! I didn't do anything!" Seamus's voice cracked. He was seconds away from tears.

Siobhan turned around and swept the boy off the steps and into her arms, hugging him tightly. "Shhh, shhh," she whispered into his ear. "You're Momma's best boy, her very best boy. Momma was just angry about something else."

Seamus pulled his head back. "So you're not mad at me, Momma?"

"Never!" Siobhan kissed her son on the forehead and set him down. Then she rushed down the hallway to the kitchen, where the stove was cold and all the supper dishes were still clean and stacked in the cupboards. And the dirty lunch dishes still littered the table.

"I know!" Siobhan spun around and caused the little boy to stumble, so close he was upon her heels. "We'll have French toast! What do you think of that?"

Seamus's eyes sparkled with glee. "Oh yes! Momma, yes! I'll go get the eggs!" The boy raced across the floor to the cold storage room on the other side of the door at the far end of the kitchen.

Siobhan pulled out the skillet and set it on the stove. She opened the cupboards and snatched out the mixing bowls and the rickety egg beater. She glanced at the clock hanging on the wall above the sink. 'Sophie, Sophie, where are you?' she wondered, a mother's apprehension making a small knot of fear in her chest.

In answer, she heard her daughter's voice through the screen door and from across the porch. Sophie was coming up the driveway. Instantly Siobhan's worry turned to fury. No after school cheerleading practice went to--Siobhan looked up at the clock again--seven o'clock! She stifled the wave of shame sweeping over her. She turned the heat of it into fury at her daughter. She whirled around, ready to challenge her daughter, when the sight of Sophie helping an old Polish woman up the steps of the porch stifled the scolding words of reproach in her throat.

Behind the old woman was a young girl of five or six. The girl seemed familiar to Siobhan, and her mind scrambled to identify her. Ah, yes! It was the Swazlowski child. Beyond the visitors, Siobhan was stunned to see the stone path carefully laid out, right down to the driveway. Had the men finished that while she lay dreaming her day away upstairs on the bed? And then there was the thump, thump of Tony's crutch against the porch steps.

Siobhan stared at him in cold fury. Now what did he want? She held the egg beater in one hand like a weapon.

It seemed to Siobhan that Sophie was especially busy about holding the door open for the old woman and ushering her to a chair, and then sliding another over for Tony while pointing to a third for the child, all the while avoiding her mother's eyes. The barrette was gone from Sophie's hair and her blouse was pulled out and hung sloppily over her cheerleading skirt.

Sophie quickly gathered up the lunch dishes, placing them on the counter next to the sink. Then she went over to sit next to the old woman.

Seamus came in from the cold storage. "Uncle Tony!" he shouted and Siobhan bent over quickly to rescue the bowl of eggs about to drop from her son's hands.

"Hey, little man!" Tony hooked the boy's neck in the bend of his elbow and hugged him close.

The boy noticed the little girl sitting next to him and shyly slid out from under his uncle's grasp. "I'm Seamus," he said.

"I'm Leocadia."

"La--what?"

The girl giggled. "Leocadia, Lah-cah-dee-ah."

"Oh. Cadia. That's a funny name." Seamus sat down beside her.

"Well, what's your name?"

"Seamus."

The girl giggled. "That's a funny name, too."

Seamus shrugged his shoulders. "Yeah, I know. But I'm used to it."

Tony slid down onto the last chair. They were all sitting and looking to Siobhan, expectation in their eyes. Siobhan, still standing, stared back at them, the bowl of eggs in one hand, the egg beater in the other.

"So you've all come here to eat, have ye?"

Tony and Sophie laughed while the little girl explained in Polish to her grandmother what Siobhan had asked. When Leocadia finished translating, the old woman looked up and glared indignantly at Siobhan. She began to stand up as if to leave but Tony reached across, patted her aged and spotted hand, and urged her to sit back down.

"I should explain. Stacia here wrote to her grandson who's in the army. The letter came back to her." Tony leaned towards the old woman and said something to her in Polish. Stacia nodded and pulled the letter out of the pocket in the skirt of her dress and handed it to him.

Siobhan set the eggs and the beater on the counter behind her and went over to take the envelope from Tony. She opened it and stared at the letter tucked inside. She looked over to Tony who nodded, and then Siobhan took the letter out of the envelope and unfolded it. After studying it for a few seconds, she said "It's in Polish. You can't write a letter in Polish. The censors just send it back. The letters have to be in English."

Tony explained what Siobhan had just said. The old woman nodded impatiently, "Ja, ja," she said, and then rattled off a string of Polish sentences.

Tony turned to Siobhan. "She knows now. She wants to know if you would write her letter for her in English."

Siobhan went to the table and motioned for Sophie to get up. Sophie stood, "I'll go get some paper, Mom."

Siobhan sat in the seat vacated by Sophie and gave the letter back to the old woman. She looked to Tony. "Stacia speaks English?"

But it was the little girl who answered. "No, no. Babcia only speak Polish. But I can tell you in English what she say and you write it for her."

Sophie came back into the kitchen and put a pad of lined writing paper in front of her mother along with a pen.

Siobhan hesitated as she stared at the pad and pen. "Well, I suppose, but we haven't eaten yet."

"Yeah!" Seamus said. "And we're going to have yummy French toast."

"I can make the French toast, Mom, while you write the letter."

Siobhan looked up at her daughter, her daughter with the disheveled hair and the blouse hanging out ragged edged over her cheerleading skirt. But that discussion with her daughter could wait. She sighed, and picked up the pen and tilted the pad of paper towards her. "All right then."

Seamus jumped up. "No, Momma, no! Sophie always burns the toast."

"I do not!"

"Yes you do! You burnt mine the last time! It was all black and I couldn't eat it." Seamus made a gagging sound.

Siobhan smiled. "Well, why don't you go and supervise. Go get the stool. You can help your sister and keep an eye on the French toast and tell her when it's time to turn it."

The boy's dimples dotted the upward turns of his smile.

Sophie rolled her eyes. "Oh, thanks, Mom."

Tony excused himself, saying he had to tend to his father, but that he would be back in a bit to pick up the old woman and her granddaughter. Siobhan looked to Stacia and, with a nod, encouraged her to dictate the letter. In a halting monotone, the old woman began to speak.

Polish--it was a swishy language with chewy consonants and diphthongs that had a bite to them.

The woman stopped and looked to her granddaughter.

The little girl sat up importantly and began to translate. "She say we all miss Edziu and pray for him and hope he good and healthy. And we all proud for him."

Siobhan began to write. It felt familiar. It was like writing letters for the market people worried about their families left back in Ireland. When she had finished writing what the little girl had translated, she looked up to Stacia and nodded, encouraging her to continue.

The old woman's eyes softened with gratitude.

They went on that way, Stacia speaking of the farm and what they had planted and how warm the spring was after such a cold winter and it was a good thing because they had just about run out of the food that they had saved from last summer's harvest.

And Leocadia translated for her grandmother.

The old woman laughed softly after saying how they missed Edziu especially when it came time to clean out the cold storage and the rotten potatoes left there from last fall. Stacia turned to Siobhan then, and patted her letter-writer on the arm as she scrunched up the wrinkles in her face to share the pungent smell of rotten potatoes.

Siobhan found herself smiling in return.

Then Stacia's face turned sad and tears trickled into the rivers time had gouged around her eyes. She told how a neighbor had shot Edziu's dog Roosevelt by mistake thinking it was the wild dog that had been killing his chickens.

Siobhan stopped writing. She looked over to the little girl. "Tell her, I can't write that. The censors will mark it out or maybe even return the letter again."

Leocadia translated.

Stacia's eyes grew big as she stared at Siobhan.

Leocadia explained. "She want to know why she can't tell that. Edziu love Roosevelt."

"Tell her I understand. But the censors don't want any sad news in the letter. They don't want the soldiers to be sad and worrying about home. It's bad for their morale."

"Morale?"

"Oh, 'morale' is the way you feel about things. You can have a good morale or a bad morale. If the soldiers feel sad and if they are sad about things back home, then their minds are distracted."

The little girl's face bunched up in puzzlement.

"Distracted? Hum...'distracted' means that they won't be paying attention to their jobs of fighting against Hitler. They would be thinking about home instead of about their fighting duties. And if they are not paying attention, an accident could happen. They could be hurt, or shot--" At the mention of shot, Siobhan found herself gulping for air.

There was an awkward silence in the kitchen. Siobhan fought to catch her breath. From his perch on the stool, Seamus turned to look at his mother. His face was solemn as he over looked to Leocadia. "My Momma is a bad morale. Because of Daddy." The girl stared back at him, her eyebrows raised in questions. Seamus nodded solemnly then turned back to watch the slices of toast sizzling in the skillet.

Sophie started to cross the kitchen to her mother but then Seamus pulled on her blouse. "No, Sophie. Watch! Watch the stove. Don't burn the French toast."

At that, Siobhan's face relaxed into a smile and it seemed the whole kitchen breathed again.

Leocadia explained to her grandmother that she couldn't put any sad news into the letter because it would make her grandson sad. The old woman nodded. "Tak, tak."

"She say yes, yes."

They finished the letter just as Sophie brought a platter of French toast over to the table. The old woman took the letter from Siobhan and nodded her thanks. She got up to leave. Siobhan pointed to the platter of toast and motioned for her guests to stay, but, through her granddaughter, Stacia explained that they had taken enough of kind Siobhan's time and that they would wait for Tony out on the porch. As they processed across the kitchen floor, Seamus said, "'Bye, Cadia." The little girl smiled. She held her right hand behind her back and she wiggled her fingers in a wave.

"Sophie," Siobhan said. "Pour them some lemonade and then Seamus can take the glasses out to them."

She watched as her daughter did as she was told and then she looked down at the table. Sophie had quietly set the table as Siobhan wrote the letter. And the French toast was not burnt. Perhaps she'd let it go, that her daughter had come home so late and in such disarray. But she'd keep an eye on Sophie, she promised herself. She was still a mother, with responsibilities towards her children. Even if Sophie no longer considered herself a child. And the next time....

Chapter Six

"Can you just take them out some water? A pitcher, five cups…maybe two or three times a day, Siobhan? Westover Air Force Base makes them their lunches. We're just supposed to provide the water."

"We?" Siobhan had her back to her brother-in-law as she kneaded the dough for bread. She was grinning. She couldn't have said why, exactly, but she was in such a habit of giving Tony a hard time about everything, she couldn't stop herself.

"Okay, 'you.' I would do it but I have my own prisoners to keep an eye on."

"And that soldier won't be doing the eye keeping-on for you?"

There was an awkward silence, and Siobhan imagined that if Tony had both legs, he'd be shifting them back and forth.

"Hi, Unk," Sophie said. She had just tumbled down the steps from upstairs. "Can't we get a fan up there, Mom? It's so bloody hot! I keep falling asleep. I'll never get this stuff memorized for the exam tomorrow." The history book made a thunk as she tossed it onto the table. She then flung herself onto a chair at the table and grabbed a cloth napkin, left over from dinner, to blot the sweat on her brow.

Siobhan dusted the flour off her hands by clapping them together. Then she turned and crossed her arms over her chest as she stared at Tony. Her chin was tilted upwards as she studied him. "And so, tell me, your soldier can't watch them?"

"Okay, here's the thing." Tony took a deep breath. She imagined him going to confession, the priest waiting on the other side of the screen in the confessional while the penitent hemmed and hawed. "I asked for ten men, five for you and five for me. But over there at Westover, they think they'll all be working for me. One guard for ten men."

Sophie sat up, amused. She looked over at Tony, then at her mother, then back at Tony.

Siobhan, however, did not look amused. "And?"

"Well, I thought the guard should be over here. You being a woman, and all."

Siobhan bit her lower lip to keep from laughing. To her surprise, it was Sophie who expressed indignation. "What do you mean, my Mom 'being a woman, and all?' You don't think she's tough enough to boss those prisoners around?"

Tony lifted a hand from the top of the chair he was resting against and he patted the air in a hopeless attempt to placate the women in front of him. "It's just, well, it's just that the Westover people think a man is in charge of the prisoners. That soldier they send over here with them is supposed to give the orders. Strictly speaking, nobody else is supposed to be talking to the prisoners. Something about the Geneva Convention. And," Tony sighed. "I don't want to muck up this chance at labor. I'm behind getting the crops in as it is."

"Your father can't help?" Siobhan asked.

Tony looked down as if he were studying the grains in the wood of the chair. He took a deep breath. "You might as well know, Siobhan. He's lost his mind."

There was a snub in Siobhan's voice. "That's not news."

Tony raised his head and looked at his sister-in-law directly in the eyes. "No, Siobhan. I mean he's not rational no more. And he's losing control over his body. He barely walks. He shakes all the time. Wets himself."

Siobhan felt a stab of pity. "I'm sorry for that. Must be all that liquor he's drunk over the years."

"No doubt. No doubt. But we're off the subject. I need to know, Siobhan, if you'll take some water out to the prisoners, two, maybe three times a day. That's all. You don't have to have anything to do with them, just give the pitcher and cups to the guard, if you want."

Sophie stood up. "I'll do it!"

Tony grinned. "So you saw them, eh, Soph? Young handsome bucks your age?"

Sophie blushed. "That's got nothing to do with it, Unk. Blessed are those who give water to the thirsty, or something like that."

"You'll do nothing of the kind, Sophie." The tone in Siobhan's voice said there'd be no debate. "If it must be done, I'll be doing it. But I'll be having nothing to do with those murderers. I'll give it to the guard."

Tony gave his niece a sympathetic smile. "You'll have to look elsewhere for a boyfriend."

"That has nothing to do with it." Sophie's face was flushed. "I was just going to make it easier for Mom. That's all. And speaking about boyfriends, what about girlfriends? You got your eye on anybody, Unk?"

It was Tony's turn to blush which surprised both Siobhan and her daughter. "You do! Okay, Unk, spill. Who's the lucky girl?" Sophie slid back down onto her chair.

Tony's ears turned red. He shook his head. "Nah. Nobody. Who'd want a one-legged man anyway?"

Siobhan couldn't help herself. "Well, if all the other parts work, what's the problem?"

Sophie's eyes went wide with surprised amusement. "Mom!"

Tony turned to go. "I'm leaving before I get into trouble." The thump of the crutches punctuated his walk across the kitchen to the screen door.

Just then Seamus came bounding up the steps and he held the door for his uncle.

"Visiting that puppy of yours?"

"Yup. She wanted to come home with me but Momma says she's not ready."

"Which 'she?' the pup's mother or *your* mother?"

Siobhan went to the door and reached down to give her son a hug. "Don't be causing trouble, Tony. More trouble, I mean."

Sophie opened her history text, then looked over to Tony. "Hey, Unk! You're not off the hook. I want to hear more about your girlfriend."

"You got a girlfriend, Uncle Tony?"

"I do not." Tony leaned against the door frame and ran a hand through his nephew's hair. "Do you have a girlfriend?"

"Yup," Seamus said. "Momma's my girlfriend. When I grow up, I'm going to marry her."

Tony laughed. Sophie started to explain how that would be impossible but her mother gave her a look that said "Let it go."

"So you'll take water out to the prisoners?"

Siobhan held his gaze, but her jaw line had softened.

"I'll take that as a yes. 'Night."

"Good night, Unk."

The three of them, Siobhan with her arm wrapped around her son's shoulder, Sophie standing back at the kitchen table, watched as Tony hopped across the porch, down the steps, and then across the stones of the newly laid path. Soon they heard the engine of the truck come to life, the crunch of the tires against the gravel, and then Tony was gone.

Siobhan set the bread into the oven for the first rising. She glanced over at her daughter still sitting at the kitchen table. The girl's eyes were focused on the ceiling, her lips moved in a mumbling murmur, her right hand clicked off the fingers of her left, one at a time. Sophie became aware of her mother quietly looking at her. "Aargh!" she screamed. "I hate history!" She shook her head ferociously, then took up her pencil and began writing in her notebook.

Siobhan glanced over at the counter. The supper dishes were washed and put away. The counters were clean. Until it was time to knead the dough again and shape the bread, she suddenly felt empty with nothing to do. Yes, there was mending; yes, there was dusting; yes, there was sweeping up the kitchen floor; but it didn't feel like those things mattered. Siobhan felt useless, like someone waiting to be given a new purpose in life. She'd had that feeling a lot of late, ever since she learned that Stan had died. She shook her head. There was plenty to do. Two children to raise and her summer garden to tend to so they would have the canned vegetables to last the winter. Now, those prisoners. Take them water? The very idea.

And yet with all there was to do, she stood paralyzed. Sophie studying; Seamus back over at the Tudryn barn--did they really need her? Nothing seemed to matter much and she found herself struggling against the impulse to slip upstairs, close her door, lie down on her bed, and move her heart and thoughts back to the past.

"Can I help?" Siobhan heard her voice ask.

Sophie looked up from her notebook, surprised. "Well, yeah, sure, Mom. I'm so tired that I'm having trouble concentrating, but here--" she turned the notebook around and shoved it towards the opposite side of the table.

Siobhan sat down across from her daughter.

"I wrote down the questions Miss Dwyer gave us, and then the answers I think she wants for each one. You can ask me them and see if I get all the parts of the answer. Okay?"

Siobhan smiled. She felt a flush of pride for her daughter. She herself had not finished high school. Siobhan and her father had crossed the ocean and worked in the market in Boston. There was no time to be spent at a desk in a classroom. Siobhan was grateful to her father for paying for the little tutoring he could afford for her at the convent.

"Okay," Siobhan looked down at the notebook. "What were the causes that led to the world war?"

Sophie got up from the table and began pacing back and forth as she recited the answers to the questions her mother asked. At one point, she looked over to her mother. "This is nice, Mom, you and me."

Siobhan flushed. She was much more accustomed to yelling at her daughter and having her daughter yell back. She just nodded and asked, "What were the reasons the United States entered into the war?"

Almost an hour had passed when Seamus raced up the porch steps and flung open the screen door. "Momma! They're here!"

"Who's here?"

Then she heard the familiar rumble of Tony's truck. She shook her head. "Now what?"

"Iggy, Momma! And Leon!"

Siobhan felt the terror her son must be feeling; she stood and wrapped her arms around him. Sophie flushed with anger. "Those boys still tormentin' you? I'll punch their lights out." She ran out to the porch and nearly knocked Tony over. Behind him stood the two terrorists, their faces pale with fright.

Silence escorted Tony and the two boys into the kitchen. Iggy and Leon made a point of not locking eyes with Sophie. Or anyone else for that matter.

"Gentlemen," Tony said, leaning against the door frame. "Don't you have something to say to this young man?" He lifted a crutch and pointed it at Seamus.

Seamus stepped away from his mother. His eyes were huge with--Siobhan couldn't have said *what* it was. Fright? Wonder? He looked so small to her. Small and scared and incredibly brave. She felt her heart shiver.

"We're sorry," Iggy mumbled.

"That's no way to do it, you coward!" Tony roared. He lifted a crutch towards the boys quivering behind him and tapped each one on the shoulder. "Get out from behind me! Stand up like men. Apologize like men, you miscreants!"

The boys scrambled out from underneath the crutch and faced Siobhan. Iggy said, "We're sorry for calling him names."

Tony whacked each boy again on the shoulder again. "Not to her! You apologize to the boy, to Seamus. He's the one you offended."

Leon took a deep breath then forced himself to look at Seamus. "It was wrong of us to call you names. We're sorry."

Tony tapped Iggy on the shoulder. The boy stumbled forward, eager to escape Tony's crutch. "Me too."

"You too what?" Tony roared.

"I'm sorry too for calling you names."

Tony nudged their backsides with the tip of his crutch. "And what else?"

Leon took the initiative this time. "And we're sorry about your soldiering Daddy."

"He was very brave. We are proud that he was a son of Hadley," Iggy added, the line delivered like a memorized poem.

Then there was silence again. Sophie stared at the two boys, her hands balled into fists. Siobhan resisted the impulse to scoop up her son into her arms. Seamus looked up at the boys. The two "miscreants" fidgeted, their eyes roaming the ceiling of the kitchen. Tony breathed heavily as he rested his body against the wall just inside the door. His face was flushed and there was the sweet cloying smell of alcohol clinging to his person. And Seamus, Seamus stood like an island, abandoned and floating in the sea. He looked up at his mother who smiled back at him. He looked to Sophie who mimed punching the boys in the stomach. He looked to Tony who nodded back at him, indicating it was Seamus's move next.

"Okay." Seamus smiled at the two boys. "Do you want to see some puppies?"

The shoulders on Leon and Iggy visibly relaxed. Their breath whistled through their teeth as they exhaled.

"Yeah, sure," they said as one.

The two boys followed Seamus out the door and across the porch.

Tony shouted after them. "Don't be long!" He turned to face Siobhan. "I promised their Mommas I'd have them back 'fore dark and it's nearly that now."

Sophie turned to Tony, flexing her fingers, stiff from balling them into a fist. "I coulda taught them two a lesson they'd never forget."

Tony grinned. "No doubt, no doubt."

"Thank you, Tony. Thank you," Siobhan said. She sat back down at the table.

"Hey, Unk! Do you want to hear about the roaring Twenties?" Sophie asked.

"Sure, why not." Tony limped across the kitchen and joined the other two at the table.

A half hour later, Siobhan looked out the kitchen window next to the table where she and Tony had been drilling Sophie for her history test. And even though dusk had made quite a dent in the long light of the early summer evening, she was horrified to see her son and the two older boys marching single file across the lawn from the Tudryn barn towards her driveway. Seamus was in the rear. They were chanting something and her ears strained to hear the meaning of it. The three boys had their right hands across their foreheads in a salute and they were swinging their left arms in a stilted military fashion. As they marched up the steps onto the porch, she heard it. "Whistle while you work! Hitler is a jerk; Mussolini is a meanie."

Icy coldness spread through her body. Seamus had lost his father; she herself was forced to use German labor to farm her lands. But beyond that she had planned to keep the war as far away from her son as possible.

Now she saw that she could not even win that battle.

Chapter Seven

Siobhan in the principal's office. The very idea! The very appalling idea! Actually not yet in the principal's office but even more appalling, outside of it. Made to wait while a secretary typed away on a black Remington and occasionally glanced up to give Siobhan a perfunctory smile.

Siobhan wasn't sure but she thought she recognized the secretary from the funeral, the sister of some brothers fighting in Germany, or it could be in Africa or even in Italy. It seemed like the war was everywhere and you never did know for sure where the soldiers were. Their letters came from overseas to the hungry hands and eyes of their families, eager to know on what ground their sons stood only to see any mention of place heavily blacked out by the censors. When Siobhan had scoffed at the censorship, Tony said ominously, "You never know where spies are."

The secretary pulled the typewritten sheet out of the Remington and inserted a blank one, spinning the carriage dial with a practiced right hand. Siobhan stared at the clock on the wall over the secretary's head. Three forty-five. She had been asked to report at three. Anger took hold of her mind again and she tensed, seething with fury. And where was Sophie? The object of the "principal's concern"?

"Shouldn't be long now," the secretary said. "I'm sorry for the wait but Mr. Banas was called out to the fields. Some of the baseball players got into a fight with a player on the team from Shelburne Falls." She tsked her disapproval. "You'd think with the war and all, we'd learn that fighting doesn't settle anything."

Siobhan's face was frozen. She couldn't chit-chat with that secretary. She had nothing in common with her and who knew what the girl really thought. 'There's the irresponsible mother of that wild Sophie Norowoski. Well, what can you expect, poor thing, her husband killed and all. She just fell apart.' That's what they thought of her, all of them, Siobhan was sure of it. And she mentally winced, thinking any criticism of her would be right, a woman who couldn't seem to bounce back from having lost her husband despite the fact that she had two children to raise and a farm, fallen into disuse, to resuscitate if they weren't going to starve. A woman who couldn't resist the call to climb the stairs to her bedroom, close the door against the present world, lie down on the bed, shut her eyes, and live in the past where her beloved Stan was still alive.

"Momma?"

Siobhan jerked. How was it that she had forgotten she had Seamus with her? The little boy had sat still beside her, his eyes roaming the walls of the office of the school where his sister Sophie went every day. But he began to get restless and swung his feet back and forth, the soles of his shoes hitting against the wall under the bench they sat on.

"Sweetheart, hold still."

"But Momma, I'm tired. I want to go. This isn't fun."

Siobhan felt her heart go tender. She embraced her son and pulled him to her. "You're right about that. It's not fun." She smoothed the boy's blond hair back off his forehead, wet her fingertips and plastered it in place. He looked like pictures of his father as a boy.

"I want to go home. I want to play with the puppies."

"I know you do, Sweetheart. Momma wants to go home too," she added, giving the secretary a stern glance.

She should have left the boy at home but who leaves a small child at home with those German assassins in the field just a few feet away from their back doorstep? And that guard didn't seem a bit reliable.

Siobhan's face tightened again. That was just another thing she was furious about. She took a pail of water out for the prisoners midmorning to Sergeant Whatever-his-name-was, as Tony had asked her to do. He was sitting at the edge of the field, leaning against a tree, cap low over his forehead and eyes, a rifle lying on the ground next to him. And what if the prisoners suddenly bolted, grabbed that useless guard's gun and went on a shooting rampage? Siobhan had kicked at the soldier's boot and he sprang awake, grabbing the gun and scrambling to his feet. When he saw that it was Siobhan, extending the pail towards him, his face broke out in a grin. "You got me," he said.

"Better me than one of the prisoners."

"Yeah, okay, relax Miss. Nothing's going to happen here. Take a look."

Siobhan's gaze followed the line of the soldier's outstretched hand as he pointed to the field. Tony had made the first pass with the plow the afternoon before and now five men were busy working the rich soil as if it were their own land, energetically, like they really cared. The prisoners took the hoes and spades and hacked away breaking up the clumps, turning under the weeds and sometimes bending to dislodge a rock which they threw to the side of the field. The field had lain fallow for two years and the soil was compacted. Silt from the spring overflows of the Connecticut River had proved a fertile ground for new weeds across the top of it all.

The soldier cocked his hat back and looked down at her, a knowing smile flirting about his lips. His eyes traveled up her body to her face. It was a familiar look, one that had happened in that lifetime ago when she worked in the Farmers' Market in Boston. She knew then how to slice the onlooker down to stumbling over his own feet and words, all with just a glance. Now she felt defenseless. What had happened to the spunk she'd had as a young girl? Suddenly, Siobhan wanted to cry, and that was not something she could ever do in front of that insolent soldier. She dropped the bucket to the ground, water splashing out over the top of it, and she turned to head back to the house. She could not let that brash soldier know how much he had rattled her, but it was all she could do to keep from running. It was a flight, nonetheless, and as she fled, she felt as if pieces of herself were falling off.

Even now, sitting in the principal's office, she felt the flush of rage and embarrassment, the soldier's laugh chasing her back to the house. Her hands were balled into fists on her lap.

"Momma?" Seamus nestled his head against his mother's arm. She smiled at him and when she did so, her face hurt. She hadn't realized how much anger had tightened her cheeks, her jaw, her mouth, the skin around her eyes.

"Momma?" Seamus asked a third time.

"Yes, my sweetheart?" Siobhan flexed her left hand, tight from the fist she had made moments before. Then she reached over and around her son's shoulders and pulled him to her. She could feel tenderness flood through her body and make her whole again. She kissed the top of his head.

"Is Sophie really in trouble? Is the principal going to yell at her?"

Some of the anger returned. "I suspect so. The principal just doesn't call you into his office, just doesn't call the mother down here for some little thing. It must be very serious."

Seamus's eyes flooded with tears. "But Momma, I don't want the principal to yell at Sophie. Sophie's my friend. My best friend."

It was true, Siobhan had to admit, and one of the most admirable traits in her daughter. Sophie loved her little brother. The boy's hair was once again standing on end. Siobhan patted down Seamus's hair. "Don't spit on me, Momma," he said, just as she was about to lick her fingers again.

Just then, she heard Sophie's voice out in the hallway. She couldn't make out what her daughter was saying, but she heard the principal answer, "It's just not something that I can ignore."

Sophie's eyebrows flew up when she saw her mother and Seamus sitting in the office. "Mom, I didn't--"

Seamus sprang up from his seat and ran to hug his sister around her waist. Siobhan stood and extended a hand to the principal.

"Yes, yes, Mrs. Norowoski. I do apologize for keeping you waiting. Let's all go into my office."

Seamus held back as the others passed through the doorway. "Come on, Pip Squeak," Sophie said.

Seamus beckoned to his sister who leaned down to listen to his whispers in her ear. She ruffled her fingers through her brother's hair destroying all of her mother's efforts. "It's okay. I can take it. And it doesn't mean you are in trouble. Not all the time." She turned to the Principal. "He thinks you only go into the principal's office if you did something wrong." Sophie wore the most innocent expression she could muster. "And I didn't do anything wrong, did I?"

"Well, let's talk about that." Banas indicated the chairs lined up in front of his desk. "Sit, sit." Seamus climbed up on his sister's lap.

"So," the principal directed his attention to Siobhan, "I asked you to come because I'm concerned about your daughter."

Siobhan shot a look at Sophie.

"Mom, really, I didn't do anything wrong."

"That's not exactly true, is it, Sophie? You missed your last period class two days last week, and this week, now, three days in a row. And I have to say you were spotted out in the field yesterday with that young Barney Mokrzecki lad, the one who, unfortunately, we had to expel last month."

Sophie jumped up, dumping Seamus to the floor. "Who told you that? Who? I know who did, that despicable Henry Kapinos, who should mind his own damn business!"

Appalled, Siobhan shouted "Sophie!" Seamus scrambled up onto his mother's lap.

Mr. Banas looked up at Sophie calmly. "Sit down, Sophie. Why don't you tell us about those missing classes?"

Sophie burst into tears. Siobhan stared at her daughter. She couldn't remember the last time she had seen her daughter cry, really cry. There were tears, yes, at Stan's funeral, but these tears absolutely flooded from her daughter's eyes.

"He, he--" Sophie began and then she was crying in earnest. She got up from her chair and paced back and forth behind Siobhan.

"I think I know what this is about." Mr. Banas spun his chair around to face behind him and took a box of Kleenex off a bookcase. He pulled out several tissues and held them up towards Sophie as he spun around to the front of his desk again. "Please, sit down.

Siobhan watched the exchange between her daughter and the principal, mystified. Unconsciously she pulled Seamus tighter against her chest.

Sophie took the tissues and blew noisily. Reluctantly, she slid back down onto the chair next to her mother.

Mr. Banas's eyes softened as he looked to Sophie. "I know this has been a hard spring for you, losing your father, and we--"

Sophie was on her feet again, furious. "You leave my father out of this! He's none of your business. This has nothing to do with him!"

A stunned silence followed. Siobhan stared at her daughter open-mouthed. Sophie had shown so little emotion after her father's funeral. The principal studied his folded hands resting on the ink blotter on his desk. Then he raised his head and looked at Sophie, compassion in his eyes.

"You are quite right, Sophie. The issue at hand has nothing to do with the tragic loss of your father. Please, accept my apologies." His gaze held Sophie's who did not lower her head. After seconds of uncomfortable silence, Sophie nodded, a nod so slight it was more like the blink of an eye.

"Okay then." Mr. Banas turned to address Siobhan. "You see, Sophie is a friend of Barney Mokrzecki."

"A friend, Mom, just a friend!" She glared defensively at her mother. "Which is way more important than being a girlfriend."

"And young Mokrzecki enlisted in the Army after he was dismissed from this school. Not something I wanted to do, understand, the dismissal, I mean, but there are rules and when you break them so many times, well, the boy left me no choice."

"Sophie--Sophie isn't going to--?"

"No, no," Mr. Banas waved a conciliatory hand in Siobhan's face. "I'm not going to expel Sophie, but her behavior has to be addressed."

"He was going to war, Momma. To war! Barney's only a year older than me, Momma, and he went to the war! Yesterday. He could be shot and killed. You know it happens, Momma, you know it! I just wanted him to know that somebody back home cares." She glared at the principal. "After he got expelled, it seemed like nobody cared about him. Nobody cared what happened to him. Like he wasn't important anymore. People made fun of him. But he's a decent guy. A human being."

The principal smiled. It was a wise smile that seemed to understand Sophie. "And you wanted to make sure before he went off to war that he knew someone thought he was a good person and would care about whatever happened to him."

"Somebody needed to be there for him. It wasn't right that he'd go off to war and nobody seemed to give a damn. I just spent a little time with him, that's all. So he knows somebody back here cares. So it's not so lonely over there."

Mr. Banas looked at Siobhan. "Perhaps you don't know the family, but the mother died years ago, the father joined the service two years ago, and the boy has just been sort of lost since then. The grandmother is elderly and can't really exercise any control over him. He acted out a lot in school, deliberately provoking people to dislike him."

"He just didn't have anybody," Sophie said. "He tried to make like he didn't care, but he was a very lonely guy. I couldn't let him be alone before he went off to war." She looked at her mother, her voice and her posture pleading. "I just couldn't."

Siobhan felt a flush of pride and love for her daughter. She reached over and caressed her daughter's cheek, flicking away an errant tear with her hand.

"Sophie, I understand and admire your compassion for your young friend, but can I ask why you didn't spend time with him after school hours? Why did it have to be during English class?" Mr. Banas asked.

Sophie was indignant. "I have cheerleading practice after school. I made a commitment. I need to be there! We are training the kids that want to try out for the squad."

"Well English class is a commitment also."

Sophie turned to her mother. "I can make that up easy. No problem. Carol took notes for me."

"Okay, so here's where we are." Banas's voice slid into official principal mode. "I can understand completely Sophie's actions. She's a good girl, Mrs. Norowoski. A bit headstrong sometimes, but her heart is in the right place, even if her judgment and common sense aren't always. Nevertheless, I can't just let the missed classes go. What would the discipline of this school turn into? Every student deciding he or she has a really good reason to disregard the rules? No, that would not be a good thing. So, here's what we are going to do. Sophie will go on probation--"

"What does that mean?" Siobhan asked.

"It means she has to obey the school's rules from now to the end of the school year which, lucky for her, is actually within sight, just a couple of weeks away. If she breaks a rule, she could be suspended or even expelled. In addition, she will stay after school every night for two weeks and she will assist the janitorial staff in whatever tasks they see fit to assign her."

Sophie's lower lip jutted out in defiance, "But you said you understood why I--"

"She'll do it," Siobhan said. She turned to her daughter. "It's a fair punishment. You'll do it."

Fifteen minutes later, Siobhan, Sophie and Seamus said goodbye to the principal. The secretary had already left and their footsteps made hollow, echoey sounds as the three walked down the deserted hallway to Sophie's locker, where she pulled out her English text for that night's homework.

It was late spring and a beautiful early evening as the three headed down Middle Street towards home. A couple of the baseball players at practice called out to Sophie. Siobhan couldn't make out what they said but Sophie's cheeks reddened. Her daughter didn't turn to respond to the boys.

"I'm proud of you, Sophie," Siobhan said, "but I'm also disappointed in you. There are right ways to do good things."

Sophie gave her mother an impish grin. "You're proud of me and disappointed at the same time?"

Siobhan nodded.

"Is it a tie?"

Siobhan hesitated. "Well, I think perhaps it is."

"Good," Sophie smiled, realizing there would be no further repercussions to her transgressions once they arrived home.

Chapter Eight

It was like a truce, the peace that was a temporary roof over Siobhan, Sophie and Seamus in the following month. There was only one skirmish and that was when Siobhan realized that Sophie was still in bed though she had been called more than once to the breakfast table. The madder Siobhan got at her daughter, the quieter Seamus got. Finally Siobhan went tearing up the steps to the second floor, fury on her face, and Seamus right behind trying to pull at the hem of his mother's housedress. "Maybe Sophie's sick," he kept saying.

Siobhan blew into her daughter's room, a tornado touching bottom, and yanked the blanket off her daughter. "Now!" she thundered. "Get up now! You are already going to be late for school. I thought we weren't going to have any more problems with you and school."

To her amazement, Sophie just giggled. That incited further fury.

"Young lady! I don't find this in the least funny! Get up right now."

Sophie turned over lazily in the bed and peered over to her wind-up alarm clock on the nightstand. "Okay, okay, Mom! I guess it's time to get up."

Siobhan's face was a murderous red. She didn't like the feeling, that feeling of once again being out of control whenever rage got a foothold in her. Ever since she got that telegram with the terrible news that her Stan had been killed, there had been those bouts of fury. She hated them; she hated feeling out of control. She had been fooled into thinking she was back in charge during the relative peace of the past month. Siobhan stood there holding the edge of the blanket in her hand and suddenly she had no idea what to do.

Sophie started to laugh, then seeing the fury on her mother's face, apprehension and worry took the place of laughter. "Mom, Mom, calm down! The kids are cutting grass."

Siobhan stared at her daughter.

"Asparagus time, Momma," Seamus echoed, climbing up into bed and snuggling close to his sister.

Brother and sister stared at their mother, waiting. Siobhan dropped the blanket, then she sat down on the edge of the bed. "Asparagus," she mumbled. "I forgot." She turned to look at her children and started to laugh.

Sophie and Seamus laughed too, but, as their mother continued to laugh, that laugh turned hysterical and within seconds Siobhan was sobbing.

Sophie and Seamus scrambled to sit beside their mother. "Mom, Mom, it's okay." Sophie stroked her mother's hair.

"It's okay," Seamus echoed. "It's okay, Momma." He petted her hand.

"We don't have asparagus," Sophie explained as if to a child. "Most of the kids at school are helping their parents cut grass. You gotta do it early in the morning, when the stalks are firm with wet. It's Late Start at school today. Today until the end of the month."

Siobhan's crying slowed to jerky sobs. "I forgot," she managed. She wrapped her arms around her children, one on each side of her, and the three sat at the edge of the bed rocking softly back and forth.

"It's okay, Momma, it's okay," Seamus kept repeating while stroking his mother's back.

Siobhan leaned down and kissed the top of her son's head. "I miss your father so much."

Sophie leaned her head against her mother's shoulder. Her face was wet with tears. "Me too, Mom, me too."

Seamus began crying in loud hiccuppy sobs.

Siobhan forgot about her own tears. "My Sweet, what's wrong?"

"I don't remember Daddy."

Sophie stood and went around to kneel down in front of her brother. "I do, Pip Squeak, and you know what? Every night from now on, before you go to sleep, I'm going to come into your room and tell you a story about Daddy. A true story. And you'll know everything about him."

Siobhan's eyes were shiny as she looked at her daughter. The outburst moments ago surprised and scared her. She thought she was getting better. She thought finally she was able to move on. It had been two weeks since she had escaped up into her room to lie on the bed and live in the past. But right at that moment, the desire was so strong, so powerful, to run down the hallway to her room, slam the door shut against the present, and fling herself onto the bed and onto the cushion of her memories.

Sophie wrinkled her nose in disgust. "Mom, something's burning!"

"Oh, dear God!" Siobhan flew up from the bed, down the hall, and down the stairway, her children tumbling after her. All three came up short when they saw Tony lifting a skillet from the stove.

"Ow, dammit, dammit, dammit!" he cried out, dropping the skillet onto another burner.

Sophie laughed, running to her uncle's aid. "Use a pot holder, Unk! Or don't you have any of those in that dump you call a kitchen?"

Tony hopped over to the sink and turned on the cold water. He stuck his hand under the stream and relief ran across his face.

Siobhan went to him. "Are you okay?"

"Of course I'm not okay! What's wrong with you, Siobhan? You coulda burnt the house down!"

Seamus ran to his uncle and pulled on his leg. "Don't yell at Momma!"

"What's wrong with *you*, Unk? You grabbed a hot skillet with your bare hand." Sophie picked up a potholder and brought the charred skillet over to the sink. She stared at the blackened contents. "What was it, Mom?"

"Pancakes," Siobhan said. "Here." She took the skillet from her daughter and she took back control of her kitchen. "Sophie, you better make some toast and then get off to school. Get the margarine, Seamus." She looked up at her brother-in-law. "I miss butter!"

"You and me both. If we had some, I could put it on my hand."

"They use butter to make bullets," Seamus announced solemnly as he went to the ice box.

"Bullets?" Siobhan asked.

"Iggy told me. But I like margarine. I like making the dot disappear. Seamus took out a new package of margarine and began massaging the food coloring into the bland blob of oleomargarine.

Siobhan set the skillet into the sink and then took Tony's hand out from under the stream of cold water. He shook his hand in pain and sprinkles of water flew at Siobhan's face. "Let's see. Oh, not too bad. I have some salve upstairs. I'll be right back."

Tony stuck his hand back under the cold stream of water.

Moments later, Sophie was off to school and Seamus headed over to the Tudryn barn to visit the puppies. Tony sat at the table and let Siobhan rub the salve onto his hand. "Looks like you might get a blister. But maybe not. What are you doing over here anyway? Don't you have prisoners to supervise?"

"The guard can handle 'em. Besides, they know what to do. As far as I can make out, one of them prisoners actually worked in forestry before the war. They are hard workers, every one of 'em." He didn't disguise his admiration.

"Hmmm," Siobhan grunted. She stood and began clearing the breakfast dishes away from the table.

"Anyway," Tony sighed and his eyes took on a faraway look. "Chester died."

Siobhan stopped midway across the kitchen and turned to stare at her brother-in-law. "Chester? Chester, your father?"

Tony nodded. He looked so sad and dejected that Siobhan set the dishes on the counter next to the sink and then went back to sit across from her brother-in-law. "I'm sorry,

Tony." She reached her arms over the table and wrapped her hands around his. His hands were big under hers. Big and rough with hardened calluses. And the right hand was slippery with the salve.

"Yup. Chester is gone. Actually he was gone a long time ago. The liquor took him after Mom died. That and probably the loneliness. Anyway," a long sigh whistled out from him, "the body went last night."

The two sat in silence, hands wrapped around each other's.

"Nobody left but me."

"And us, Tony, you have us, Sophie, Seamus and me." Siobhan was surprised to discover that she meant it. Just a month and a half earlier, she would have had nothing to do with her brother-in-law, lumping him in with all the rest of Polish Hadley who had never welcomed her into their hearts. But since Stan died, well, so much had changed in her life.

Tony slid his hands out from under hers and stood. "Anyway, just wanted to tell you that the funeral is this Saturday."

"At St. John's?"

Tony grinned down at her. "At Holy Rosary. You know that."

Siobhan sighed. Another Polish Mass to suffer through. "Well, we'll be there."

Tony made as if to leave, at the screen door, he turned back to face Siobhan. "Oh, you know those fields Stan bought down at the Meadows across from the river?"

"He was going to plant them after he came back from the war."

"I'm thinking we'll use the prisoners to get the fields ready. The soil is good there for potatoes. So I'm thinking that's what you should plant there. We can sell them to the army. John Mish told me about it. He's got a contract with the government."

"Doesn't it flood there a lot?"

"Earlier in the spring, yes, when the snowpack up north melts off and swells the river. But it's the end of May, Siobhan.

There shouldn't be any danger by the time we get the potatoes in."

"Unless we get another hurricane."

Tony shook his head in exasperation. Siobhan bit her tongue. She had to learn not to keep finding fault with everything Tony said. "Not likely. In my lifetime, that only happened once! So what do you say, Siobhan? Okay to plant potatoes there?"

She felt a pang of helplessness. "I don't have the seed money, Tony."

"That's okay. I thought about that. I'm going to get a loan. For the potatoes and for the prisoners. We can pay it back after the harvest."

There was nothing Siobhan could say so she just nodded. "Take care with that hand. If it blisters you don't want it to get infected. Wait, let me get a clean cloth and wrap around it. That way it'll be protected."

Moments later, Siobhan sat at the table, listening as Tony's crutches made thumps across the porch floor and down the steps. Then she was surprised to hear the thumping again as Tony made his way back into the kitchen.

"Forget something?" Siobhan asked.

"Yeah. I was thinking. I'm having trouble keeping up with the grass this year. The prisoners don't get here until a little later and by then sun's well up. The stalks start to wilt. You want to have them firm with water. The earlier in the morning the better with asparagus. Do you think Sophie could help out?"

Siobhan grinned. Sophie's sleep-in would be over. Her daughter'd have to get up even earlier than she did for the regular start of school.

"She'll be happy to help. I'll let her know."

Chapter Nine

Siobhan cleared the food from the supper table. Sophie was already at the sink filling the dishpan with soapy water. "Hop to, Pip Squeak," she shouted over to her brother who was still sitting at the table and, in her opinion, stalling for time by making Francie sit up and beg. After a long debate, Seamus had decided to name the dog "France" in honor of the country where his father's final battle took place.

"Look, Mama, I taught her how to ask for a treat!"

Seamus beamed. The boy surprised them all by housebreaking the dog in a week's time after she was weaned. In the beginning, Tony spent a lot of time with Seamus teaching him how to train the dog. Now the boy was coming up with his own signals for Francie and he spent hours with her, drilling her over and over and rewarding her with nibbles of stale bread.

Siobhan looked over at her son from the icebox where she was storing the leftovers. "You did, or Tony did?"

"*I* did, Momma. Tony taught me how to do it, and then I taught Francie. She is a really smart dog. Look, Momma! Look, Sophie!"

Exasperated, Sophie glanced over her shoulder at Seamus. "'Taught,' not 'teached.'"

"What?"

"You don't say 'teached.' There's no such word. You say, 'Tony taught me how to do it.' Not 'teached' me. You're talking in the past tense."

"What?"

Siobhan ducked her head down behind the door of the icebox to hide her grin. Sophie rolled her eyes. "Oh, never mind! Quit stalling! It's your job to get the dishes over to the sink. I'm ready to wash and look! No dishes. I already washed Momma's."

"That's because Momma took her dishes over. Why didn't you take your dishes over?" Seamus heaved a grown-up sigh and stood up. "We'll play later, Francie." He took his own plate over to Sophie who plunged it into the soapy water.

"What about your milk glass? And my dishes?"

"I don't see why you don't take your own dishes, Sophie. Like Momma does."

"Then how would you ever learn what's supposed to be done? Besides it's your job to bring the dishes over."

Seamus slumped his shoulders and turned to Siobhan. He dropped his arms dramatically and the dish towel dragged on the floor. "Momma?"

"What did I tell you?"

"But Sophie should take her own dishes over when she gets up!"

"But what did I tell you?"

Seamus's recited in a sing-song, "The more you complain, the longer it takes."

Siobhan took the dish rag from Sophie's hand and went over to wipe off the table.

"Hey! How am I supposed to wash without a rag?"

After she finished, Siobhan said, "Catch!" and tossed the rag over to Sophie, who missed and the rag landed on the floor.

"Mom!"

"Oh, bend over and pick it up. Don't be such a martyr!"

Siobhan went to get the broom to sweep the kitchen floor. Seamus was back over at the table petting Francie who rewarded him with big sloppy kisses on his cheeks. Seamus giggled. "That tickles!"

"Pip Squeak! You're not done. Get over here and dry the dishes. I already did you a favor and dried Mom's."

Seamus dragged the stool over to the sink and stepped up. He picked up the towel from the counter and then took a soapy dish from his sister. "Hey, you have to rinse the dishes! You have to get all the soap off or we'll get sick!"

"I'm thinking you are getting so big, Little Man, that you could take over the job of rinsing the dishes before you dry them."

"Momma!"

"Rinse the dishes, Sophie. You know better."

"Mom, do you realize you always take his side?"

Siobhan ignored Sophie. She went into the front room and came back with paper and pencils. She looked over to Sophie who was blowing soap bubbles in Seamus's face while the boy batted at them, pretending to be annoyed. "When are report cards ready for pickup, Sophie? And stop that. You're getting suds all over the floor."

"Yeah, Soapie Sophie, stop that!" Seamus burst out in a fit of giggles. "Soapie Sophie, Soapie Sophie!"

"Next Monday, I think, Mom. You are going to be surprised at how good my grades are."

"That *will* be a nice surprise."

"Mom, you don't need to be sarcastic. Besides, now that I decided I'm going to college and get a degree, I understand how important it is to get good grades. Before, I couldn't see the point. But I'm not gonna end up some Polish farmer's wife. I'm going to have a career."

Siobhan hid a smile. Getting Sophie to take her schoolwork seriously had been a battle since elementary school. She had to admit that after Barney Mokrzecki left for the service, she had noticed a real determination in her daughter. Not once did she have to remind her to do her homework, or study for exams.

"Hey, stop that, Little Man!"

Seamus had cupped his hands around some soap bubbles and blew them up in his sister's face. He giggled. "Stop calling me Little Man. And Pip Squeak. Next Monday is my birthday and I'm gonna be six and all growed up."

"'Grown up.' And wipe that plate again. It's not dry."

Seamus picked up the plate. "You'll have to call me Big Man after my birthday."

87

"You'll always be my Little Man, Pip Squeak. You'll never catch up to me." Sophie emptied the dish pan and Seamus peered over into the sink. He liked to watch how the water swirled around the drain before disappearing. Sophie handed the dish pan to her brother to dry, and she looked over her shoulder at her mother. "Are the ladies coming tonight, Mom?"

"Yes, the W's, Mrs. Windoloski and Mrs. Waskiewicz." Word had gotten out and Siobhan now regularly helped several mothers and grandmothers write letters in English to their beloved boys in the Armed Forces.

Sophie stood on her toes to peer out the little window above the sink. "Oh, I see them coming down the street now. Come on, Seamus, let's get these dishes done so we can get out of here."

Seamus didn't need urging. He didn't like how Mrs. Waskiewicz smelled--like old cabbage, he said--and she always pinched his cheeks.

Sophie dried her hands on the end of Seamus's towel. He tugged at it trying to get it away from sister. "Can I go over to Millie's for a while, Mom?"

Siobhan just nodded as she got up to greet Sarah Waskiewicz. The elderly lady used a cane now. She was severely bent over, but every week she came by to have Siobhan write a letter to her grandson.

Seamus and Francie were all set to sprint across the porch and go out to the backyard to play, when Siobhan stopped him. "Go and help Mrs. Waskiewicz up the steps."

"But Momma! She is a really scary old lady. She's got a big bump growing out of her back."

"Nonsense. She's just old. It's all the years of hard work that have her bent over."

Seamus's eyes went wide. "Will you get a big bump in your back when you get old, Momma?"

"Most likely."

Seamus scrunched up his face in disgust and shuddered.

Sophie punched her brother playfully and then bent over imitating the elderly woman's way of walking. "You'll get one too."

"Not me! I'm never getting old! Come on, Francie!"

"Good evening, Mrs. Waskiewicz." Siobhan had to shout as the old woman was going deaf. She gave her son a gentle nudge and Seamus went across the porch. He held out a hand to the old woman. Francie followed the boy, wagging her tail.

"What do you say, Seamus?"

"Good evening, Mrs. Waskiewicz," Seamus shouted. Francie barked.

Sophie slid by her mother. "Hi, Mrs. Waski," she said and then she was gone, down the steps and out the driveway. Released from duty, the boy and his dog bounded out the door to the back yard. Seamus had a ball in his hand. He was teaching Francie to fetch.

Moments later, Siobhan was seated with Sarah Waskiewicz and Anna Windoloski at the table. Anna was much younger and she translated for Sarah who had never learned much English. Siobhan actually didn't need her to translate because the older woman's letters to her grandson were always the same. "How are you, Michael? I am fine. Your mother and sisters are fine. We are very proud of you fighting against that devil Hitler. How is the weather where you are? The weather here is nice. We love you and pray for you every day. Lots of love, Babcia."

Anna's English was quite good but she had only gone to school for a few years in Poland before she arrived in Hadley and had never learned to write in English.

Siobhan got up to make tea for the women before she began Sarah's letter. The women preferred coffee but it had gotten scarce when the German U boats attacked the ships from Brazil. Even store-bought tea was not to be found. Siobhan wondered briefly what women who weren't farmers used to make tea. 'This damned war,' Siobhan thought.

She looked over her shoulder to the women. "Anna, you have some of those prisoners working your fields, don't you?"

"Tak, tak! They are good workers, those Germans. Good workers."

Siobhan carried the tea cups over to the table. She hesitated, then asked what she had been dying to ask the ladies the past two months. "Doesn't it bother you? I mean, they killed and wounded our soldiers. Doesn't it bother you to have them on your fields? Doesn't it make you angry?"

Anna's eyes opened in surprise. Sarah Waskiewicz didn't hear Siobhan's question. She busied herself pouring some milk into her tea, then added several teaspoons of sugar, a real treat as sugar was very scarce and they didn't have any where she lived with her son and his family. Siobhan herself had very little sugar left, and, even though she had some red rationing stamps to buy more, there hadn't been any sugar the last two times she went to the store. She hoarded it for social occasions, which, other than her letter writing nights, were non-existent.

"Angry?" Anna took the cup from Siobhan. "Thanks, dear. Why, Siobhan? Why would I be angry? Without their help we wouldn't be able to get our crops in. And then where would we be? Besides that, those Germans are very hard workers."

Embarrassed, Siobhan sat back down at the table. She hadn't prepared herself any tea. There was so little left from last summer that she rationed herself just one cup a day. "Well, yes, I have noticed that. They do work very hard. And you're right. With Stan gone--"

And it happened again.

Each time she was sure that the next time she mentioned her husband's name, she would be able to do so without tears flooding her eyes and a lump clogging her throat. Siobhan prided herself on resisting the temptation to slip upstairs to her bedroom to live in the past. It had been a full three weeks since she had last given in to the temptation. But the tears, she didn't seem to have control over them. They surprised her when she was least prepared.

Anna reached a hand across and squeezed Siobhan's. "It takes time." Touched by the woman's sympathy, Siobhan nodded her thanks, then grabbed for the skirt of her apron to blot her eyes.

Sarah looked up, startled. She asked what was wrong, and Anna spoke loudly, telling her in Polish that they were remembering Siobhan's husband. "Ah, tak, tak." Sarah also reached across to Siobhan.

Siobhan stared at the old woman's hand wrapped over her own. It was a rough hand, speckled, the joints permanently swollen. As Sarah's hand pressed over hers, Siobhan could feel that the palm and fingertips were hardened with those whitened calluses from years of working in the fields. Then she slid her hand out from under Sarah's and once again picked up a pencil. She always wrote the letters first in pencil and then after the women left, she would rewrite them in her best penmanship.

"But," Anna said, "you ask for prisoners. No, no I don't hate. They don't make the war. Hitler make the war, not prisoners. They suffer, like us."

Even though Tony had said the same thing several times, Siobhan had not been able to accept that line of reasoning. She thought that her brother-in-law was just saying that to get her to accept the prisoners working in her own fields and to get rid of her hateful feelings. But these women, Polish women, whose families back in the old country were at that moment suffering from the occupation by German troops, that these women could accept the prisoners and not blame them, well, that did indeed give her pause.

Two hours later, Siobhan sat back down at the table to write the good copies of the letters the Polish women had dictated to her. The women had left, and Seamus had had his bath and was tucked into bed. Siobhan pretended not to see Francie go up the stairs when she heard Seamus's loud whisper calling the dog to come to bed with him.

She looked at the clock on the wall above the sink. It was getting late. Perhaps she should call over to Millie's. At that moment Sophie came bounding up the porch steps. "Still working on the letters, Mom?"

"I'm almost finished. How's Millie?"

"Who?"

Siobhan looked up at her daughter. "Millie? The girl you just spent the evening with."

"Oh." Sophie turned her back on her mother as she headed to the icebox to get a drink of cool water. "She's fine. Whoa! There's not much left in the pitcher. I'll pump some more tomorrow, Mom." She stopped by her mother at the table and bent down to give her a kiss on the cheek. "Night, Mom."

"What's Millie been up to?"

"Oh, the usual."

Sophie left the kitchen and bounded up the steps to her bedroom.

Siobhan shook her head. How many times had she told her daughter to go up the steps lady-like and not wake up Seamus?

She turned back to finish the letter she was copying. Tomorrow she, Seamus and Francie would walk down the street to take the good copies to Anna and Sarah for them to mail.

Chapter Ten

It was a hot June, hotter than usual for that early in the summer. The prisoners had finished plowing and planting the fields behind Siobhan's barn and were now working on the other side of the river in the Meadows where Stan had purchased an additional field to expand their farming income. The tires on Stan's old car had dried and cracked and split open. Siobhan had had them patched so many times that there was no point in doing it again. She was hoping to get new ones with the rationing stamps she'd saved, but preference was given to tractors and other farming equipment. With the scarcity of rubber, there were no tires left for "pleasure" cars. When Tony's truck finally broke down, she lent him Stan's. So now if she needed to go some place, she had to walk.

It was a long trek over the bridge to the Meadows, especially carrying a huge jug of water in each hand for the prisoners, but there was no remedy for that as Tony had taken the truck to Boston to the markets. They needed the money, both of them, from selling the early crop of beans, so the night before she'd assured him it would be no problem for her to take the water over. He'd promised to see if he could get some sugar while in Boston.

Siobhan set the jugs of water down on the roadside and lifted her apron to blot the sweat off of her face. Up ahead, Seamus also stopped. "Sit," she heard the boy command Francie. He stood straddling the bar of the old bike Tony had given him for his birthday. Tony had rescued it from the back of his barn. It had been his bike when growing up, then Stan's, and now Seamus's.

She remembered looking out the window over the kitchen sink to see Tony hop alongside the bike, one hand on the back of the seat as he guided Seamus. "Pedal fast, faster!" she heard Tony shout. Francie ran alongside barking. And then he was doing it! Tony pulled his hand away and Seamus was riding the bike by himself, his little legs pumping fast. "Don't watch your feet!" Siobhan had heard Tony shout. "Watch where you are going!" Seamus looked up and in the nick of time he swerved to avoid hitting the corner of the barn. There was a wobbly moment of uncertainty when it looked like boy and bike were teetering towards a fall, but Seamus was able to right the bike and pedal off. He turned to look back at Tony, his face beaming joy. "I did it, Uncle Tony! I did it!" When he turned towards his uncle, instinctively he yanked sharply on the handlebars in Tony's direction. The bike tipped and tossed the boy onto the grass. Siobhan watched as Tony hobbled across the lawn, his crutches punching wildly into the ground. She heard Seamus giggle and watched as Francie licked the boy's face. "Don't, Francie, that tickles!" Tony bent over and picked up the bike, steadying it with the end of one of his crutches. Seamus was rolling on the ground, burying his face in the grass trying to elude the dog. "Quit fooling around, you two! Seamus, you always have to look where you are going!" Siobhan had let the tears fall. She couldn't help it. Grateful as she was to Tony, it should have been her son's father teaching him to ride a bike.

"Momma? Are you crying?" Siobhan looked down at her son. He had pedaled back to where she had stopped on the road. She leaned over and picked up the two water jugs again.

"No, Sweetheart, I was just sweating."

"Me too, Momma, but when I pedal fast, the wind makes me cool on my face."

Siobhan grinned. "Now remember what I told you and Francie."

Seamus turned the bike around and remounted. "I know, Momma, I know. Stay on the side of the road in case a tractor comes."

They had just gone over the bridge when a battered truck pulled up alongside Siobhan. "Ride?" the driver asked. She recognized him. It was Sarah's husband and he was even older and deafer than his wife. She pointed to the boy and the dog just up ahead and shouted up to the driver. "I need to keep an eye on my son."

The old man cupped his hand around his right ear. "What?"

"I need to--" She pointed to Seamus and Francie.

The old man put the truck in park, opened the door and slid out of the sagging seat. He took the two jugs and headed back to the bed of the truck. Siobhan felt a pang of pity as she watched him. He was bent over and with each step he seemed to stagger from one side to the other. He grunted as he reached up and put the jugs in the truck. He turned back to Siobhan and pointed to the fields where the prisoners were working. "Okay?"

"Okay," Siobhan nodded. She waved as the farmer drove off. Even though the situation wasn't funny, Siobhan grinned at the comical sight of the truck limping on ahead. Its tires were bald and the rear right one was badly patched with old rags. It ran lower than the others giving the impression of an elderly man gimping along. She ran to catch up to Seamus.

Twenty minutes later she was down in the fields where the old farmer had parked his truck. Nodding and smiling, she took her two jugs from him and went down close to the river where her workers and the soldier were sitting on the ground, opening up their packed lunches. She saw a couple of POW uniforms lying on the bank next to the river and looked out to see several of the men splashing about in the water to wash off the morning's layer of dirt and cool off. The men eating their sandwiches all had wet hair which glistened under the hot sun. When they saw Siobhan, they stood. One came over to her and reached to take the jugs from her hands. She felt an instinctive shudder of repulsion when the man's hand brushed against hers. Instantly she felt ashamed, remembering Tony's words, 'They're just soldiers. Following orders. Just like Stan was.' And Anna had said, 'They're good workers, those Germans.'

The soldier beckoned to Siobhan to sit beside him under the sparse shade of a scrawny tree, near the river. Seamus had already left his bike there and he and Francie were running towards them. "Momma! Can I put my feet in the water? Can I? I took my shoes off." The boy pointed to his shoes which were behind him lying on the grass next to the soldier. Without waiting for a reply, the boy and dog ran to the river's edge.

"No, Seamus, that's not a good--"

"He'll be okay," the soldier said. "We'll keep an eye on him."

"I don't--"

"Look, he's just sitting down on that rock and dangling his feet in the water. That's all."

"Well--"

"He'll be okay. I promise."

Siobhan turned to look at the soldier. He was a different one, not the brazen one whose eyes scraped across her body whenever she had taken the water out to the fields behind her barn. "Captain Shaney, ma'am," he said, extending a hand.

Tentatively, Siobhan held out her own hand. She didn't give him her name, however. He seemed like an old man, but probably not as old as his scarred and battle-lined face looked. Captain Shaney stepped back and swept his arm out, indicating a place where she could sit. Siobhan noticed the revolver lying on the grass at his feet. That's when she saw that one of the Captain's arms dangled uselessly from its elbow. Siobhan remained standing until her son came sprinting up from the riverbank. "Momma, that water is nice and cold. I'm going to learn to swim. Tony can teach me and then when I'm all teached and it's really, really, really hot, I can swim in the river."

Siobhan's face went white at the thought.

Captain Shaney chuckled. "That'll be a while yet, Ma'am."

But Siobhan didn't see anything funny about the situation. "People drown in that river. There's a fast and tricky current out there." She turned to look at her son. "And he's growing up way too fast."

"Yes, Ma'am. I'm sorry. I didn't mean to make light of it."

He was still standing and Siobhan realized that if she didn't sit down, neither would the soldier. She sat at the edge of the shade and pulled Seamus down beside her. Some of the prisoners had finished eating and were kicking a ball back and forth. Siobhan turned to the Captain, "Why do they kick that basketball?"

"Oh, that's not a basketball, Ma'am. It's a soccer ball. They play soccer a lot on the continent. You play it with your feet. The Red Cross gave the prisoners some balls."

Francie got up from the boy's side and ran chasing the ball. Just as she would get near it, a prisoner would beat her to the ball and kick it to another prisoner fifty feet or so away.

Seamus watched the men with wide open eyes following the flight of the ball. He turned to his mother. "Can I play, Momma? Can I? Please."

Siobhan was shaking her head 'No' when Captain Shaney said, "It's okay, Ma'am. Nothing bad will happen. These guys are still pretty much kids themselves. 'Cept that one." He pointed to the only older man among the prisoners. "When we came over this morning, that one showed me a picture of a little boy. I gather it's his own son. He tapped his heart and then he slid the picture back into a plastic cover, put it in his chest pocket, and zipped it up tight."

Siobhan looked for her son, but he and Francie had already joined the impromptu game. She felt her heart tighten as she watched him, her baby, running around among the German prisoners. They were shouting and pointing to the boy as to where he should be. Siobhan didn't understand a word the men were saying but Seamus seemed to understand the universal language of sport. In spite of the tightness in her chest, she felt proud when Seamus kicked the ball back to one of the prisoners, that older prisoner who had shown Shaney a picture of his own son. She was touched by the joy that lit up that prisoner's face.

As she watched, Siobhan noticed that the prisoners had split up into sides and some sort of game was going on. Seamus was on the team of the older prisoner. She watched as a ball was kicked towards Seamus and the boy ran to meet it. He gave the ball a kick so hard that Seamus landed on his back. Siobhan was on her feet instantly, her eyes on her son, but Seamus leapt to his feet just as fast and ran towards the river, shouting, "No, Francie, no!"

The dog had followed the flight of the ball which was now floating on the river's surface. It was drifting out to where the current was considerably faster. Francie splashed into the water and began paddling out after the ball. Despite his handicap, Shaney jumped up, grabbed his gun and sprinted towards the water's edge. The older prisoner beat him to the river and plunged in. The ball was nearly out into the middle of the river and spinning quickly downstream. Francie was losing traction as the current began to suck her away from the shore. With swift, strong strokes, the older prisoner reached the dog, wrapped his arm around her, and began to swim back to shore. It was tough going with only one arm free to stroke against the current, while the other held tight to the squirming dog. One of the other prisoners also jumped in. He swam out to the older prisoner and took the dog from him.

When all three, wet and bedraggled, came ashore, the others stood cheering at the bank's edge. The soccer ball disappeared down the river.

Seamus grabbed Francie from the soldier and hugged the dog tight. Francie squirmed under the boy's grip. "Francie, bad dog! You almost drownded."

Siobhan was at her son's side. He sat down on the bank and loosened his grasp on the dog but did not take his arms from around her neck. Francie shook herself and Seamus let go, dodging the shower of water coming off the dog. Then Francie licked his face with sloppy kisses. The dry prisoners stood around the other two slapping them on the back and congratulating them. Siobhan glanced back at Shaney who stood apart from the scene, watching and smiling. Behind them stood the old farmer, Sarah's husband.

Siobhan turned towards the prisoners again. She caught the eye of the one who had rescued Francie, and nodded to him. "Thank you," she said.

The prisoner waved his hand as if rescuing dogs from swiftly running currents was something he did on a daily basis. He came over to Seamus to pat the boy on the top of his head.

Smiling, he bent down and patted Francie also. She barked her thanks at him.

Siobhan felt someone's hand on her shoulder and turned to face Sarah's husband. He motioned for her and Seamus to follow him. Not once had that man shown any expression whatsoever, not when he stopped them just past the bridge, not when he handed Siobhan back her two jugs at the field, and not then either, when he escorted them back to his truck. Not even, despite grunting out his effort, while lifting up the boy's bike to put it in the back of the pickup.

Chapter Eleven

Seamus ran screaming up the side porch steps, the dog bounding along at his heels. "Momma! Momma!" He yanked open the screen door and ran into the kitchen. The puppy got shut out as the door sprang back in her face. She yelped, then, whimpering, pawed at the screen.

"Momma! Momma!"

Siobhan turned from the stove where she had been preparing a stew for dinner...lots of vegetables and some broth to hint of meat. Her face went suddenly white with worry. "What? What happened? Are you okay?"

Seamus bent over dramatically, panting loudly. He put out a hand telling his mother to wait until he caught his breath.

Siobhan knelt beside him. "Sweetheart! What's wrong? Did something happen to you? To Francie?" Siobhan looked up to see the dog on the other side of the screen door. She called out sternly, "No, Francie, no!" The dog stopped pawing at the door and sat back on her haunches. Siobban turned back to her son. "Are you hurt?"

Seamus shook his head. "No, no Momma, but something terrible happened!"

Fear clutched at Siobhan. "Sophie?!"

"No, no, Momma. Sophie's fine. She went down to the river, too. Lots of people are going. Even Iggy and Leon. They told me all about it. Can I go, too, Momma? Please, Momma?"

Relieved that the 'something terrible' didn't directly involve her children, Siobhan stood and led Seamus to the kitchen table where she sat down. She turned the boy to face her. "Slow down now, Seamus. Tell me what happened."

"He mighta drownded! They don't know for sure. People are swimming out to save him."

"Who, Sweetheart? Start from the beginning. Who might have drowned?"

"A prisoner, Momma, one of the prisoners!"

"A prisoner tried to escape? He jumped into the Connecticut River?"

Seamus, exasperated, jumped from one foot to the other in impatience. "No, Momma, no. Uncle Tony lets them swim in the river after work. While they're waiting to go back to the army base. Lots of farmers let them swim in the river. To have a little fun. And they get washed up that way."

"I didn't realize they did that. And so what happened?"

"One of the prisoners swam out too far, and he got caught in the current, just like you said, Momma, when you told me never, never, ever, ever to go into the river, and now they don't know where he is. He mighta drownded. Can I go, Momma, please? I can ride my bike. Me and Francie. Everybody is going."

The boy jumped up and down in excitement. Francie barked from the other side of the screen. Siobhan turned to look at the dog. "You too! You want to go, too?" Francie jumped up and swished her tail back and forth so fast it was a blur. Siobhan laughed. She looked back at her son whose whole body begged for permission; his legs danced back and forth. Siobhan stood, untied her apron, put it over the back of the chair, and walked over to the stove where she turned the burner off and slid the pot off the heated coil.

"I think we should both go," she told her son. "To see if we can help."

"Yayyy!"

"But not on your bike. You stay with me. Right by my side. Especially if there are lots of people and lots of trucks. You and Francie. Maybe you should put a rope on her."

"No, Momma." Seamus opened the screen door. "She obeys me. Watch."

The boy snapped his fingers and patted the right side of his pants. The puppy trotted over to Seamus's right side and accompanied mother and son as they crossed the porch, stepped down onto the stone path, and then headed across the street to the Meadows about a mile away.

"See Momma, how good Francie is. I trained her!"

"You should be very proud. I know I'm proud of you."

Siobhan looked down at the puppy. It was hard to say who the sire was. The mother was a long-haired collie, but her growing pup was short-haired and all spindly legs. She'd be a tall dog. But Siobhan had to agree with her son. Francie was a smart dog.

Siobhan looked up to see that others were also heading from their farmhouses down to the river. She recognized some of the women for whom she had written letters to their soldiering sons. They nodded in her direction. Siobhan was surprised by the flush of pleasure she felt at their quiet greetings. She gave a little wave back. That's what they did in her country; you waved. But she was beginning to understand and appreciate the understated Polish way. What she had thought was snobbishness just a few months ago was just the natural Polish reserve.

Every time Francie made as if to prance ahead of them, Seamus snapped his fingers and the dog obediently trotted back to the boy's side. Seamus would stoop to rub behind Francie's ears. "She likes this, Momma, look! She's smiling." And it did indeed look as if Francie were smiling.

Mother and son had crossed the bridge and met up with the dirt road that led down to the fields in the Meadows.

They turned when they heard a horn beep behind them. Siobhan, Seamus, and Francie climbed up into Tony's truck. The dog sat on Seamus's lap.

"That dog be gettin' too big for your lap."

Seamus grinned up at Tony. "That's okay. She can sit beside me then when she's growed up."

"So what's going on, Tony?" Siobhan asked.

"Well, a prisoner got caught in the current out there. Probably drowned. Or made to drown," he added with a sly wink.

Siobhan's eyes went wide. "Made to drown?"

"There's talk some of the prisoners had it in for one of the guys. None of them would talk to him and he didn't talk to any of them. Kept to himself, you might say. Eddie Tudryn, the kid that just got back from the war on leave, said he could be an SS guy or SS sympathizer. The regular German soldiers don't want anything to do with them guys."

"SS?"

"Stands for Schutzstaffel or some such thing in German. They're like special forces under Hitler, like his personal bodyguards. Nazis, all of them guys."

Siobhan was stunned. "These prisoners, they're not *all* Nazis?"

Tony laughed. "No, Siobhan, the guys working your fields aren't Nazis. The rank-and-file soldiers, as far as I can tell, were just drafted and sent to war. Like our guys."

The truck hit a deeply carved rut in the dirt road and bounced into the air. Siobhan's hand instinctively flew across her son's body and the dog's to keep them from sliding off the front seat. She braced herself with the other hand against the dashboard.

Tony let fly a string of Polish swears. He glanced over at Siobhan after wrestling with the steering wheel and getting the truck under his control.

Siobhan was puzzled by the look on Tony's face. It was a half-smile and half-question. "What?"

"Just admiring your motherhood is all, Siobhan."

"Look!" Seamus shouted. "Look at all the people!"

There were indeed a lot of people along the banks of the river. The German prisoners were easily identified with their gray uniforms and the large PW stenciled on their backs. They were closest to the bank, all of them staring out at the river. But there were farmers too, hot and dusty after a day's work, and, increasingly, more women and children flocked to the field.

"Would you look at that!" Tony jumped out of the truck and pointed to one of the prisoners who was cradling a rifle in his arms, not holding it like a weapon, but as if he were holding a baby.

"What's with that guy?" Tony turned to a farmer Siobhan didn't know and nodded towards the prisoner.

"Shoulda seen it! The guard just threw the rifle at him and jumped right into the river to go get the prisoner that was in trouble." The old farmer laughed. "But look at him out there! Splashing around like *he's* going to drown."

It was true. They watched as the bedraggled guard made his way back to shore.

"That current in your river is a bitch!" he announced as he climbed out of the water. "He's got to be gone. Drowned. You can't fight that kind of force. But we have to be sure." The soldier shook the water off his uniform. The prisoner carrying his rifle walked forward and surrendered the weapon. The soldier nonchalantly took it back, but his attention was still focused on the river. His face wrinkled with worry. "We've gotta find him. We gotta have the body. We can't have any escaped prisoners getting out into the local area."

"Mom!"

Siobhan turned to see Sophie running across the field towards her. Loping along at her side was a tall young lad. Siobhan recognized him as one of the basketball players she'd seen on the court when she went to watch her daughter cheer in the old Hopkins gym. Jim? Joe? No, John something. John Callahan! She remembered because he had an Irish last name and she was impressed to find out the boy's dad was a lawyer, not a farmer. Though she hadn't met the boy's parents, she felt a kinship and was proud of their shared Irish heritage. She was later disappointed to find that the boys' parents hadn't come directly from Ireland. Nor *their* parents. She wouldn't be able to share her memories. The discovery had made her feel lonely all over again.

Seamus and Francie ran to meet Sophie and her companion.

"Mom!" Sophie gasped for breath. "A prisoner escaped!"

"So I've heard. How are you, John?"

"Fine, Ma'am."

"So Mom, what do you think is going to happen? They've been searching for him but so far there's no sign of him anywhere."

Siobhan shaded her eyes against the glare of the late afternoon sun on the river. She could actually see the rush of the water out in the middle. Even though the danger of flooding had passed, the river's current was still running strong from all the snowpack that melted up north in Vermont and beyond.

The crowd turned at the roar of oncoming trucks, army trucks, rumbling down the dirt road to the river's edge. Soldiers jumped out and within minutes were setting up flood lights. It would soon be dusk, then dark. They were determined to find the missing POW...or his body.

Tony went over to the driver of one of the trucks. "What if you don't find the body?"

The soldier glared at Tony for a few seconds and then barked, "We have to find the body. We can't have German prisoners escaping. It could jeopardize this whole work program."

Tony shrugged. "Oh, okay then, well, good luck. Anything we can do to help?"

The soldier's expression relaxed. "Well, yeah, okay, you know the area better than we do. We'd like to send search squads down along the riverbanks. That Kraut's been gone quite a while. No telling where he might have crawled out. Maybe you guys could guide us along the riverbanks. We'll break up into four teams, north and south on both sides of the river. Once these flood lights are set up here, we'll take the trucks and go back over the bridge and hit the other side of the river. Maybe you could see about which farmers might be willing to help us."

"Well, honestly, I don't think you need to go far up in the northern direction. That current's pretty strong. It sweeps everything south."

"Well," the soldier hesitated. "Just to be sure, though. We'll go in both directions."

"What if he didn't escape? What if he drowned?"

The soldier shrugged. "We've gotta have the body."

Some of the farmers sent their sons home to retrieve flashlights.

Tony looked behind him, across the fields, at the setting sun. It was big and heavy in the sky, blazing red-orange. It would be gone in another half hour, forty-five minutes at the most. "They're going to need some food. Something to drink. Hell, these guys have been out in the fields working all day. This search could go on into the night."

Tony turned to head off towards the farmers standing along the river bank. Siobhan pulled on his shirt. "Tony? Could I take your truck back? Some of the woman were thinking we should have some food here. Our guys haven't eaten dinner and they're gonna be hungry. We could make some sandwiches, maybe some iced tea, and set up a refreshment area here."

Tony nodded. "You can drive a truck?"

Siobhan held out her hand for the keys. She smirked. "How do you think we got to the market every day in Boston?"

She motioned to Sophie who had wandered off with John a way down the river bank. "What?" the girl shouted up impatiently to her mother. But Siobhan just motioned for her to come back up. Sophie grimaced, then turned to her friend who shrugged his broad shoulders. The two then jogged up the embankment.

Siobhan explained that she and some of the other women were returning into town in Tony's truck and would be bringing back food for those staying to help the soldiers look for the missing POW. "I want you to come with us and get that old table out of the barn and put it in the bed of the truck."

Sophie glanced up at John.

"Yeah, sure. Be glad to help." His wide grin made Siobhan understand Sophie's attraction for the tall boy. And stiffened her resolve to keep an eye on her daughter. "I can ride with you in the back of the truck, Mrs. Norowoski."

"Me too! Can I, Mom, can I? Me and Francie?"

Siobhan was about to tell the child it was too dangerous when John said, "I'll keep a tight hold of him, Ma'am. He'll be safe."

Siobhan turned to her daughter. "I suppose you want to ride in the back, too?" She was surprised to see Sophie blush. Amused too, to see her daughter hide the blush by being the first to lead the troop back to the truck.

Waiting at the truck were three other women, all of whom had come to Siobhan to have their letters written in English to their sons abroad. They had been matter-of-fact in their gratitude to Siobhan, confining it to a nod of the head and a hint of smile. Now they stood in front of her, that same matter-of-fact approach written in their demeanor. "We help," one of them said. Siobhan was surprised that the women knew what she was up to and then she just smiled. Somehow, the Polish women always seemed to know what was going on. And now she had to admit that their generous hearts were most always in the right place. The three women wedged themselves into the front seat, the younger one in the middle, sitting forward of the other two. They were careful to leave a sliver of space for Siobhan behind the steering wheel. Siobhan watched as John hoisted Seamus into the bed of the truck, then passed up the wriggling dog to Seamus's outstretched hands. John held out his hand to Sophie who slapped at it good-naturedly and hoisted herself up and over. Once in the bed of the truck, John wrapped his arms around Seamus while Sophie held on to Francie. "Sit!" Seamus commanded.

Siobhan pointed a finger at John. "The road is very bumpy. You keep a good grip on my son."

There was that red flush of embarrassment on her daughter's face again. "Mom," Sophie lectured. "He knows what to do. Nothing bad is going to happen."

"But bad things do happen," Siobhan muttered as she headed to the front of the truck.

When Siobhan crawled up into the truck and sat behind the wheel, Mrs. Rytuba patted her on the arm saying, "Dat's da kids. Dey tink nothing bad happen. We know different, don't we?"

Siobhan felt a sudden flush of tears at the unspoken sympathy behind the old woman's words. But she wouldn't cry.

No, she wouldn't. Not in front of those ladies. Who knew what hard times they'd suffered, hard times that had just begun with leaving Poland, their homeland. Siobhan nodded briefly and busied herself about starting up the engine.

She dropped the women off at their homes promising to come back within the hour to pick them up along with their contributions to the refreshments. The two older women said they wouldn't be returning down to the river but they would have food ready for her.

Back in her own kitchen, she warmed up the stew in the cast iron Dutch oven and sliced the bread she had baked that morning. Seamus and Francie had been sent out to the barn "to supervise." Siobhan smiled when she looked out the window. Sophie was giggling as she and John maneuvered the old table out the barn door and staggered under their awkward load towards the truck. Their laughter reminded Siobhan of herself and Stan, and she felt a blow of sadness so hard that she leaned against the counter, bent over. She couldn't breathe for several seconds.

"Momma, what's wrong?"

She looked down to see Seamus staring up at her, blue eyes huge with concern. When had he come back from barn? The dog was at his side and she also stared up at Siobhan with the same look of concern. It was comical. Siobhan laughed. "Nothing, my sweetheart. Nothing's wrong. Momma was just taking a two second rest. Speaking of which, it's almost your bedtime." Siobhan was going to tell Sophie to stay behind with her brother and make sure he went to bed on time. She heard John's laughter at that moment and thought better of it. "Listen, my sweetheart. You can go down to the river with us but as soon as we drop off the food and set up the table, Momma's bringing you back home to get to bed."

"But Momma, I want to stay till they find the prisoner!"

"That could be a long, long time. The current could have swept him way down the river. All the way to Connecticut."

"But Momma--"

"No more buts. It's already dark out. Besides, Francie is tired. She's still a growing puppy and she needs lots of rest."

Seamus looked down at the dog hoping for moral support, but Francie just gave a whimper.

"See, what did I tell you. Francie's tired. Here, take these plates and napkins out to the truck."

"Momma?" Seamus looked up at his mother, his forehead wrinkled in worry.

"What, my sweetheart?"

"I like the prisoners. Is that okay?"

Siobhan felt a sharp pang at the boy's question. How was it that he had come to like the prisoners? She led the boy and the dog across the kitchen floor to the porch. "Why do you ask?"

"Well, they're nice to me. And--"

Another shiver went through Siobhan. "What do you mean they are nice to you? When have you been talking with the prisoners?"

At his mother's sharp tone, guilt and defensiveness flashed across the boy's face. "Momma, I didn't do anything wrong!"

"I'm not saying that you did, Seamus. But when did you talk to them?"

Mother and son went down the steps and headed towards the truck.

"I didn't talk to them, Momma. They don't know how to talk my kind of words."

"But you said they were nice to you."

"Yes, Momma, they are. When it's time to take the water out, I help the guard. The prisoners always smile at me and one of them patted me on my shoulders."

Siobhan stood in front of the open door of the truck, uncertainty gripping her. One of those assassins touched her son? She took a deep breath. Tony was constantly pointing out to her that those prisoners weren't the ones who shot her husband. And even if one of them was, he was just doing his duty. Then last week, there was that older prisoner who jumped into the river to save Francie. "And we don't know how many enemy soldiers Stan killed. Nor how many German wives and mothers were left weeping."

At Tony's words, Siobhan's blood had run cold thinking of her husband shooting someone, killing him, even if he was a Kraut. Her husband had been such a gentle man. Everything he touched was with a light and easy hand. "War is a terrible, terrible thing, Tony." Siobhan had said to her brother-in-law. "Even if you're in the right and the other side is in the wrong." Siobhan shook her head. She didn't like thinking about the prisoners. It confused and bewildered her.

Seamus tugged on his mother's skirt and brought her mind back to the present. "Did I do a bad thing, Momma? Is it bad to give the prisoners water?"

Siobhan placed the Dutch oven and the bread on the floor of the truck in front of the passenger's seat and bent down to hug her son. "No, sweetheart. You were being nice to them. You should always be nice to people. You are just like your Daddy. He was always nice to people."

The boy beamed. Francie barked. That was happening a lot lately; whenever Seamus looked especially happy, Francie would bark.

"I hope the prisoner is okay, Momma. The one out in the river. Don't you?"

"Well--" And at that moment, Siobhan surprised herself. "Yes I do. But he's been gone a long time." It was a good feeling, that feeling that rippled through her. She discovered that no, no she didn't wish harm on that escapee. Or on any of her prisoners. Her prisoners! She marveled at how much her feelings had changed. How she didn't feel so bitter anymore. It had been weeks since she had slid away from the present and fled upstairs to her bedroom to live in the past, back before the war and back before German prisoners.

Siobhan shook her head. "Now, where is your sister?"

"She's in the barn with John. Momma, can you boost me into the truck?"

After her son and Francie were both ensconced into the bed of the truck, Siobhan turned to head to the barn, a frown on her face. She heard Sophie's giggle and quickened her step. At that moment, the two appeared in the doorway of the barn.

Siobhan couldn't help noticing the flush on her daughter's cheeks. What had those two been up to?

John Callahan sprinted ahead of Sophie. "Anything I can help you with, Ma'am?"

"You two can get in the truck. We need to get going." The words came out sharper than she had intended.

Siobhan shot her daughter a stern look which Sophie saw but ignored, pretending to be busy about boosting herself into the bed of the truck. Once on board, she sat on the opposite side of her brother and John Callahan and glanced up at her mother. "Well, are we going?"

"By the way, Sophie, there's a letter from Barney Mokrzecki for you on the kitchen table."

Her daughter's face lit up with pleasure. "Really?" She made as if to stand up. "Maybe I'll just--" then she caught John Callahan's look of curiosity and sat back down. "It can wait," she said, pretending the letter was no big deal.

"Mokrzecki?" John Callahan frowned. "That guy writes to you?"

"Yeah, so? We're friends. He's serving our country. It takes courage, you know."

John Callahan shrugged his shoulders and looked away.

Siobhan drove over to the Rytubas'. She had barely pulled into the driveway when John Callahan shouted, "I'll get it, Mrs. Norowoski!" and leapt out of the bed of the truck, startling Siobhan. The truck had not yet come to a full stop. He headed for the back door and came back carrying a large container of kielbasa and cabbage. Pauline Rytuba stuck her head out the door and waved to Siobhan. As soon as John Callahan set the dish into the bed of the truck, Francie broke free from Seamus's grip and headed straight for the food. Sophie grabbed the dish and held it high above the dog's head.

"Hey, Stupid!" she grinned down at the boy. "And they call *us* dumb Polacks! Put this up front with Mom!"

Red-faced, John Callahan handed the food to Siobhan. Francie whined.

Twenty minutes later, Siobhan was once again headed back to the Meadows. She had picked up food at the Zgrodniks' and then headed over to the Wilgas', where Audrey joined her in the ride back down to the fields. Because the front of the truck was filled with food and containers of water, John Callahan jumped out and linked his hands together to make a step for Audrey who then joined the others in the back of the truck.

Sophie gave the boy a smirk. "Ever the gentleman, eh?"

Dusk was giving way to the fast-falling night. John Callahan and Sophie set up the table under the floodlights that the army had brought and then helped Siobhan carry the food from the truck to the table. Within minutes several hungry farmers gathered around. Grateful, they offered to spell the others who were out still searching along the riverbanks.

Siobhan noticed the drooping eyelids of her son and Tony led him back to the truck. Seamus lay down across the front seat, his arm around Francie who busily licked the boy's face and then stretched out against the boy's body.

Tony petted the dog. "Who's your Daddy?" he mumbled. "You're going to be a big one." Then he went back to help Siobhan at the table. A new batch of farmers were standing hungrily at the table as Siobhan passed out plates with food.

"Any sign of the escaped prisoner?" Siobhan asked when Tony came back to the table.

"No. I overheard the soldiers. They're determined to stay all night if that's what it takes to get the guy."

"All night?"

"Don't worry, Siobhan. When you want to go back, I'll take you and Seamus. I'll stay until the food is gone then load up the table and the pans."

"--and Sophie."

"What?"

"You'll take us all back, me, Seamus and Sophie."

Tony grinned. "Worried about Sophie and that Callahan boy, are you?"

"She's too young."

"Isn't she sixteen? Didn't you get married at seventeen?"

"That was a long time ago. Things were different then. Besides, when Sophie finishes school, I want her to go to college, or nursing school. Whatever she wants to do. I don't want her getting married right out of high school."

"Aren't you getting ahead of yourself? She's just having a little fun. Exploring what it's like to have a boyfriend."

"Boyfriend?!" At the shocked look on Siobhan's face, Tony shrugged his shoulders and headed down the bank to where a group of farmers and two soldiers sat chewing on hunks of bread.

A short while later, Tony led another group of farmers and two more soldiers back to the table. Siobhan marveled at how well her brother-in-law got around on his crutches despite the uneven slope of the riverbank. She overheard him brag about his brother Stan who had given his life for the cause of freedom. Siobhan pretended not to notice when Tony pointed in her direction. She didn't want to hear expressions of sympathy. Siobhan stepped away from the table and tapped Tony on the arm. "As soon as these guys get something to eat, I'd like you to take us back. It's way past Seamus's bedtime. And where did Sophie get off to?"

Tony nodded to the right of the table where his niece was busy pouring water into cups for the farmers.

"She's going back with us."

Tony frowned. "Now Siobhan, why do you want to embarrass her like that in front of the Callahan lad? Like as if she had to go to bed when her little brother did? I'll bring her back in a little bit. I promise it won't be late."

"But--"

"And yes, I'll keep an eye on the Callahan boy. He gets out of line, I'll whack him over the head with my crutch and beat him to a pulp. And when I'm finished, I'll turn him over to Sneakers Callahan and she'll finish him off."

In spite of herself, Siobhan laughed. She'd heard the tales of how tough the widow Callahan was. The workers complained that they never knew when she was coming up on them because she wore sneakers and, before they knew it, she was lashing them with a colorful tongue for slacking off.

Fifteen minutes later, Siobhan gathered up the empty pans and plates belonging to the farmers' wives who had sent food back with her. She wrapped them in an old blanket Tony had in the back of the truck and then climbed on board and gently lifted her sleeping son onto her lap. Francie insisted on wriggling her way onto Siobhan's lap as well, but after she kept sliding off, she settled her increasingly lanky body between Tony and Siobhan.

Siobhan was surprised at feeling content, peaceful even, as they drove back to her farmhouse. She was surprised too at how easy it felt to breathe...in, then out, no pinching in her chest. She glanced over at Tony who was skillfully avoiding the worst of the ruts in the dirt road. And she was surprised again to notice that she didn't feel like her guard was up against her brother-in-law any longer. Siobhan looked down and caressed her boy's soft flaxen hair, nearly white like her Stan's had been. She laughed lightly as Francie nudged her hand looking for a caress of her own.

Tony glanced over at her. Siobhan couldn't make out his face in the dusky darkness of the cab but she felt the glance. "Don't think I ever heard you laugh before, Siobhan. It's a nice sound coming from you."

Instinctively Siobhan tensed. She said nothing for a few seconds, and then she took a deep breath. "Well, don't get used to it."

Chapter Twelve

"But Momma, I don't like my shoes! They hurt my toes!"

Siobhan looked down at Seamus from the sink where she was washing up the breakfast dishes. She had on her Sunday dress, an all-purpose gray. Earlier that morning she had had to repair the hem, again, and she found herself wondering how long she had had that dress. She stood in front of the mirror assessing herself. She'd lost weight after Stan died and now the dress hung out on the edges of her hip bones. Siobhan had lost her curves. She was all hard angles now. Whatever it was inside mirrors that slid down had happened to the one above her dresser and as she stared at her distorted image, Siobhan thought it was a perfect reflection of who she had become. And what was that exactly, she wondered. It might be time to think about stitching up a new dress. But why? she found herself wondering. Who did she have to get dressed up fancy for? Old drab gray. That suited her just fine. And for another funeral? Perfect.

Her son's voice pierced the melancholy mood that shrouded Siobhan.

"They really, really, really hurt, Momma. Look!"

Francie whined.

"I'm six, now, Momma. I need six year old shoes!"

The mood was broken and Siobhan laughed watching her son walk around the kitchen as if he were stepping barefoot on cut glass.

"Don't laugh, Momma!"

Siobhan dried her hands on a towel and then bent down to straighten the collar on her son's shirt. "I know, Sweetheart. You are getting so big! This is the last time you have to wear your good shoes. Today. But maybe Sunday church too. And then we'll see about getting to Northampton and buying you some new shoes."

At the mention of "buying," a shadow of concern fell on Siobhan's face. Luckily a check arrived the day before from the US Army. That would help, but money, or rather the lack of it, was beginning to be a problem. Tony was right to insist she plant her fields. All of them.

At the mere thought of Tony, she heard his truck pull up, crunching the gravel on the driveway. Moments later his crutches punched across the porch floor. Siobhan stood up as Seamus ran across the kitchen floor to greet his uncle. She noted that the tightness of his Sunday shoes didn't seem to bother him at that moment. And she noted also that Tony almost seemed handsome in a black suit she had never seen before. Not even at Stan's funeral.

"Don't mess up my hair!" Seamus admonished just as Tony extended his free hand towards the boy's head.

"Why not?" Tony's hand was suspended above Seamus's head as if he were about to bless the child.

"Cuz then Momma will have to comb it again and I don't like that comb."

"Okay. Fair enough." His hand dropped uselessly at his side. Siobhan thought that Tony looked unsure what to do with himself. The sudden awkwardness of her brother-in-law amused her. Tony caught Siobhan's smile and seemed to blush under the ruddy tan he'd acquired from the early summer sun. "I can't stand these kinda days. Let's go."

Francie barked again. Siobhan crouched down to pick some dog hairs off her son's pant legs and then eyed the dog suspiciously. "Seamus, did Francie sleep with you again last night?"

Seamus turned away from his mother. "I'll just go on out to the truck, Uncle Tony."

"Oh, what's the harm, Siobhan?"

"A dog belongs in the barn, not upstairs, and certainly not in the boy's bed." Siobhan left the kitchen and went into the hallway. She opened the door to the stairs. "Sophie! Come on down. It's time to head to the church. Tony's here and we're all waiting on you."

Sophie appeared at the head of the stairs. She had on her Sunday dress but her face was flushed and reddened. "Do I have to go, Mom?"

Siobhan found herself rushing up the steps. "Sophie, dear, what's wrong?" She put her hand on her daughter's forehead.

Sophie brushed her mother's hand away. "I'm not sick, Mom."

Siobhan had been hearing that sharp tone from her daughter a lot recently. "Then what, Sophie? Did Barney's letter have bad news?"

To her surprise, Sophie burst into tears and collapsed onto the top step. "I just miss him so much, Mom. So much."

Siobhan was startled. Until yesterday, Sophie hadn't even mentioned Barney Mokrzecki since that day in the principal's office last spring. She didn't think Sophie had even written him a letter, but then there was a lot she didn't know about her daughter lately. Siobhan sat down on the top step beside her daughter and reached over to stroke her Sophie's hair. "I know. You miss your friend. We can pray for Barney."

Sophie pulled her head away from her mother's touch. "It's not that, Mom. Well, yes, that, too. No, Barney seemed okay in the letter. There were parts blacked out, like where he was stationed and where he's fighting 'n stuff." Sophie was suddenly furious! "How dare the Army read private letters! How dare they censor! I know that's who did it, Mom, because Millie said her uncle's letters were like that. Did you know that?"

Siobhan nodded slowly. It was something she had never shared with her children, that Stan's letters sometimes had black strokes over parts of them. "I asked about that at the Post Office. They said that the government does that to protect the soldiers."

Sophie's head whirled around to face her mother eye to eye. Her face was a mixture of shock and rage. It was tear streaked. "What!? How does interfering with your right to communicate to your very own family, the people who love you, how does blacking out what they say to you protect them? Huh? Tell me that! How!?"

Siobhan tried again. She placed her hand over Sophie's and gripped it tight. Her daughter didn't pull away. "If the letters ever fell into German hands, they could give away valuable information to the enemy. They could know where to ambush our soldiers."

Sophie wilted. Just as quickly as it had come, her rage was gone. "Oh, I never thought of that." She leaned her head against her mother's shoulder.

"So what did Barney say that has you so upset?"

"Oh, he didn't say anything really upsetting. Nothing, really. He just said the food was crappy and we should appreciate the fresh food we have here because of the farms. That he misses me, even his grandmother. Even Principal Banas." Sophie laughed lightly.

"And that's what made you sad? That you missed him?"

Sophie shook her head and tears once again coursed their way down her cheeks. "It's today. It's the funeral," she managed to gulp.

"The funeral?" Siobhan was puzzled. She was pretty sure that Siobhan didn't know Tony's father, enough, anyway, to be saddened by his death. And then it hit her, and tears filled her own eyes.

"You're remembering Dad."

Sophie nodded, sniffing loudly. "When I was getting dressed, I just started thinking about the day we went to Dad's funerals." She gulped. "I just don't think I can go. Please don't make me." She squeezed her mother's hand tightly.

Siobhan flicked away her own tears and then took a handkerchief from the pocket of her dress and blotted her daughter's face. "But Sophie, dear. We should go, for Tony. He's done so much for us. Going to his father's funeral would mean a lot to him. We're the only family he has now."

"I know, Mom. I keep telling myself that. Getting to know Uncle Tony is like the only good thing that came out of Dad's dying. But every time I think of myself sitting there in church and everything being about death, I think about Dad and I just start crying again."

Siobhan was touched. Since Sophie had shown so little emotion at the time of Stan's funeral, she had wondered if her daughter missed him at all. "I know, Sophie dear, but this is clearly different. Tony's dad was old. He was sick a long time." Siobhan sat there stroking her daughter's hair. "It's not like it was for your Dad. He--" Siobhan felt her throat catch.

"She doesn't have to go."

Startled, both looked down to see Tony standing in the doorway at the foot of the stairs. He was leaning against the doorjamb. Silence held their gazes as they stared at one another, Sophie and Siobhan at the top of the stairs, Tony at the bottom.

Suddenly Sophie stood. "Yes, yes I do, Unk. I have to go. For you."

Siobhan blinked. Keeping up with Sophie's mood changes was getting to be a challenge.

Sophie stepped around her mother's body and bounded down the steps two at a time. The skirt of her dress billowed up behind her as if it were racing to catch up. 'Now, Sophie,' Siobhan thought, 'she's the one who deserves a new dress. Something bright and young and womanly.' She thought about that dress she had been working on, before that horrible day when Yantik came. It was still in the basket alongside the sewing machine. Siobhan resolved to get back at it, and get the dress done.

Siobhan watched her daughter throw her arms around Tony's neck and give him a kiss on the cheek. Then the two of them turned and headed down the hallway towards the kitchen. Again her daughter had surprised Siobhan. Stan would have been so proud to see how grown up his daughter was getting to be.

Sophie's face appeared back in the doorway that led up to the top step where her mother was still sitting. The girl's elbows jutted outward; her hands were balled up into fists against her hips in mocking severity. "Well, are you coming,

Mom? Everybody else is already in the truck. We're all waiting on you."

Francie whined as Siobhan nearly closed the kitchen door in her face. "This is one time you are not coming. Go to your bed." She pointed at the rumple of old blankets next to the door that led out to the storage shed. Francie obediently trotted over, pawed at the blankets rearranging them in a pattern that made sense only in her doggy mind, circled once, and then lay down, her head resting on her front paws. She stared soulfully at Siobhan who shut the screen door and headed out to join the rest.

Siobhan crowded in next to her daughter. Seamus was sitting on Sophie's lap. After Siobhan pulled the door shut behind her, Tony put the truck in gear. "They found the body."

Puzzled, Siobhan asked, "Whose body? Your father's? But I thought--"

Sophie and Tony laughed. "No. That missing prisoner's."

"Oh! When?"

"Early this morning. The soldiers had given up around dawn. Packed everything up and went back to Westover. But some of the farmers kept looking. The young bucks. The body had washed up along the Hatfield side."

"Oh, so he wasn't trying to escape. Just got caught in the current."

Sophie faced her mother. "Well, Mom, he coulda been trying to escape but that river just got the best of him."

"I hope it wasn't one of our prisoners. I like our prisoners." Seamus turned to look up at his mother. "None of our prisoners shot Daddy, Momma. They are too nice."

Words leapt to Siobban's lips but in the end she couldn't find any right ones. She reached over and squeezed her son's hand. "Ow, Momma. Don't squeeze me so tight." He looked up at Tony who had a grin on his face. "She always squeezes me soooo tight. And hugs me really, really, really tight. Sometimes I can't hardly breathe."

"That's because she loves you, little man."

"Yeah," Seamus nodded. "She loves me."

"And me, too." Sophie avoided her mother's eyes. "She loves me and she loves you." She reached around to tickle her brother's stomach. He wiggled away from her touch.

"And Uncle Tony. Momma loves Uncle Tony, too," Seamus added.

There was an awkward silence until Tony said "Well, I wouldn't go that far." He reached over and pinched the boy's knee.

"No, don't, Uncle Tony! That really, really, really hurts."

They had reached the church parking lot. For a moment, all four of them sat staring at nothing out the front window of the truck. Then, silently, they climbed down and walked across the parking lot and along the sidewalk towards the front door. Sophie held Seamus's hand while Siobhan and Tony walked side by side.

As they rounded the front corner of the church, Siobhan was startled to see John Callahan standing there in the entrance, tall and handsome in his navy blue Sunday suit. His hair was still damp from when the boy had brushed the unruly mop into place. Siobhan glanced over at her daughter and was not really surprised to see two dots of a sudden blush redden her cheeks.

"Good morning, Mrs. Norowoski." The boy nodded in her direction.

"Good morning, John. I'm surprised to see you here. I didn't know that you knew Chester Norowoski."

The lad stepped over to stand beside Sophie whose glance seemed suddenly focused on John Callahan's shoes. "I didn't, that's true. But I wanted to be here to support you and your family in this time of sorrow. Your family has suffered a lot of losses lately."

Siobhan felt her eyes flood with unexpected tears. She shook them away. She remembered how Sophie had bragged about John Callahan, that he was going to college, hopefully to that famous football school, Notre Dame, and follow in his father's footsteps. 'That boy is going to make a fine lawyer some day,' Siobhan thought.

Silently they entered the church and followed Tony down the center aisle. He stopped in front of the casket draped with a pall and placed a hand on top of it. His lips moved in a silent prayer. Then Tony and the others slipped into an adjacent pew.

Chapter Thirteen

Siobhan was used to it now, the thump of Tony's crutches against the floor of the side porch. It didn't even get her guard up anymore. She thought about that for a minute. Her body didn't snap up straight with tension strangling her breath. She shrugged her shoulders and hid her smile; her back was to Tony as she busied herself at the kitchen sink. "Sophie!" she yelled.

Seamus tumbled down the stairs, Francie right on his heels. "Watch this, Uncle Tony. Sit, Francie!" he commanded. The dog's hind legs immediately slid forward and her rump fell to the floor; her eyes never left the boy. "Down!" Francie hit the floor. "Crawl!" Seamus ordered, and the dog began to slink across the kitchen floor.

"See!" Seamus whirled around to face his uncle. "Francie could be a war dog! She could sneak right up into the front lines and scout out the enemy. That way no one would get kilt! Francie could save the soldiers."

Seamus ducked away from Tony's hand as it reached forward to ruffle the boy's hair.

"You're right! They should use smart dogs like Francie in the war."

Siobhan turned to face the hallway as she dried her hands on a towel. "Sophie!"

"She's still in bed," Seamus said. "She says she doesn't want to be a farmer."

"Sophie!"

"I hear you, Mom! Stop yelling. I'll be down in a minute!"

Siobhan turned to Tony. "What's the job for today?"

"Clipping onions."

Siobhan grinned. "She's not going to like that."

"I wouldn't be so sure. I got the Callahan boy working for me today."

"Oh, Tony, is that a good idea?"

"Onions. They're doing onions. It's a hot day. Sweaty hot job. You don't have anything to worry about."

"That's exactly what I'm worried about. When *you* don't worry, I know it's time for me to take over. Want some coffee?"

Tony's face brightened. "Sure! Did you get some sugar too?"

"A little. But what I didn't get is shoes for Seamus."

Tony sat down at the kitchen table. Seamus and the dog ran out of the kitchen, across the porch and out to the back yard.

"No?"

"They were so expensive and he's growing so fast, it just didn't seem worth it."

Tony took the cup from her. "But what are you going to do? Cut the toes out of his good shoes?"

"I have an idea about that." She sat down across from Tony. "There's lots of kids in town and other mothers must have that same problem. You know, kids growing out of their shoes so fast. So I was thinking, what if we had a shoe swap. People would bring in their kids' shoes that don't fit anymore and swap them for a pair that did."

Tony's eyes widened with appreciation. "Great idea. Where you going to do this?"

"Well, I thought about church, but then--"

"Yeah, you got to get a neutral site."

"Well, I think we could still use the churches to spread the idea and collect the shoes. Then I was thinking maybe we could use a room at the Town Hall, say one day a week, and maybe have a booth or something and mothers could come and get new shoes for their kids. We could use the church groups to clean up and polish the shoes."

Tony nodded. "You've given this some thought."

"I can talk to our pastor at St. John's about announcing the program but I was wondering if you--"

"Sure, I can talk to Father at Holy Rosary, but I'll probably get further if I talk to his housekeeper."

"Okay!" Siobhan felt enthusiasm swell within her. "And then there's the Congregational Church. Do you think they'd go for the idea?"

"Don't see why not. Tell you what. I'm going to see Norm Barstow about taking some lettuce and stuff to Boston. I'll ask him. I think he's a big shot in that church."

Siobhan slapped her hand against the table. "Sophie!"

"Mom, you don't have to shout. I'm right here."

Siobhan jumped at her daughter's voice behind her ear.

Tony stood. "You ready?"

"As I'll ever be." Sophie rolled her eyes dramatically. "Let's go."

"Not without a decent breakfast, you don't."

"Mom, I'm not hungry. Don't you know you're supposed to listen to your body? It tells you if you are hungry or not."

Tony hid a smile. He enjoyed those morning skirmishes between mother and daughter. Siobhan wrapped some bread in a napkin and held it out to her daughter.

"What am I supposed to do with this out in the field? Ants'll be all over me!"

"Eat it now, in the truck, on the way to the field. For God's sake, Sophie! Why must you turn everything into an argument?"

Sophie took the bread, unwrapped it, then tossed the napkin back to her mother. It hit Siobhan in the chest. Then Sophie took a big bite out of the bread and chewed it with her mouth open. "Sa--tish-eye'd?" she mumbled through the bread to her mother. Sophie let the screen door slam behind her as she headed across the porch, down the steps, and out to the truck where Tony already had the motor running.

The napkin fell to the kitchen floor. Siobhan stared down at it. "Fetch!" she heard Seamus yell. Then Francie barked her play-bark and snatched the napkin up off the floor. She ran in circles around the kitchen, Seamus right behind her, giggling. The boy grabbed a ball from Francie's bed and ran out across the porch into the back yard. Francie dropped the napkin and raced out after Seamus. Siobhan rescued the napkin from the floor.

The desire was so powerful, so sudden then, that Siobhan grabbed for the kitchen chair and bent over gasping for breath. Her legs wanted to run from the kitchen, run from her children, run from her life. Run upstairs, close the door, fall to the bed, shut her eyes and live in the past where all of life's problems had solutions and everywhere there was Stan. Stan smiling, Stan with his shirt wet clear through from working in the fields, Stan cradling her in his arms.

Siobhan collapsed back onto the chair and gasped for breath. She took in huge swallows of air. She fought, fought hard against the tears, fought hard against the desire to run away into the past. She bent over the table and let her head drop into the hole made by her arms crossed in front of her. Violent sobs shook her shoulders.

She was a mother. She had children to raise. She had responsibilities. She had to earn their living now. But why did it have to hurt so hard? Why did it have to be so lonely? She cried.

Siobhan didn't know how long she had sat that way, hunched over the kitchen table, her head buried in her arms. But it must have been a while because her eyes were now dry and achy. She was conscious of someone patting her on the back. 'Seamus!' she thought with a sudden urge to hide her sorrow. She bolted upright.

"Oh, good, good!" she heard someone behind her say, but it wasn't Seamus. He was standing at her side looking up at his mother, worry written on his face. Francie sat dutifully at the boy's side, head cocked in companion concern.

Siobhan whirled around in the chair. She looked up to face Sarah, the old woman who came every week to write to her grandson in the Navy. "Oh, I'm sorry, Sarah. Was it today? Did I forget?"

The old woman patted Siobhan's hand. "No, no." She pointed to a pile of clothes on the table. "For you. For the store."

Siobhan turned to stare at the mound of clothes on the table. When had that happened?

She stood.

Sarah pointed again to the clothes. "For you. For the store."

And then Siobhan remembered discussing the idea of a shoe exchange among the townspeople when Sarah and her daughter had come for the letter writing two days ago.

The old woman went around Siobhan to the table and began searching through the clothes. "Ah!" she said, triumphantly. She held up a pair of shoes, a kid's small shoes. Sarah pointed to Seamus. "For you."

The boy's eyes lit up with joy. "Momma! Look!" He took the shoes, sat on the floor and began to fit one of the shoes over his grass-stained bare foot. Francie grabbed the other shoe and pranced around the kitchen holding it proudly in her mouth. Seamus leapt to his feet, and limped across the floor after her, his foot half in, half out of the shoe. "No, Francie, no! Bad Francie! Drop it! Drop it!"

Disappointed, the dog let the shoe fall to the floor. She eyed it longingly as if it were a big bone, chunks of meat still attached to it. Seamus picked up the other shoe and once again sat on the floor.

"No, no!" Sarah went through the pile of clothes again until she found a pair of socks. She held them up to Seamus.

Siobhan, as if coming out of a trance, took the pair of socks and then squatted down on the floor next to her son. "You have to put socks on first. You don't want to ruin your new shoes." She picked up Seamus's foot and looked at it. "But first you have to wash off those feet. You don't want to ruin your new socks either, do you?"

"Okay!" The boy leapt up and ran down the hall to the stairs. Francie bounded after him.

Siobhan held the shoes and socks in her hand and looked up at Sarah. "Thank you! Thank you so much." She got to her feet and went over to the table. "Of course! Why didn't I think of that? Kids need more than shoes. We can make it a clothing exchange."

"Tak, tak!" Sarah nodded. The deep wrinkles made several parentheses around her smile.

Siobhan bent over to hug the old woman. "Thank you, thank you so much. This is wonderful!"

"Tak, tak." Sarah slid out from under Siobhan's embrace. "Good, good." Then she walked over to the screen door and, without even glancing backward at Siobhan, she left.

Chapter Fourteen

Siobhan, Sophie, Seamus, Tony and the ever-present John Callahan walked into the back of the Hopkins Academy gymnasium. John tapped Siobhan on the shoulder. "See those lights up there, Mrs. Norowoski? You have to know just where to shoot from because if you hit those lights, the ball is out of bounds." Siobhan gave a polite smile of acknowledgement. She knew that. She had been to several games to watch her daughter cheer. But she couldn't recall the Callahan boy making many baskets. The star of the team had been that Brown boy. The one who played Taps at Stan's funeral. He was short, that kid, but he could shoot.

The gym was nearly full, the place buzzing with greetings as farmers said hello to one another and talked over the state of their corn and squash crops. Their hands were rough with callouses, knobby knuckles swollen; their shoes, worn and cracked, were dusty with dirt from the fields; the underarms of their shirts were dark and stained; and, though they had brushed their hands against their pant legs and stomped their shoes before entering the gymnasium, it was clear the farmers had come in from the fields, grabbed a quick bite of supper, and then headed with their wives, tired and sweaty from a day of canning, over to the Hopkins Academy gymnasium.

Principal Banas stepped up on the stage platform, Frank Zalot right behind him. The chatter changed to a murmur of urgency as people began to take their seats. Tony stuck his crutch out across two chairs at the end of a row towards the back, reserving them for him and Siobhan and shutting out two kids who gave him a dirty look.

"We're going to go sit in the bleachers," Sophie said.

"Me, too." Seamus started to follow his sister when Siobhan reached out and grabbed her son's shoulder.

"No, Seamus. You sit with Momma and Uncle Tony."

"But--"

"No buts, young man. You listen to your Momma."

"But there's only two seats, Uncle Tony."

"You can sit on my lap. That way you'll be taller'n anybody and you can see good."

Seamus brightened at that and followed his mother and uncle into the aisle towards what seemed like the only remaining seats.

Siobhan hadn't wanted to come in the first place. She didn't want any of them to go. She didn't want any of them thinking about the war and she especially didn't want to hear any soldier glorifying it. Young men looking to escape the drudgery of a lifetime struggling with the soil thought being a soldier was glamorous and exciting. Serve Uncle Sam and see the world! What a load of crap! Siobhan knew what war was about. It was about dying, getting shot and killed and never coming home again, and it wasn't glamorous.

"But Mom," Sophie had insisted. "I want to know what it's all about. It makes me feel closer to Dad. To know what he went through." At that Sophie had stopped; her lower lip bounced as she struggled to control her emotions. "Besides," she said, finally, "Guys I know from school are over in the war. Barney's over there fighting for our country. It's like--" She stopped, looking in the air for the words to express her feelings. "Well," she looked her mother square in the eyes. "it's like if I go to the talk I'm supporting our troops. I'm behind our boys."

In the end Siobhan gave in. Tony had said he was going. So Siobhan said they'd all go. That way she'd know what was said, she'd know what her children were thinking, and if they were thinking the wrong things, she could set them straight. Siobhan looked up towards the makeshift stage. The basketball hoop had been raised and the United States flag was hung on the wall behind the podium. Principal Banas was sitting next to Frank Zalot, the young man dressed in his uniform. Frank, just a few years older than Sophie, was the featured speaker.

Siobhan remembered hearing from Sophie how Frank turned seventeen the day Pearl Harbor was attacked. The next day, Frank went to classes in the morning, and in the afternoon he left Hopkins, and his father drove him to Springfield to enlist in the Navy. Then, the very next day, he left for Boot Camp. He didn't finish his senior year.

There was a rumble as farmers, students and children alike got up from their chairs and stood for the Pledge of Allegiance. The Hopkins Academy band played the national anthem. Siobhan fought her tears as she listened to her brother-in-law sing the words, his voice husky with emotion. She smiled as she heard him sing "At the twilight's last *beaming*." She glanced up at the bleachers and saw her daughter singing along. Siobhan had asked Sophie to teach her the words. It was time to learn them. She was never going back to Ireland and, she realized with surprise, she didn't even want to.

Everyone stood again and gave thunderous applause when Principal Banas introduced the speaker, "One of our own, Signalman First Class Frank Zalot, here to tell us firsthand about his harrowing rescue at sea off the coast of New Zealand."

"Where's New Zealand?" Seamus whispered.

As if the young sailor had heard Seamus, Frank asked the principal to hold up a map of the world. "We're over here in Hadley." He pointed to New England on the map. "Our boat, the U.S.S. American Legion, was just off the coast of Paekakariki beach, waaaayyy over here." Frank brought his arm across the map.

"Pie-what?" John Callahan called out from the bleachers.

Everyone laughed, including Frank.

"Paekakariki." He said it several times slowly and then he had the whole audience say it.

"That's one of the things about being in the Navy. You really do see the world. I was excited about that opportunity. I never thought I'd see much more than the asparagus and corn fields in Hadley."

Everyone laughed. Everyone but Siobhan. "He's making it sound like an adventure. Like fun," she hissed.

"Anyway," Frank turned back to the map. "Our ship was over here."

"Wow, that's really far away, isn't it, Momma?"

Siobhan nodded to her son.

A boy sitting next to John Callahan called out, "What's a Signalman do?"

"Well, just like the word says, I was responsible for giving signals from our ship to other ships. Visual communication. You use hand flags and or flashing lights in Morse code, to spell out the messages."

"Your ship didn't have a radio? Why didn't you just radio messages?"

"Well, we did have a radioman, but radio messages could be and often were intercepted by the Japanese. So that's why we needed Signalmen."

"Oh." The boy sat back down.

"Anyway," Frank continued, "the American Legion was an attack troop transport ship and a training ship. We had 1600 Marines on board the day I'm going to tell you about. We were supposed to do some practice landing exercises on Paekakariki beach. We had 35 LCVP boats to do the job."

"What are they?" somebody called out.

"LCVP boats? Landing Craft, Vehicle and Personnel, LCVP. These boats had a ramp that you could lower for the Marines to disembark or you could unload cargo or supplies. As a Signalman, I was part of the 'beach party.'"

"Party?" another voice shouted out.

"Not really a party," Frank said. "Just the LCVP that took about 25 sailors, including me and the Radioman to shore first. We were going to set up the landing positions for the rest of the LCVP's. These boats, if it weren't a practice exercise but the real thing, would bring in all the personnel and then they would start bringing in the supplies. Thousands and thousands of crates of food, clothing, medical supplies, gasoline and fuel for vehicles, arms, and ammunition. Enough to last for two weeks.

"So it was also the responsibility of the 'beach party' to unload all the supplies. Then all the others would leave and after the landing was completed, we would also head back to the ship. The 'beach party' was the first to arrive on shore and the last to leave.

"Well, anyway, it was really early in the morning and still dark when we climbed down from the American Legion on ropes to get into these smaller boats. For you guys it was summer here, but where we were was below the equator and it was winter. It was blowing like crazy, pouring down ice cold rain, and because of the wind, the waves were really huge. The boats were bouncing up and down on top of the waves and our rope ladders were swinging back and forth in the wind. We couldn't even see the boats below us. We had to kind of aim for them and hope for the best. Well, we were soaking wet in a matter of minutes, before we even got to the boats.

"It just seemed like everything went wrong from the start. Not only was the weather terrible, the beach at Paekakariki is one of those where it gets deep gradually, making it tough to land an LCVP, especially with the tide going out. And, as our bad luck would have it, we were at low tide. So about a hundred feet from shore, our coxswain lowered the ramp, stopped the boat and told us to get out."

A man near the front interrupted Frank. "What's a coxswain?"

"Oh, he's the one that's the pilot of a landing craft, the LCVP. He ordered us out of the boat. We thought he was crazy. The water was ice cold, forty degrees if that, but the coxswain said he couldn't get any closer because it was too shallow and the boat would get stuck.

"It *was* shallow, about twelve inches deep, but the waves right behind us were breaking at eight feet or better. We took off everything from the waist down, our shoes and socks, too. We held up our clothes and equipment over our heads, jumped in and headed for shore. Halfway in, we were hit from behind by a huge wave."

Frank's body shook as he shivered from the memory. "We were in frigid water up to our armpits." He brushed his hands against each other as if to say 'Well, that's over.'

"I can tell you we were in a pretty foul mood by the time we staggered ashore. Since it was a training exercise, no supplies were delivered, but by now it was low tide and the propellers of our thirty-five LCVPs were stuck in the sand. We were stranded. I radioed back to the ship for help. Later, a lot later, a New Zealand company sent over a vehicle that had huge rubber tires and a huge crane. The crane lifted up our boats, one by one, and then set them back down in deeper water. It was a very slow process. As was the protocol, our boat was the last to leave, but by that time it was dark again, past nine p.m. The tide had come back in so, luckily, we did have enough depth to move out on our own.

"But," Frank sighed, "it was that kind of day. Our motor wouldn't start. We waited a couple more hours until an LCM1 arrived."

One of the kids sitting in the bleachers on the opposite side of the gym shouted out, "You need to know your alphabet if you're going into the Navy."

Even Frank laughed, but he amended the boy's statement. "For any branch of the Armed Services! LCM1 stands for Landing Craft Mechanical. The Mark 1 version was made by the British. It had an eight-inch hawser."

Siobhan recognized her daughter's voice. "What's a hawser?"

"That's a thick cable that they fastened to our stern as a towline."

"Stern? Isn't that the back end of the boat?"

"Yes, it is," Frank nodded with a grimace. "We were being towed backwards and the waves kept coming at us. Since we were being towed at the stern, we were having a tough time riding the breakers. Actually we *couldn't* ride the waves, only smash right into them and get swamped with water. So Mulcahy, our Chief Bosun's Mate--and before you ask me, the Chief Bosun's Mate has lots of duties but in this case was in charge of operating and maintaining the equipment used in loading and unloading cargo, ammunition, fuel, and so forth. Anyway Mulcahy yelled at me, 'For god's sake, Zalot, tell them to stop.' I jumped up on the motor deck and started sending the message on my signal gun, but the LCM kept going. If it had only paused between swells, we would have had enough slack in the towline that we could have climbed the swell and ridden over the oncoming waves.

"But there was no pause and the next wave was a big one. It threw our boat upside down and dumped us right into that icy, swirling sea. The LCM kept towing our boat which was now submerged. It was pitch black, which was probably why no one could see my signals and probably why they didn't realize we had been tossed into the ocean.

"It all happened so fast that at first I didn't realize where I was. Then I felt a kick to my head and realized I was under water. I grabbed onto a shipmate's belt-buckle and started towards the surface. When I broke the surface, it was like a nightmare. Men were screaming, 'Help, help! I can't swim!' I-- I--"

At that point, Frank just stopped. He stared up at the basketball hoop which had been raised to accommodate the assembly that evening. It seemed as if everyone in the Hopkins Academy gym stopped breathing at that moment. It was a hot, sweltering August night in the gymnasium, but Siobhan shivered in the forty-degree water off the coast of New Zealand. She heard the sailors screaming. Her hands instinctively flew up to her head and she covered her ears.

After a minute, Principal Banas stood, poured a glass of water from the pitcher on the table next to him, and took it over to Frank who gulped it down. "Would you like to sit for a while? Take a break?"

"No, sir. Thank you, sir. I'm okay."

Frank turned to face those in front of him.

"Those screams of those brave men who died, they're still in my head." He tapped his forehead. "I hear them every night before I go to sleep, screaming and screaming. You know, I used to think only women screamed. Now I know different." Frank paused and raised his head. "So maybe we could all remember them in our prayers."

It was as if everyone had stopped breathing. Siobhan imagined they were all saying a silent prayer for those who had drowned, just as she was doing. She looked over to her brother-in-law and saw his lips moving.

"Well," Frank gave a light laugh, "obviously I made it, so you are probably wondering what happened next. I took a deep breath and went under the water again. When I came up, I heard Chief Mulcahy yelling, 'Hang on, Zalot--we'll make the beach.' He grabbed a life jacket that was floating by and shoved his arm into one of the arm holes and I put mine through the other. I still had all my equipment on, and it kept pulling me backwards and down into the water. I started ripping it off, a backpack and a canvas sack with two heavy cell batteries for the signal gun. But my binoculars were the first to go and, despite the roar and pounding of the waves around me, I clearly remembered hearing what the Quarter Master had said when he issued me the binoculars that very morning: 'These cost $125 bucks. Don't come back without them.'

"By that time, the tide was going out again and we couldn't make it to shore. Every stroke we tried to take forward towards the beach was just so puny. The waves were so powerful that they just yanked us backwards out to sea.

"The LCM had arrived back at the ship; our boat was still attached to it but it had sunk deep into the water below. When they realized what had happened, the captain sounded a general alarm and all available boats were launched to look for us survivors.

"It was the middle of the night and most of the guys on board had already gone to bed. Can you imagine what that must have been like? Those guys, exhausted after that grueling landing exercise, and then being startled out of a sound sleep by the alarm screaming at them, the storm still howling around the ship?"

The farmers around Siobhan, their faces creased with years of squinting against the sun as they tugged crops from stubborn soil, nodded their heads in sympathy. She couldn't help but think that they, too, knew all about exhaustion.

"Meanwhile, Mulcahy and I were out bobbing around in the ocean in the middle of the storm. We would be sitting precariously on the crest of a wave for several seconds, then all of a sudden we'd be plunged to the bottom of a swell and then yanked up to the next crest. Over and over again. Those swells were at least ten feet high.

"Our life-jacket became so waterlogged that we were no longer above water when the waves crested. We had to use our free hand to cover our mouths and noses to keep from swallowing water. We were so exhausted we couldn't hold our breath. It was so loud, really, really loud..."

Frank paused for a moment. It was as if he were back tossing about in the waves of that angry sea.

"...so loud, that wind, and so dark."

Everyone imagined themselves being thrown about on stormy waves, thrown further and further away from shore. Siobhan shivered.

"I remember I wanted a pen and paper and a bottle to put the note in. I wanted to write to my mother...let her know I was thinking about her right up to the very end. I know. It sounds crazy, but that's what I was thinking. That I didn't have those things, that paper and pen, seemed to me the cruelest part of what I thought was going to be my dying moment at sea.

"And then I must have passed out. Yes, I was rescued, but I don't remember seeing or hearing the boat that rescued us. One of the sailors in that boat said he saw my hand. It was sticking up out of the water so he tossed a life-ring over it and pulled me to the boat."

"Thank God," Siobhan heard Tony mumble. His arms were wrapped tight around Seamus and his knuckles were white. Seamus didn't seem to notice. Siobhan followed her son's gaze back up to the stage where Frank stood.

"I do remember the two sailors leaning over the boat and trying to lift me over into it. A sailor yelled, 'We can't budge him' and then another one must have spotted Mulcahy. I heard that sailor shout, 'There's a guy hanging onto his leg.'

"Two other guys grabbed Mulcahy and we were both tossed into the boat like sacks of potatoes. I landed on my back and every time a wave broke over that boat, the water would crash over me. I knew what was going on. I could hear and see, but I just couldn't move. I couldn't talk. I remember thinking, 'They pulled me out of the ocean and now I'm going to drown in the boat.' One of the sailors was bringing me a cup of hot coffee and just then the boat lurched and he lost his balance. That coffee splashed down on my face. But I didn't feel a thing. My face, my body, everything was numb. He did put a life jacket over my face, though, and so I didn't drown in that boat."

Frank laughed lightly. It was a nervous laugh, but no one in the Hopkins Academy gymnasium laughed. He cleared his throat and went on.

"When we got back to the ship, I was taken to Sick Bay where the doctor gave me a glass of whiskey." Frank licked his lips, remembering. "Three Feathers Whiskey. I lost consciousness. I'd shake, then stop, then shake all over again. Two of my closest friends stayed at my bedside. I was technically unconscious but I could hear my own voice yelling out. When I came to, one of my buddies said, 'Boy, were you having a conversation! Who were you talking to?' I told him. I was talking to God. I saw Him. He was on a white cloud, an angel on either side of him. I was thanking Him for saving me."

It seemed as if those in the Hopkins Academy gymnasium all breathed a collective sigh of gratitude. But the gratitude was short-lived.

"Fifteen of us survived and I don't know how we ever did. Nine sailors reached the shore and the remaining six of us were picked out of the sea by rescue boats. But ten valiant soldiers died that day, one officer and nine enlisted. One of the men, Seaman First Class Joseph Lorbietski, was even an excellent swimmer. And yet Mulcahy, who couldn't swim at all, ended up saving my life. He was awarded the Presidential Unit Citation for doing so."

No one said anything for a minute or so. Then Sarah's husband struggled to his feet and began to applaud. Seconds later, everyone in the gymnasium stood and joined him. Even Siobhan.

Frank's face flushed with embarrassment. He waved both hands back and forth, saying 'No.' "I accept that applause on behalf of Mulcahy and the ten brave men who died that day."

The young man sat down. The applause continued and then gradually, one by one, everyone in the audience sat back down. When it was clear that no one was thinking of leaving the gymnasium, Principal Banas turned to Frank. "Would you consider taking a few questions?"

Frank nodded and stood. The silence was awkward until a man Siobhan didn't know raised his hand. Principal Banas nodded in his direction.

"Well, first off, I applaud your service for this country. And I don't mean to take away from your bravery or nothin' but, if you don't mind me sayin', it seems kinda crazy that it was a stormy night, and you guys being sailors and all, and in the Navy, and not wearing life jackets..."

There was an odd mixture of laughter on the part of some members of the audience, but more than a few, and not only the women, glared at the man making the comment.

"You're absolutely right, sir. It was crazy of us to be doing all that without wearing life jackets. They were in our boats, of course, and I don't know whether we thought nothing would happen and we didn't need to be putting them on, or that if something did happen, we would have time to get to them. I just don't know. At any rate, the Navy learned a lesson from our tragic experience. After that, it was mandated that all members of a shore party had to wear life jackets while in a boat. And keep them on."

The man nodded, satisfied, and then sat down.

Sophie's friend Millie was the next to raise her hand.

"Why didn't the guy in charge of the boat towing you guys, the coxswain, is that the right term?"

Frank nodded.

"Well, why didn't that coxswain in the boat towing you guys slow down over the big waves after you signaled him?"

"That's a very good question. And one that was asked by the Board of Inquiry about two weeks after the accident. I think it was just a confusing time, what with it being night and the storm blowing and the message just never got received or understood. I'm not sure. In the end it was ruled an accident, a series of events where everything went wrong."

"Another question?" Principal Banas asked.

One of the basketball players from Sophie's class stood up. "I know you said it was dark and nighttime and all, but do you actually know what time the boat capsized?"

"Yes, Sir. I do. My watch stopped at 11:17 pm. when I was thrown into the ocean. They should make waterproof watches! They told me later that I was rescued shortly after midnight. Of course to me and Mulcahy, it seemed like hours that we were in the water."

A chubby woman stood up, her face flushed as if she had just been leaning over a hot stove.

Tony leaned over to whisper in Siobhan's ear. "That's Bibiana Tomaszewski. From North Hadley. Stan was sweet on her in high school."

"Are you sure? Stan never mentioned her to me."

Tony just smirked. Siobhan leaned forward to study the woman as she phrased her question.

"Did you get to meet any of the local people in New Zealand while you were stationed there?"

"Yes, ma'am. I sure did. Very nice people. They were very grateful for the American servicemen in protecting them from the Japanese."

Siobhan whispered back to Tony. "She doesn't seem to be Stan's type."

"Not now. She's put on a lot of weight. But back then--" Tony gave off a low whistle.

The man sitting in front of Siobhan and Tony turned to glare at them.

Bibiana was still standing. "Did you actually get to know any of the people, though, like make friends with them?"

"Yes, Ma'am. I was especially close to the O'Brien family. They ran a milk bar."

"Milk bar?"

"Yes, it was a sort of drug store that also served food. Anyway, when I went to say goodbye to them before our ship left to move closer to Japan, Mrs. O'Brien asked me if I had heard anything about the tragedy at Paekakariki. I said, 'Did I hear about it? I was in it!' and I told her what happened. Her face got kinda white and I said, 'But don't worry, I'm okay now.' And she said, 'You know, there was such a storm that night that we closed up early and I went to bed. I had a dream you were in terrible trouble and that dream woke me up. I got out of bed and prayed to God to see you safely through any danger. I prayed on my knees for a long time, about forty-five minutes. It was midnight when I crawled back into bed.'"

"Wow!" Bibiana said above the murmur of voices in the auditorium.

"I want to know more about Frank's ship." Seamus looked over his shoulder at Tony. His small boy's voice, however, carried over the heads of those present to Frank standing on the stage.

"Oh, my ship? The American Legion. When I joined the Navy, I had a vision of being on a brand-new shiny ship so at first I was disappointed when I was assigned to the American Legion. It was old, built in 1919 as a cargo ship and then refitted for war. But she was a sturdy ship and she did well in all the battles we faced. I'm proud to be on her."

Seamus's face blushed with pleasure that the hero Frank had answered his question.

Siobhan recognized her daughter's English teacher as she rose to ask, "So you've had some battles with the Japanese?"

"Yes, ma'am, I have. But for security's sake we are not to disclose that information at this time. But I will tell you this. We will beat the Japs! We will win! And we will avenge the attack on Pearl Harbor!"

All those assembled leapt to their feet in loud applause.

Frank sat back down. He seemed exhausted.

Principal Banas reached over to shake Frank's hand. "Well, I'm sure you all join me in thanking this young man, a brave son of Hadley, for sharing his story with us, and for serving our country so courageously."

There were enthusiastic murmurs of agreement and more loud clapping. Frank fidgeted in embarrassment.

"So before we go," Principal Banas continued, "let's all stand and each in his or her own way, let's have a moment of silent prayer, a prayer of thanksgiving for God's watching over one of Hadley's very own, and for all of our brave soldiers who have died in this terrible war, and for those who continue the valiant fight."

A few minutes later, everyone began to exit the gymnasium, prayerfully as if they had just attended a Sunday service. Seamus rubbed his sleepy eyes as he rested against Tony's shoulder. John Callahan reached over and took the child from Tony and hoisted him high over his shoulder. Seamus rested his head on top of John's and wrapped his arms around the lad's neck. In seconds he was sound asleep. No one spoke as they walked down Middle Street back to Siobhan's home. It was as if their minds and hearts were busy with thoughts too sacred to voice.

Chapter Fifteen

This was the third morning that Siobhan looked out to the screened-in porch and saw John Callahan standing there, looking bewildered, shifting his body nervously back and forth on his long lanky legs. Twice last week, and here it was 7 a.m. Monday morning. Siobhan had heard her daughter running water in the bathroom sink at six and had smiled to herself at how responsible Sophie had become, getting up on her own to head down to the fields across the river to help Uncle Tony dig up potatoes. And while she worked alongside those German prisoners, Siobhan was comforted both by the fact that Tony had promised to keep an eye on her daughter, and, grudgingly, by the fact that that Callahan boy was also working in Tony's fields. Even though she thought Sophie was much too young to get involved with John Callahan, or any boy, at least he wasn't a German prisoner. "Just keep your priorities, straight, young lady," Siobhan frequently reminded her. Never mind, as Sophie often threw it in her mother's face, that Siobhan herself was only a year older when she married Stan. "Times were different then," Siobhan would respond. "There was no thought of a young girl going off to college, to have a career...as you are going to do."

"But you loved, Dad, right? You would marry him over and over or so you've said," Sophie would retort. And that would end the debate, her daughter having the last word.

But this was puzzling, John showing up on the porch, expecting to walk Sophie down to the fields, especially when her daughter had shouted up the stairs, "Bye Mom, Bye Pip Squeak," a half hour earlier.

"Sorry, John, but Sophie already--" Siobhan began, but she stopped when the boy shook his head emphatically from side to side.

"She's not there. I checked. I went straight to the fields, thinking she might have gone like last week. But she's not there."

"Well," Siobhan stammered, taken aback. "Maybe she stopped by Millie's first..." Her voice trailed off as that Callahan boy turned, opened the screen door, and let it snap decisively behind him as he punched his boot clad feet down the stairs. Siobhan watched as the boy stormed down the driveway.

Apprehension pressed against her chest. Where was her daughter? Where was she going so early in the mornings? Siobhan slapped the dish towel against the counter alongside the sink and stepped into the hallway to shout upstairs. "Seamus! Seamus!"

First the dog's face appeared around the corner at the top of the stairs, and then the child's, scrunched up with worry. Instantly, Siobhan's heart softened. Her son thought he had done something wrong, when in fact her precious boy never did anything against her wishes. She was beginning to think that wasn't necessarily a good thing. Tony had said, "Yeah, he's a good kid, but it ain't right. He should do something wrong now and again. Disobey. It's part of growing up." Siobhan had the suspicion that her sadness at Stan's death had something to do with it. That for some reason, Seamus felt responsible and so he tried especially hard to make his mother happy. And the truth was, Seamus did make his mother happy. Siobhan smiled up at him and his shoulders relaxed. "Did Sophie tell you where she was going?"

"When?"

Impatience flooded back into Siobhan. "This morning?"

Dog and boy tumbled down the steps. "Don't be mad, Momma. Don't be mad. Sophie didn't do anything wrong. You always yell at Sophie."

It was true. Lately, Siobhan and her daughter seemed to end every conversation yelling at each other.

Siobhan knelt in front of her son and hugged him close. "I'm not mad, Sweetheart. I just wondered if she said anything to you about where she was going this morning."

The boy shook his head solemnly and Francie sat down beside him, tilting her head in concern. It was remarkable how the pup seemed to respond to every shift in her young master's moods. Then Seamus grinned, and Francie opened her mouth, letting her tongue hang out. Siobhan couldn't help thinking the dog also was grinning. "Momma, it's Monday. She went to work in Uncle Tony's fields, remember?"

Siobhan reached across to ruffle up her son's hair. "Of course. I just forgot."

Seamus pulled his head out from under her hand. "Momma! Stop doing that. I'm not a little boy no more."

She reached to hug her son but he dodged her arms and boy and dog bounded back up the stairs. "I'm teaching Francie to pick up my pajamas and put them in the basket. She already knows how to pick up my socks and put them away."

Siobhan shook her head and walked back into the kitchen, her mind traveling to the possible places her daughter might have gone. She stood in front of the window over the kitchen sink and her eyes absently traveled across her own fields to Tony's a quarter of a mile away. She could make out the backs of several POWs bent over cultivating the soil of the rows between Tony's beans. Then her gaze sharpened, her eyes squinting. Suddenly, she could see, she could see with a mother's eye, the way a mother's eye could see something where before there had been no sign, no evidence, no premonition.

Siobhan turned and dashed back down the hall. "Seamus! Seamus!"

Again the boy's worried face appeared in the doorway above her. "Bring me your binoculars. Okay? Bring them down right now."

"Why?"

Siobhan bit her tongue not to yell at her son in her impatience. "I just want to look out of them, okay? Please Seamus, right now."

As the boy still hesitated at the top of the stairs, Siobhan reassured him. "Nothing's wrong, Sweetheart. I just want to look through them. Like you do."

"Okay."

Moments later, Siobhan trained her vision through the binoculars out the kitchen window, across her fields to Tony's, and to where the POWs were working. She saw the guard sitting, his back against a tree, cap pulled low over his forehead. "Some guard, that one," Siobhan muttered. With her index finger, she dialed the binoculars into sharper focus and trained them on each of the five prisoners, one by one. When she got to the last prisoner, she nearly dropped the binoculars. That final prisoner was not bent over like the others; he was standing, leaning against the hoe propped next to him as if he were listening to someone facing him. And there was Sophie! Her back to the lens, but no matter. Her mother knew every inch of her daughter, front and backside, right from the day she held her newborn in her arms and all the days in between. Sophie's arms were waving large circles, no doubt translating her words into gestures so that the young POW would understand what she was saying. Siobhan dialed in the focus even closer. The POW was one of those young ones. He looked about 16 or 17, as old as Sophie. He was smiling at her daughter. Cold fingers clutched Siobhan's heart. She moved the binoculars over slightly. The girl's shoulders were shaking and she could tell her daughter was laughing at something.

The air went out of Siobhan and she bent over the sink. Sophie, her very own Sophie was befriending one of those assassins. Befriending him and--she let her thoughts slide over to a certain realization, a realization that chilled her. Sophie was infatuated with one of those killers! Maybe she even fancied herself in love with him. And suddenly John Callahan's anger made sense. He must have suspected what Sophie was up to.

Siobhan's mind spun. What to do with that knowledge? She couldn't confront Sophie. How would she explain it? She couldn't reveal she'd been spying on her daughter, with binoculars no less. But there's no way she could tolerate her daughter thinking she had some kind of romantic relationship, some kind of doomed romantic wartime love. Siobhan shook her head, remembering her own wild unfettered feelings of love when she herself was Sophie's age. "But that was different!" Siobhan declared out loud, her hands setting the binoculars carefully on the kitchen counter.

She hadn't fallen in love with some soldier, some enemy soldier determined to kill Americans. She had fallen in love with her beautiful Stan, a wonderful, noble, hardworking man with whom she shared her values, her religion, her...her everything.

"It was different," she said aloud again.

"What was different, Momma?"

Startled, Siobhan whirled around to see her young son and the ever-present Francie, staring up at him.

"Oh, sweetheart, nothing. It's nothing. Momma was just thinking about, oh, when she was, uh, when she was working in Boston at the market. How, uh, how it was so different from working in the fields like your sister is supposed to be doing."

"Different how?"

"Well, instead of working in the fields to make the food, the farmers would already have the food harvested and put it in trucks. Then they would bring it out to Boston, waaaaaaayyy across the state of Massachusetts."

Seamus climbed up on the stool next to his mother.

"Where the ocean is?"

Siobhan nodded. "Where the ocean is. And then your Grandpa, the one you are named after, and I would sell the food to the people in Boston who didn't grow their own food."

"Well, if they didn't grow their own food, what did they do all day?"

"Lots of things. Like maybe they were teachers or doctors or--"

"Momma, I've been wondering something."

Siobhan grinned. The boy's attention didn't last long on one subject unless it was something he could actually see or imagine. "What?"

"You know when bean plants make flowers, and then the flowers grow into beans?"

"Uh-huh."

"Well, potato plants make flowers, too."

"Yes."

"But the flowers don't turn into potatoes. The potatoes grow under the ground. Are there flowers under the ground too?"

"I don't think so."

"But what are the flowers for up top of the ground? If they don't turn into potatoes?"

"You know, that's a very good question. I don't know the answer to that. We'll have to ask Tony."

"Okay." Seamus slipped off the stool and motioned to the dog who had settled down on the cool floor at the boy's feet. "Come on, Francie. We have to practice your tricks. We're working on fetching, Momma. Francie doesn't want to bring the ball back to me. She wants to lay down on the ground and chew it, or sometimes, she wants to run away from me with the ball in her mouth and have me chase her to get it back. But Uncle Tony told me a trick. He said to tie a rope onto the ball and when Francie gets the ball in her mouth, I should pull on the rope towards me." Seamus was acting out throwing the ball and then tugging on the imaginary rope. Francie cocked her head, puzzled, studying her young master. "Then, Uncle Tony said, she'll get the idea to bring the ball back. And I have to give her a little piece of bread when she brings it back. It's like a reward."

"Okay, Sweetheart, but take a break if she gets tired. She's still a puppy, no matter how big she has gotten. She should rest every so often."

Siobhan watched as dog and boy bounded across the kitchen and out through the porch door. She turned slowly and deliberately picked up the binoculars, her lips forming a tight grim line across her face. But Sophie was gone. Siobhan sought out each figure on Tony's field. All five prisoners, backs bent over, were hoeing between the rows of beans. The guard, position unchanged, was no doubt snoozing under the tree. And no doubt he never noticed the young girl flirting with one of the prisoners, or if he did, he took no note of it.

What to do about her suspicions? If she told Tony, he would laugh it off and say she was making a big deal out of nothing. "After all," she could hear him say, "it's not like they can talk to one another, spend time with each other. He's a prisoner, for Chrissake. Talking in German." What would Tony know about young love? Actually, Siobhan really knew nothing about Tony as a young man. She wondered now, surprised that she never had before, if Tony had ever been in love.

But what to do about Sophie? That would take some serious thinking. Siobhan glanced over to the calendar on the wall next to the icebox. August already. 1944. The war had been going on since Pearl Harbor, and years before that. Forever, it seemed. Would it ever end? She longed for the day when those German prisoners would be sent back.

The answer came in the afternoon's paper, just after she had convinced Seamus and Francie to take a nap. It came in a blazing black headline: *Allies Cross Siegfried Line.* Siobhan's eyes couldn't race fast enough over the printed lines that told her what she always had known: that Hitler's murderers would be beaten, that they would pay for the bloody, futile loss of lives they caused.

Sophie!

They would be gone! The prisoners would be off her soil! Out of Sophie's life!

Siobhan folded the paper hastily and tucked it under her left arm as she ran down the hallway, through the kitchen, and out across the porch, letting the screen door slam behind her. Her feet flew down the steps and around the house. She ran. She ran across her fields, and somehow her feet did not stumble in the clumps of dirt turned over in the newly cultivated field. She didn't think about the dirt brushing against the bottom of her skirt. She just ran. She ran to Tony's fields, and her heart jumped in jubilation as the German POWs suddenly stood, stunned to see a woman running across the rows of beans. She took the newspaper and swatted it at the soldier dozing against a tree. He grabbed for his rifle and stumbled to his feet. Taken aback to see Siobhan standing before him, waving the newspaper, he struggled to find his composure.

"Tell them!" she yelled.

Siobhan pointed to the newspaper headline. "Tell them! Tell them they're beaten! Tell them they're going back."

The soldier took the newspaper from Siobhan. She watched as his eyes ran across the headline and down the article. It was a slow smile, at first, then it grew until the soldier threw back his head and laughed. "Yes!" he shouted, hoisting his rifle aloft in the air. Then he waved to the prisoners, beckoning them to come over and see what was in the newspaper.

The prisoners looked at one another; then they dropped their hoes and hesitantly made their way over to the guard.

The guard waved the newspaper in each of the prisoner's faces, punching the headline with his index finger. The prisoners stared at one another, bewildered. The soldier knew a little German and managed to find the words to tell them that their famed Siegfried Line had been crossed.

The prisoners shook their heads, and two of them even laughed. Propaganda, they told the guard. The Siegfried Line could never have been penetrated. They gestured with their hands showing how bunkers had been built, how there were miles of tunnels, and how thousands of cement mounds-- *Hocker,* dragon's teeth, they called them--had been constructed to tear the bottoms out of the Allied tanks. They waved their arms showing how the Siegfried line went for miles and miles, and that there were thousands and thousands of tank traps. No, no, they shook their heads. It was a lie, they told the guard, avoiding Siobhan's eyes. Propaganda, they insisted, just to keep up the American's spirits. They even dared to look sympathetic at the soldier's naiveté.

But the guard just shook his head, and his grin cracked open his face from ear to ear. He pointed again to the headline in the newspaper. "We don't lie to our people!" he shouted.

Siobhan's eyes sought out the young German prisoner she had spied through the binoculars. Sophie's prisoner. He was the one hanging back behind the other four. While the others were laughing and joking among themselves over the simple Americans who actually believed that their mighty German bunkers could be crossed, both doubt and belief flickered across that young prisoner's stricken face.

And Siobhan was stunned. While she was racing across the fields, she couldn't wait to show that prisoner, that special particular prisoner, that he was beaten, that he would be going home, that he wouldn't be dreaming about a young American girl. When Siobhan showed him the newspaper, he would know he was a fool.

But now, as she watched the shock in the young boy's face, she felt an enormous swell of sadness and pity for him. He was little more than a child. Her own Sophie's age. The age of that Callahan boy. A plaything that Hitler had sent off to fight his stupid war. What would happen to that boy who in his young life had found himself across an ocean, far from his family, far from the classroom he should have been sitting in, dressed in the drab garb of a prisoner of war, hoeing around rows of beans that were not his own, standing in the dirt of a foreign land? What would happen to him? Siobhan couldn't help thinking that the young prisoner was wondering the very same thing. That nothing was certain in his life, that most likely nothing good would come to him from Hitler's eventual surrender. And he *would* surrender. He would be beaten, Siobhan was sure of that. And this young prisoner? Sophie's prisoner? A young life ruined because of a maniac's deranged dream.

Siobhan reached over and took the newspaper from the guard. She folded it carefully and then she walked down to the street, shook the dirt from her skirt, and headed back to her home.

"Yes, Siobhan, it means something, but it doesn't mean everything." Tony shook his head. He was sitting at the table and holding the newspaper in his hands, hands that were embedded with dirt, nails broken and black. Siobhan had shoved the newspaper at him, ordered him to sit, as soon as Sophie had gone upstairs to wash off the sun and sweat and dirt from an afternoon in the corn fields. Tony had given her a ride home.

"But it's the end of the war!"

Tony shook his head. "Maybe. Don't get me wrong. It's a terrific win for the Allies, but it's far from over. And honestly, Siobhan, I know because of Stan..." and Tony broke off, unexpected emotion catching his breath.

Siobhan was moved. Tony hardly ever mentioned his brother. Sometimes she thought he didn't even miss him. He was so much older than Stan. It was a problem for her, his seeming lack of feeling over the loss of his brother. That suspicion of Siobhan's had always been between her and her brother-in-law.

Tony ran his hands through his hair. It was turning gray, Siobhan noticed with shock, and thinning. As often as Tony had sat in her kitchen, nearly every day since the afternoon Yantik delivered that telegram, she suddenly realized that she didn't really know Tony. She hadn't ever really looked at him. She'd been so busy looking into herself. Even her children, Sophie especially, had seemed to slip away from her.

Siobhan abruptly pulled out a chair and sat down next to Tony. Her hand reached up to...to what? She didn't know. Hug him? Caress him? Her hand just hung in the air an inch above Tony's shoulder.

Tony picked up the newspaper again. He shook his head. "I don't mean to discourage you, Siobhan. Yes, it's good news. Wonderful news, but you know for Hadley, we're so focused on the other war. Our young boys are in the Pacific, fighting the Japs. But maybe..." Tony rested his chin in his hand, elbow propped against the tabletop. "If we get Hitler, it'll get easier for us to beat the Japs." He turned abruptly and reached for his crutch. "I gotta go."

This time Siobhan did put her hand on Tony's arm. "Wait. There's something else. I, uh, well--"

Tony grinned. "Not like you to stumble around for words."

Siobhan glanced around the kitchen, and towards the hallway. She tilted her head, listening. She heard Sophie's footsteps overhead, back and forth, and visibly relaxed. "It's Sophie. Have you noticed anything?"

Tony frowned. "Like what? She's been very responsible, working hard. I know you thought she wouldn't be, but she has been."

"She hasn't been late to the fields?"

Tony shrugged. "Once or twice, but that's nothing."

"She, uh, well, how does she relate to the prisoners?"

"The prisoners?"

Siobhan's voice snapped with impatience. "Yes, Tony, the prisoners."

"Well, she smiles at them once in a while but she keeps her distance." Tony laughed. "John Callahan keeps a close eye on her. Fancies she's *his* girl. Fancies himself a knight in shining armor where Sophie's concerned. She thinks it's funny. She mocks him for it. I tell him to take it easy."

"But?"

"What's on your mind, Siobhan? Spit it out. I'm tired, dirty, and hungry, and I want to go home."

"It's just, I noticed something."

"You are going to make me drag it out of you piece by agonizing piece? How long is this gonna take?"

"Maybe it's nothing."

Tony got to his feet. "Well, when it *is* something, I'm sure you'll let me know."

Siobhan watched Tony's back as he left. His shoulders had rounded over the summer, and were more bent over his body. She hadn't thought of it before, but she realized that her brother-in-law worked hard. It was literally back-busting work.

Sophie tumbled down the steps and into the kitchen, strands of wet hair flying out behind her. She looked at the empty table. "You haven't started supper yet, Mom?"

Chapter Sixteen

Siobhan never knew when Tony was going to show up. She heard the cough of his truck as it bucked to a stop just beyond the screened-in porch. The muffler was shot but even if there were money for a new one, Tony explained, just like new tires, spare auto parts were not to be found. "The war, you know," he shrugged when she asked about it.

She knew about the shortages, the scarcities, the just plain non-existent. She was experimenting with how to get a sweetener in her baking, now that the German boats were attacking the ships from South America and sugar was added to the list of rare commodities.

Siobhan heard the familiar clump-slide, clump-slide as her brother-in-law came across the porch floor. She busied herself at the sink, not turning to face Tony, not willing to let him see the smile on her face. She wasn't sure when her body had stopped bristling at the sounds of Tony's impending visits; she wasn't sure when her body had actually relaxed at the sound of the clump-slide; nor was she sure when the moment happened that she looked forward to Tony's stopping by; and not even when it happened that her body slumped in disappointment if a day passed by without a visit from her brother-in-law.

"You're too late. Sophie left already."

Siobhan heard the whoosh that seemed to come out of Tony's body as he collapsed onto the chair at the kitchen table. She took the towel that was lying next to the sink, dried her hands, and turned to face Tony. "To what do I owe the pleasure? Shouldn't you be at the fields, supervising the assassins?"

Tony grimaced. "Time you stopped calling them that. They're Prisoners of War just like ours are over there. Victims as much as ours are. You would want our guys to be treated well."

Siobhan went to the stove to warm up the water in the tea kettle. She'd made a kind of potion of herbs from her garden that served as a passable tea. With a little honey, it actually made a brew that was soothing to drink, a treat in the relative cool of the morning hour despite the impending heat that would be suffocating as the day wore on. In front of Tony, she put a teacup. It had a small chip on the lip of it, but if you turned the handle around to the opposite side, you could sip from the cup and not cut your tongue. She was reluctant to throw the cup out as it was the very last one from her mother's set, the one she had brought with her from the old country. Siobhan set the tiny strainer on top of the cup and slid the honey over towards Tony.

"Aren't you afraid the assass--the prisoners will escape if you're not there?"

"I got them going on the potato fields. And the guard is there. But honestly, where are they going to go if they escape? Anyway, I'll be back soon. But I got to thinking about what you said."

"I've said a lot of things." The whistle blew on the tea kettle and Siobhan went back to the stove.

She heard Tony's chuckle behind her back. "Yup, that you have, Siobhan. Said a lot of things. But about Sophie--"

Tony stopped as he heard boy-plus-dog tumble down the stairs from the bedroom. Francie dashed over to Tony and began licking his hands. Her wagging tail thumped against Siobhan's skirt as she leaned over to pour the hot water into her brother-in-law's teacup.

"Hi, Uncle Tony." Seamus slid onto the seat of a chair next to Tony. The boy dragged the dish of raspberry jam--a treat *he* hadn't been offered at breakfast--over in front of himself. Then he reached to take the bread which his mother had set out for his uncle, but Tony rapped Seamus on the knuckles.

"That's mine."

Siobhan turned and put the tea kettle back on the stove; then she went over to the sink.

"Thank you, Siobhan. Why don't you sit a spell and have a little tea with the boy and me?"

There was a hint of smile in Siobhan's voice. "Unlike you, apparently, I have work to do."

As he lifted the teacup to sip from it, Tony raised his eyes and glanced over to the counter next to Siobhan. His eyes widened in pleased surprise. "Are those Stan's binoculars?"

"Yup," Seamus said. "Daddy gave them to me when he went to the war."

Siobhan reached out for the binoculars as if to hide them. She turned to face Tony and held the binoculars in her hands, guiltily, as if she were a thief caught hands full of stolen goods.

Seamus leaned over and broke a piece of bread off of the hunk that Tony held in his hands. "Mommy is keeping an eye on your prisoners, Tony, while you are at your other fields. So they do the work right."

Siobhan felt the red flush of embarrassment heat up her neck and face. She turned quickly and set the binoculars back down on the counter, yanking her hands away from them as if they were prickly with thorns.

Tony's eyes danced with amusement. "That so, Siobhan?"

Siobhan turned on the faucet and let the water run full force. "What?"

"You been watching my prisoners, Siobhan?"

Siobhan turned the water off and turned to face Tony, wiping her hands on her apron. "Seamus, aren't you playing with your new friend today? What's his name?"

The boy dipped his bread into the jam. "Oh, you mean Eddie Fighting Cabbage?"

"What did I tell you about calling him that?"

Seamus had taken to imitating his sister's roll of the eyes. "Momma, everybody calls him that. Fighting Cabbage."

"I don't care what everybody else does. I want you to call him by his right name. Fydenkewicz."

"That's too hard. Everybody calls him Fighting Cabbage. Anyway, Eddie can't play today. He has to help his grandmother go on the bus to Northampton. To see the doctor. She's old and might fall down if Eddie doesn't help her."

"I'm waiting, Siobhan, to hear about why you have been spying on my prisoners."

Siobhan took the dish rag and went over to wipe the raspberry jam off her son's face. "Why don't you and Francie go outside and practice your new tricks?"

"Yes!" The boy jumped up and turned to face his uncle. "We are going to put on a show for you, Uncle Tony, when Francie knows all her tricks."

"I look forward to it." Tony watched the boy and dog bound out of the kitchen and across the porch floor.

It seemed to Siobhan that a lump clogged her brother-in-law's throat. When he spoke, his voice was husky. "Stan would be so proud."

Abruptly, he turned to face Siobhan, at once full of business. "Okay, spill. What's this about you spying on my prisoners? Is there a problem?"

Siobhan went back to the sink where she ran some water and then rinsed out the washcloth. She turned and leaned her back against the counter. "It's probably nothing, but..."

"Spit it out, Siobhan. What's on your mind?"

She took a deep breath, then launched into a confession of her suspicions. "Before heading down to your fields in the Meadows, Sophie has been going over to see your prisoners. One in particular, that young boy. Hans, I think his name is. Blond like they all seem to be. With red cheeks. Handsome." Her voice dropped with bitterness. "All innocent looking. I thought you said the rules were that we weren't supposed to talk to the prisoners?"

Tony seemed surprised and then nodded, his mind fitting the pieces together. "Ah, that's what's got the Callahan boy in a funk of a mood."

Both fell silent, Tony's fingers drumming out a march on the tabletop. "Hmmm. Maybe I'll get that young German boy, Hans you said his name was? switched over to my crew. That way I can keep an eye on him. And on Sophie. See what's going on."

Abruptly, he stood and took his plate over to the sink. "Gotta get back. I want to get a lot of work done before it rains again and turns my fields into a mud-swamp. I'll talk to that soldier who's in charge of my prisoners. Walter, I think his name is. Sergeant Walter Something-or-other. See if we can get that young buck reassigned."

Siobhan felt her eyes flood unexpectedly. She reached a hand out to Tony's shoulder but he didn't notice and slid away from her towards the door. "Always something," she heard him mumble.

But it bothered Siobhan all day, the fact that Tony might say something to Sophie. Sophie would be outraged that her mother had been spying on her; worse, that her mother and Tony had been conspiring against her. In the end, Siobhan decided, what harm could there be in Sophie befriending one of the prisoners. Even if it was supposedly prohibited, nobody seemed to pay attention to that rule. Why just last evening, Anna Windoloski said one of her prisoners knew a little Polish and she had asked him about conditions in her homeland. And, Siobhan reasoned further, it wasn't like Sophie and the German prisoner could really communicate, spend time together. Even if the guard was rather lax in watching over the prisoners, he was still a guard; he was still always present. No, she concluded, it would never come to anything, Sophie and that prisoner, and it wasn't worth totally destroying her relationship with her daughter. Siobhan decided that, despite the wet sticky heat of the late afternoon and the threat of rain, she'd walk over the bridge and down to Tony's fields to tell him just to forget the whole thing, that she had thought better of it. She was just letting a mother's concern run away with her.

Siobhan and Seamus were soaked with sweat by the time they got to the fields. Her wet hair was glued to her head, heavy like a helmet. The prisoners were just coming in from the fields and the army truck was already there to take them back to

Westover. Her eyes roamed the fields looking for Tony. She turned when she heard the rumble of the tractor and saw Tony driving in. Several prisoners made a dash for the tractor and two of them won out, hopping aboard the fenders of the tractor to hitch a ride in from the field.

Siobhan shook her head in disapproval as Tony parked the tractor and the prisoners hopped off. They joined the others around the truck hoping to convince the guard to wait a bit longer until they had a chance to cool off with a swim in the river.

As if he read her mind, Tony said, "Oh, what's the harm, Siobhan? So, I give a couple of prisoners a ride in from the fields."

Francie barked her approval as she pranced over for Tony to rub behind her ears.

"Well, they are prisoners. It's not like we're supposed to be making it easy on them."

"Then for sure you wouldn't like what Iggy's Dad does."

Siobhan raised an eyebrow.

"Yesterday, when he was bringing back his prisoners on the wagon, he stopped at Sullivan's."

"The bar?"

Tony nodded. "And he went in and bought a bunch of beers and--"

"He just left those prisoners unattended in the wagon? They could have escaped!"

"For Chrissake, Siobhan, where are they going to go? It's not like Germany is just across the river. Anyways, Janusz came back out of the bar and gave each one of the guys a bottle of beer."

Siobhan's mouth made a perfect O of shock.

Tony grinned. "Don't have anything to say to that? So maybe my letting a couple of guys hitch a ride on the fender isn't such a big deal after all."

Siobhan just shook her head. "It's not right."

"There's a lot not right in the world today."

She stood staring at Tony, biting her lower lip.

Tony cocked his head to one side. "What's really on your mind?"

Siobhan explained her concerns about making a big deal out of Sophie talking to a German prisoner. She glanced around. "Where is Sophie, anyway?"

"She and John and Andy and Millie asked if they could get off early and go for a swim. I didn't see the harm." He shook his head and drops of sweat spun off his forehead. "I wouldn't mind a swim myself."

Siobhan shrugged. "Well, maybe we should just drop the whole thing. I mean about that young prisoner who works for you."

Tony shook his head. "Already a done deal. I talked to the soldier in charge. Told him we needed more help down here with the potatoes, young strong help, and he agreed to switch Sophie's young buck over here where I can keep an eye on him."

Despite rankling at the expression "Sophie's young buck," Siobhan felt relieved. "But you didn't say anything to Sophie, did you? About me, my concerns?"

"What do you take me for, Siobhan? A fool? Of course not. As you said, it's probably nothing anyway. I'm driving the tractor back." He grinned. "You want to hop on the fender and ride home?"

Siobhan was tempted, but she looked down at her skirt and then at the curve of the fender over the tractor wheels and decided not to risk getting her clothes caught in the wheel and ripped off her body. She shook her head.

"Can I, Momma? Can I ride on the fenders?"

"No, young man. You and Francie stay right here with me."

"Suit yourself." Tony hopped back up on the tractor and headed off. The wheels spun up a cloud of dust that settled over Siobhan.

"Perfect," she grumbled. "Just perfect."

Seamus reclaimed his binoculars, saying he would keep an eye on Tony's prisoners for him. It was a better view, he added, from his upstairs bedroom window. Siobhan felt a wash of relief that the binoculars would be gone from the kitchen counter. Not only had she wasted enough time staring at the prisoners across her fields, but there was also the risk that Sophie would ask what her Dad's binoculars were doing on the kitchen counter. Sophie was pretty clever at reading her mother and Siobhan wasn't sure she would have been able to bluff her way out of an interrogation.

Besides, Tony had said Sophie's "young buck," would be working down in the Meadows now and Sophie didn't dare risk raising her uncle's suspicions. Siobhan felt a little guilty. She remembered how her own young heart bumped inside her chest whenever Stan drove his truck into the Boston market. Siobhan shook her head. "But that was different," she said aloud.

"What's different, Mom?"

Startled, Siobhan felt her face flush and she began to stammer.

But luckily Sophie was distracted by Francie. The dog was sitting next to her chair, her front paws raised, begging.

"Pip Squeak! Call your dog! I'm getting tired of this. Every morning she's right here, wanting my food."

Seamus looked around, to his right and to his left, and then swiveled his head to glance behind him. "Who are you talking to? My name is Seamus."

"Oh!" The girl tossed her head in annoyance. Strands of black hair flew across her face and stuck to her reddened cheeks. She spit at her hair. "This is ridiculous. Mom, tell him to call off his dog." She yanked her hair out of her face. "And this stupid heat is also ridiculous. I think I should take the day off from working in the fields."

"Well yeah, but your boyfriend will be out there." Seamus made kissing noises.

Siobhan perked up. She turned her back to her children and pretended to be busy snapping the ends off the beans she planned to can that day. But she was holding her breath, waiting to hear what her daughter would say to her Seamus.

"John and I are just friends."

"Not talking about John. It's that Hans guy. Over at Uncle Tony's. Iggy told me. Leon said he saw you." And Seamus made more kissing noises, no doubt the same noises Tony's miscreants had made when recreating the scene for the boy.

Siobhan heard Sophie's chair scrape against the floor as her daughter leapt to her feet. "You don't know what you're talking about. You don't know anything. So why don't you just keep your mouth shut!"

Then there was a terrible silence.

Siobhan froze, the grip of her hands snapping a bean in two, her heart sinking at the confirmation of her suspicions about Sophie and that young German prisoner.

Seamus's voice was small and frightened. "Sophie?"

"I mean it, you little Pip Squeak!"

Siobhan ached for her son's fear that he had broken the link between himself and his sister. She ached for her daughter's embarrassment. She heard Francie whine and Siobhan saw a way to rescue both of her children.

Francie had relocated to beg at Seamus's side, hoping to catch bits of toast that the boy was in the habit of tossing her. Siobhan turned and put a scowl on her face.

"I asked you, young man, not to give the dog treats at the table. Francie is to lie down on her bed while we're eating."

At the sternness of Siobhan's voice, the dog stood, tucked her tail between her legs, and, obeying the direction of Siobhan's finger, trotted meekly over to the rumple of rags which served as her bed. She pawed at the rags, circled twice and lay down, resting her head on her paws and giving Siobhan a soulful look.

Sophie grabbed another slice of toast and headed for the door. "I'm late." She spat the words at her brother, flashing him a glance full of threat.

Siobhan ran after her daughter and caught her at the bottom of the steps just beyond the screened in porch.

"Mom! I don't have time for this!"

Siobhan pulled some hairpins and a rubber band from the pocket of her apron. "Sweetie, it's going to be brutally hot today. Let's pin up your hair." She busied herself swooping up the strands of her daughter's damp hair and pinning them in place.

It was hard to know which emotion it was that ran across her daughter's face, relief or gratitude. "Well, gee, thanks, Mom."

Siobhan watched as her daughter ran on down the driveway. Her lips were moving. "You better watch over her, Tony. She has no father to do it."

Siobhan couldn't help herself. Seamus making kissing noises had revived her fears. The image of Sophie talking with that German prisoner kept playing in her mind--her daughter's posture, tilting her head sideways, flirtatiously, the grin on Hans's face, the two standing so close together. It was an impossible situation. But, at Sophie's young age, an impossible love would be just the allure of it all.

All that day and well into the night, Siobhan was plagued with worry. Her heart ached for her daughter. Beyond her resentment of the prisoners, beyond her mistrust of them, Siobhan felt a mother's heart crack at the thought of her daughter's own heartache when the flirtation would get serious and Sophie would imagine herself in a love affair for all the ages. It was a no-win situation. Siobhan had already spotted the signs. Sophie walked around as if in a trance. Just that morning, Siobhan had told her daughter that she herself would bring Sophie's lunch down to the fields. That she shouldn't take the lunch bag with her. The heat would spoil the egg salad in the sandwich. And yet, when Sophie went to the door to head down to the fields it was as if she hadn't heard a word her mother had said. Sophie turned and held out her hand, impatiently. A sharp tone of reproach accompanied the gesture. "Mom, the lunch bag?"

Seamus, still smarting from the hurt of the reproach his sister had leveled at him the day before, stuck his tongue out at Sophie. "Duh! Momma just told you she'd bring the lunch down."

Sophie's eyes had spit fire at her little brother. She turned, letting the screen door snap loudly behind her, and sprinted across the porch floor.

Siobhan herself worked as if in a daze, worried about her daughter. Even after taking down Sophie's lunch and observing her daughter sitting on the ground under a tree next to John Callahan, she couldn't help worrying. And so Siobhan found herself heading out again in the late afternoon heat just as the workers would be quitting the fields. Lifting her skirt, she wandered out into the field, her feet making sucking noises as she lifted her shoes up from the muddy fields. It had rained overnight and, while it was good for the crops, it made for messy work. And lots of laundry. Once again Siobhan's heart fell as she saw Sophie working side by side with Hans. The lilt of her daughter's laughter floated across the fields.

Moments later, Siobhan heard the rumble of the tractor coming towards her across the fields. She raised a hand to shade her eyes against the slant of the late afternoon sun. She saw the workers stop what they were doing and begin to head back towards her. Her eyes searched again for Sophie and she felt a small whoosh of relief when she spotted her daughter and John Callahan coming in together. But where was Hans?

She scanned the field and shook her head in disapproval. Once again, the prisoners were running towards Tony, hoping to hitch a ride on the fenders of the tractor. And yes, there was Hans leading the pack, no doubt his youth giving him an advantage. She saw him gain on the tractor and Siobhan was startled to find that she was holding her breath, hoping that the young German prisoner would make it. That he would be the one to win the race and get a ride in from the muddy fields. She was equally startled to find her own legs running out onto the field so she could get a closer look.

Even though Tony had not turned to watch the prisoners making the dash towards him, he seemed to be aware of it and, as if it were a game, he slowed the speed of the tractor ever so slightly. Sophie and John stopped and turned to watch the race. Sophie shouted out, "Go, Hans, go!" and despite the heat, she jumped up and down, clapping her hands and cheering the boy on. The others turned to watch as well. Hans was well ahead of another prisoner. Siobhan recognized him. Ludwig or Luddy they called him. Just as Hans caught up with the tractor, and just as he was about to hop aboard the fender, he turned and shouted something to Luddy. His concentration broken, Hans misjudged his speed as he jumped onto the tractor. Siobhan watched in terror as the boy slid backwards on the fender. The boy realized his error and flipped onto his stomach clutching the sides of the fender. But still, he slid downwards. Unaware of what was happening, Tony continued driving the tractor.

Siobhan whirled around, her eyes searching for Sophie. But her daughter had seen what was happening and Sophie was running across the field screaming, "Stop, stop!" Siobhan found her feet flying across the field behind her daughter.

Then she stopped in horror.

Hans lost his grip on the fender and bounced off the wheel sideways. The edge of the fender ripped open his pant and sliced into the flesh of the leg. Siobhan saw a spray of blood arc upward into the air. The boy hit the ground with a hard thud.

Sophie was directly in the path of the tractor frantically waving her arms. "Stop, Unk! Stop!" With his right hand, Tony yanked back on the clutch and practically stood up straight on the foot brake. Sophie pointed to the ground where Hans lay writhing in pain.

Siobhan ran to the boy. Hans was holding onto his leg with both hands and rolling from side to side in pain. The skin of the boy's leg had been peeled back to the bone. There were gushers of blood. Sophie stood screaming behind her mother. Siobhan ripped off her apron and knelt beside the boy.

She heard Tony behind her. "We have to make a tourniquet!" Siobhan began tearing her apron into shreds. It was bizarre but at that moment she marveled that she had the super strength to tear the cloth as if it were paper. She glanced at the boy's face. Hans was white-pale, biting his lower lip so hard that he drew blood.

Tony lifted the leg and Hans groaned. Siobhan slid some of the shreds of apron under the leg. Then Tony gently set the leg back on the ground. Siobhan glanced up at the boy's face. Hans's eyes seemed to roll backwards, only the whites showing. Siobhan felt the boy grab her left arm. He gripped so hard Siobhan had the momentary fear that he would break her arm. Tony tied the shreds of the apron tight around the leg, above the cut. They heard voices and glanced up. The prisoners were running down the field towards the army truck which had just pulled in.

Later, that night, when the scenes kept replaying in Siobhan's mind, she marveled that the army truck had a stretcher on it, and a first aid kit. The guard who had been watching the prisoners, the one with a gimpy leg, and the soldier who drove the truck in, headed down the field with the stretcher. Some of the prisoners grabbed the stretcher from the army officers and ran ahead of them to where Hans lay writhing in pain in the muddy dirt between rows of potatoes.

The prisoners brushed aside Tony and Siobhan. Tenderly, like mothers tending an injured child, they lifted Hans onto the stretcher. Hans was very still.

Sophie threw her arms around her mother.

"Is he--he's not--"

Siobhan hugged her daughter. "No, no, he's not. He just fainted. No wonder with all that pain, and loss of--" She stopped short. No need to tell the gory details. They had all seen them firsthand.

Four prisoners lifted the stretcher. Hans moaned. They headed back to the army truck, each cautioning the others in German. Siobhan imagined them to be saying, "Careful, careful."

Tony, Siobhan, John, Millie, and Sophie watched as the prisoners carefully loaded Hans into the back of the truck, and then all of them jumped aboard. There would be no swim in the Connecticut that afternoon.

The truck pulled away. The sleeve of Siobhan's dress was soaked with her daughter's tears and sweat. Anger flushed through Siobhan and she whirled around to face her brother-in-law. "What were you thinking to--"

Tony's stricken expression stopped her. She saw him, leaning against the tractor, his one good leg supporting him.

Siobhan turned back and hugged her daughter. "Let's go home. We can pray for Hans. That's something we can do for him."

"He didn't cry. He didn't cry." A note of pride made its way through Sophie's tears.

At first puzzled, then Siobhan realized. It was true. Other than a moan of pain when Tony lifted the boy's leg, Hans had never cried out in pain.

Chapter Seventeen

Siobhan and the others watched as the Army truck pulled out of the fields and onto the road. The wheels spit up clumps of mud behind it as if the vehicle were bidding good riddance. Those left behind were silent, the only sound the quiet sobbing of Sophie as she rested her head on her mother's shoulder. The sudden sputter of the tractor as Tony started up the engine startled the remaining workers, and they began walking in from the fields. Siobhan too began walking, head high and shoulders squared back against another casualty of the war. Sophie stumbled along beside her. They stopped as the tractor went by and even though they wanted to avoid it, they couldn't help looking over to see where the fender was bent, dirty except where the scarlet of blood marked the jagged edge, a scarlet that was quickly drying to match the muddy brown splatters of soil from the fields.

Siobhan and her daughter were conscious of heavy thumps as someone came running up behind them. John Callahan reached a hand out to Sophie's shoulder and she shuddered out from under it as if from the threat of a reptile touch.

"Come on, Sophie. Yeah, it's too bad. But it was stupid of Hans to---"

She whirled around and spit at the boy, "Shut up! It was an accident! A terrible accident! You can't tell me that you didn't envy those guys running to ride in on the tractor! Hans had more guts than--"

John Callahan shouted back at her. "For Chrissake, Sophie! He's a prisoner! A war criminal!"

Sophie let out a strangled shriek. "He's a human being!"

"He's a Kraut! He killed our guys! You--"

Sophie screamed at him, her body shaking with fury. "We kill *their* guys!"

Siobhan pulled her daughter to her. "Come. Come. Let him go." She turned to the boy. "Just go home, John." She felt her heart soften at the bewildered hurt and anger on John Callahan's face.

Sophie stumbled after her mother.

"Sophie! Mama! Sophie!" Seamus came running down the fields towards them, Francie bounding on ahead.

Siobhan glanced up at Sarah's husband, who just shrugged. Seamus had been told to wait with the old farmer and he'd been happy to do so, crawling up onto the front seat to sit behind the wheel and pretend to drive the truck.

"I saw him! I saw Hans!" the boy blurted out breathlessly. "I saw him when they put him into the army truck. He was all bloody. Did he died, Sophie? Did he died?"

Sophie burst into a wail and her little brother flung his arms around her. "Don't cry, Sophie. Don't cry. I'm sorry I said he was your boyfriend. Don't cry."

Siobhan felt her reserve crack at the pain in her son's voice. She knelt and hugged both of her children close to her. Francie licked at Sophie's tear-stained face. When Seamus stopped trembling, Siobhan stood. "Come. Let's go home. We'll pray for Hans. We'll pray soooo hard for Hans that God will just have to take care of him."

"Does God like German Krauts, Momma?"

"God loves all people, even when they make mistakes."

"Yes, okay, come, Sophie." The boy reached up to take her hand and began walking ahead of her, tugging to make his sister follow him. "Let's go home and pray for Hans."

"We can pray now. We don't have to wait." Siobhan said. They stepped up off the fields onto the road and Siobhan and Seamus stomped their feet to knock the mud and dust from their shoes. Siobhan looked back at Sophie. Her daughter was standing stone-like at the edge of the road. Siobhan reached out a hand to Sophie and gently tugged her forward. As they walked towards the bridge that would take them across the river and on to home, far from the fields, Siobhan began reciting the prayer in a soft but firm voice, "Hail Mary, full of grace...." Seamus's sweet voice sang out as he prayed along with his mother. Siobhan glanced at Sophie. The girl's lips were moving but no sound came out of her mouth.

The prayers had faded by the time the trio reached home. Their footsteps made clumping sounds as they stepped up to the screened-in porch, Francie bounding on ahead. Sophie slumped onto one of the chairs at the kitchen table. Seamus busied himself setting the table and pouring glasses of milk for himself and his sister, and a glass of water for his mother. Siobhan heated up the soup she had made earlier in the day, a mixture of vegetables from her garden together with bits of chicken she had cleaned from the carcass of the bird that they had eaten yesterday for Sunday dinner.

They said grace, Siobhan reaching out for the hands of her daughter and her son. After dinner, Sophie slipped away from the table and went upstairs while her brother and mother cleared the table and did the supper dishes. It was bath night and Siobhan heated water in the kettles on the stove and pulled out the large wash basin from the storage room. Wordlessly, Seamus shed his clothes and climbed in. He didn't even dodge his mother's hands when she set to washing his ears.

After putting Seamus to bed, Siobhan made sure that Francie lay on her nest of rags alongside the boy's bed. Francie raised her head, glanced up at Siobhan, then assured there was no reason to worry about her master, dropped her muzzle back down over her paws. Siobhan had finally given in to her son's pleas to let the dog sleep in the boy's room. "That way, Momma, I don't have to lie to you. You are helping me to be honest."

How could she resist that argument? "Well, yes, I want you to be honest, but honest all the time. Not just when it's easy. As for Francie, now that she's housebroken--"

"Yes, Momma, it's been like forever and forever since she peed in the house." Seamus didn't mention the runny poop he had found in the hallway the day before, poop he mopped up hurriedly before his mother came down the steps.

Yet it was baffling how mothers knew everything. "Well, maybe almost housebroken. There was that accident yesterday morning."

The look of guilt on her son's face was endearing. "But Momma, I cleaned it up!"

There were beads of sweat on Seamus's face as he sat up in the bed to better protest innocence.

"Yes, that was good of you, to take responsibility for your dog." She decided not to mention the smelly mop propped against the kitchen wall that gave Francie and the boy away. Cleaning the mop afterward, and the mess it left on the kitchen floor, was a lesson for another day. As was enforcing the admonition, "Francie can stay in your room, but only if she sleeps on the floor."

An excited Seamus had jumped up and down, "Yes, okay!"

But when Siobhan looked in at her son before going to bed, she invariably found the dog back in Seamus's bed, her muzzle resting on the boy's thin white arm. And then one day the dog was just too big for Seamus's bed and it was Francie herself who chose the comfort of the rug and the relative coolness of the floor.

Siobhan kissed her son on his damp forehead, patted the dog on her head, and then left, quietly closing the door behind her.

It was time to check on Sophie.

The girl lay fully dressed on her bed, her face towards the wall. Gently Siobhan tugged at her daughter's pant legs. Then she brought in a washbasin, washcloth, and towel, and dabbed at the dirt and mud on Sophie's feet and ankles. Suddenly the girl turned and sat up. She looked up at her mother. Tears had washed rivers down through the dust on Sophie's face.

"Mom, do you think he's dead? Do you think Hans is dead?"

Siobhan held the washcloth in her hands and looked into her daughter's face. 'She's older,' she thought with surprise.

Siobhan saw her daughter's woman face as it would emerge a few short years later. "I don't know, Sophie." Seeing the disappointment in her daughter's face, she added, "Honestly. I don't know. It didn't look good. He lost a lot of blood."

"It's so stupid," Sophie said angrily. "To get through fighting in the war and die because he fell off a tractor."

Siobhan reached over and dabbed at the dirt on her daughter's face. Sophie took the washcloth from her mother. "I can do it, Mom."

Sophie tugged the tee shirt over her head and Siobhan took it from her.

"Thanks, Mom." She dipped the rag into the wash basin and then wrung the wet out of it and began wiping her face. "You know what I keep thinking, Mom? That everybody has a mother. Even German soldiers. And somewhere, Hans's mother is worrying about him, not knowing even where he is."

"Well, our government has sent word to Germany. They know the names of the prisoners and that they are here in America."

Sophie gave her mother a skeptical look. "Do you think Hitler plays by the rules, Mom? Anyway--" The girl began washing her arms, periodically dipping the cloth back into the wash basin. The water quickly turned brackish. "Anyway, what I was thinking is that I have you and Seamus. I still have you guys even though Daddy died. Hans, wherever he is, he doesn't have anybody."

"I'm sure the army is taking care of him."

Sophie rolled her eyes. "That's not the same as family, Mom."

Siobhan bit her lip to keep from smiling at being lectured by her daughter.

"I just think about Hans being all alone." The girl stopped suddenly, her lower lip bouncing as she fought to control her emotions. "And his Mom somewhere over there in the middle of all that fighting, wondering about her son, and not even knowing about this terrible accident."

"Oh--" Siobhan suddenly remembered. "Uncle Tony stopped, by asking if you were okay. I told him you'd gone up to bed. He feels terrible about--"

"He shouldn't have allowed the prisoners to jump up on the tractor wheels."

"He knows. He knows that now. But it was just a game. And Tony doesn't think of them as prisoners. They're just boys far away from home caught up in something they didn't even start. He only thought of it as letting them have a little fun. Like letting them go for a swim in the Connecticut River."

Sophie sighed. "I know. I know. I don't really blame him. Uncle Tony is a really good person. It's just--"

Siobhan thought her heart would break as her daughter shed tears again. They were silent tears now, free tears, the shaking of sobs gone. Peaceful tears, if there could be such a thing. Siobhan had begun shedding those peaceful tears herself lately, just before sleep when the loneliness of missing her husband threatened to overwhelm her. Siobhan reached over and pulled her daughter close, resting Sophie's head against her shoulder.

After a few minutes, Sophie drew her head back. "Thanks, Mom. Thanks for understanding." She tilted her head and smiled, a sort of chiding smile. "Thanks for not saying that that assassin deserved what he got."

Siobhan herself smiled. "I think Tony's getting through to me. He has forbidden me to call them assassins anymore."

"Yeah, working alongside them, I realize they are just people like us. They are also suffering from this war. And Hans is a really nice guy. His smile--" Sophie stopped, her lower lip bouncing up and down as she fought for control.

Siobhan sought to lighten the mood. "And quite good looking."

Sophie blushed through her tears. "Well, yeah, maybe, but that's not the point I'm trying to make, Mom. He's just a really nice person. Not like an evil Hitler Nazi at all. I can't even imagine him ever shooting somebody. Although, I guess he must have, he was a soldier, but," she shook her head emphatically, "if he did, shoot somebody I mean, he was doing his duty. He would be honorable like that. He was just doing what he thought was the right thing to do. Like our soldiers shooting at them."

Siobhan reached for her daughter's hand. "I know." And she was startled to realize that she meant it. She trusted her daughter's judgment of Han's character.

It was a comfortable silence, that which flowed between mother and daughter. Comfortable until it wasn't anymore.

"Okay, Mom." Sophie took on a business-like tone. "I can finish cleaning myself up. Go on. Go to bed. You have to be tired too."

"Sure?"

"Sure."

Siobhan stood and walked to the door. She glanced back at her daughter. "I'm proud of you. Always. I don't say it very often but I am."

There was a tease in Sophie's voice. "You don't say it *ever.* But, I'm proud of you too, Mom."

An hour later, Sophie knocked lightly on her mother's door. "You awake?"

"Yes. Come in."

"Can I sleep with you tonight, Mom? Like when I was a little girl. When you and Dad would let me come in after that big hairy ape-man would scare me in my nightmares."

Siobhan threw back the covers and patted the empty space beside her.

Chapter Eighteen

The days simmered on. At first Siobhan worried that Hans's accident would permanently change her daughter. Sophie seemed to sleepwalk through the first week or so. Gone was the galloping tumble down the steps announcing the imminent arrival of a disheveled daughter who seemed to crash land into her seat at the breakfast table. Siobhan even missed the bickering between Sophie and Seamus that heralded growing up in her young son. He'd begun to fight back if he didn't agree with something Sophie said, instead of quietly accepting it. Siobhan had applauded that change in her young son, even though she hated the bickering. She had begun to worry that Seamus would grow up too docile, peace at any cost, a boy ripe for the bullying of others. After Hans's accident, Seamus had reverted to tip-toeing around his sister, anxious to soothe her grief, yearning to have his big sister back. He would sit at the breakfast table, listlessly stirring his cereal and staring across to the empty spot where Sophie's ghost sat.

Siobhan would be wondering if she should call Sophie again for breakfast, warn her that she'd be late to the fields, or if she should just let her sleep in, sleep away her grief as Siobhan herself had tried to do after Yantik brought that telegram announcing the end of *her* world. But sleeping away her life hadn't worked. It was only when Siobhan forced herself to get up and focus on her children that she had begun to heal. So then, Siobhan would turn from the sink, ready to march down the hallway and yell up the stairs to her daughter only to find that Sophie had silently slipped into her seat to sit stonily at the table. But Seamus would take that stony presence as a good sign and would dig into his cereal bowl and start yammering away telling his sister about Francie's newest tricks or what Iggy and Leon were up to. Encouraged by the wan smile on Sophie's face, Seamus would rattle on and on, barely intelligible talking through mushy bites of cereal, not worrying that Sophie would chastise him, "Pip Squeak, don't talk with your mouth full."

They had tried to find out about Hans. One of the soldiers said that he was at the Veterans Hospital in Leeds and Siobhan had even gone with her daughter on the long trip, three buses over, two transfers, and then the whole long process back home again. Tony had promised to keep an eye on Seamus, taking him to the fields with him, and, despite Siobhan's misgivings, she gave in. "I'm a big boy, Momma. I can take care of myself!" But before she and Sophie had set out on the trip to see Hans, she made her daughter walk down with her to the fields. Just as she thought, Tony was out in the field, far from boy and dog, running the tractor and supervising the potato harvest. The soldier, bored with guarding prisoners who needed no guarding, was a willing participant in Seamus's dog show. And when boy and dog tired under the scorching sun, all three sought the shade of a tree and Seamus sat enthralled with the soldier's tales, exaggerated no doubt, about army days and how he got injured in the war. When Siobhan tried to scold the soldier for filling the boy's head with nonsense about how glorious war was, Seamus interrupted. "Momma! It makes me know Daddy. I can picture in my head how Daddy was." She shrugged her shoulders, gave a final glaring warning glance at the soldier, and walked away. Sophie was waiting, impatient to see Hans.

When they got to the hospital, a long sign-in process awaited them. There was a burly guard at the front desk, a hefty man whose stomach bulged over the belt of his khaki pants and whose arms pits sweated dark smelly stains through the shirt of his uniform. He practically snarled, "You are waiting to see who?"

Siobhan bit her lip to keep from correcting the guard, 'to see whom.'

It was Sophie who took him on. Siobhan was glad to see a bit of the spitfire come back into her daughter. Sophie stepped up to the desk and glared at him. "Hans, the prisoner who fell off the tractor and had his leg cut open. Almost severed clear off!"

The guard's eyes flashed with amusement. He glanced down at the papers on his desk and faked a bewildered, "Hans who?"

Sophie flushed red. She didn't know Hans's last name. But that didn't stop her. "How many prisoners named Hans have been brought in here two days ago with a gashing wound in their legs? Huh?"

"Have a seat, ladies." He gestured brusquely towards a bench along the wall. "And I'll see if we have any prisoners named Hans here." He looked up at the two and lectured, "You know this is a hospital for *our* boys, our American boys, not a hospital for Krauts."

Siobhan put a hand on Sophie's shoulders to keep her from a retort that no doubt would have had them evicted, under armed guard no less, from the hospital. "Come. Let's sit. We'll wait while this nice gentleman finds out about Hans."

Sophie rolled her eyes at her mother, but she did follow her to sit at the bench which actually resembled a church pew.

It was a good forty-five minutes until a nurse came to get them. The guard had returned to sit at his desk. He never said another word to them, just busily shuffled papers around his desk from one side to another, or so it seemed to Siobhan. She glanced over to her daughter, but Sophie's eyes were closed, her head rested against the back of the bench, and her lips were moving ever so slightly. 'She's praying!' Siobhan marveled. She reached across and squeezed her daughter's hand. Sophie squeezed back but she didn't open her eyes or change her expression. She did open her eyes though when a soldier came through the front door, an elderly man with an impeccably clean and pressed uniform and with a row of medals glinting over his breast pocket. Mother and daughter hid smirks as the pudgy guard leapt to his feet, bumping his stomach against the table and sending sheets of paper to the floor. He snapped himself to attention with a smart salute. "General!" The general asked to see someone and the guard said, "Of course, Sir. At once, Sir," and the two men turned, marched down the hallway and disappeared into the smell of antiseptic cleanliness.

Siobhan stood and picked up the papers that had fallen and stacked them neatly onto the guard's desk.

Sophie rolled her eyes as her mother sat back down. "Really, Mom? He might lose a little weight if he bent over once in a while."

"You do the right things, Sophie. Always. Even if it seems like the other person doesn't deserve it." Siobhan winced. Even to her, she sounded sanctimonious. She glanced over at her daughter expecting to see another roll of the eyes. Instead her daughter smiled.

"You are a nice person, Mom."

Since an embarrassed Siobhan didn't know what to say to that, the two sat in silence, until finally a pretty nurse came down the hall and addressed them. "I understand you are here to see Hans Drescher, the German prisoner who was injured the other day?"

Sophie sprang up from her seat. "Yes, yes, we are! Can we see him? Is he okay?"

"Come with me."

Sophie and her mother followed the nurse down the hallway and they turned onto a long corridor. "Is he okay? Is Hans going to be all right?"

The nurse turned towards Sophie and tilted her head. "I'll be honest with you. We don't know if he's going to make it. He has a bad infection. I understand he was injured on a tractor?"

Sophie nodded. "Yes, he fell off of the fender. It cut open his leg."

"Well, it was probably rusty and dirty and it caused an infection. We haven't been able to bring his temperature down. He is in and out of consciousness a lot. I'm not sure if he even knows where he is. And of course he mumbles a lot in German and we can't understand him."

Sophie's face went pale. "But he'll be okay, won't he?"

"I can't say for sure. The doctor wasn't going to give you permission to see Hans--he is a German prisoner, after all--but then he thought maybe if the patient heard a familiar friendly voice, it would put some fight into him."

Sophie nodded, determined to give Hans some fight. She mumbled to herself, "Drescher, Drescher," trying on Hans's last name.

"I noticed your name tag," Siobhan said. "Lacadia Blyda. Are you Polish? We live in Hadley and there are many Polish families there."

A smile lit up the nurse's pretty face. "My parents are still there. On West Street. I grew up in Hadley. It's so beautiful there. Well, here we are. Like I said, I don't know if Hans will know you are here but you can talk to him. Talk to him like he's listening."

A soldier sitting on a chair next to Hans, snapped to attention. The nurse chided him, "I don't think the patient is going anywhere. Why don't you step outside and take a break?"

"No, ma'am. I can't leave my post. The doctor said that I have to be here while he has visitors." The soldier glared at Sophie and Siobhan. "So they don't try to slip him something."

It wouldn't have helped matters, so Siobhan struggled to suppress a giggle. 'Slip him something.' The very idea. Her heart softened as she saw Hans lying there, his heavily bandaged leg suspended up at a 45-degree angle, his face nearly as white as the sheet he lay on, his eyes swollen and shut. Siobhan felt her heart clutch as Hans was so still, but then she breathed as she saw the boy's chest lift and fall ever so slightly. She glanced over at her daughter. Sophie's face was nearly as pale as the boy's.

Sophie reached across to take the patient's hand but the guard stepped up. "No touching, Miss."

The guard was treated to one of Sophie's sarcastic rolls of the eyes.

But the guard just glared back at her.

"Okay, okay. Relax. I'm not going to bust him outta here."

Sophie and Siobhan watched silently as the boy lay there with his quiet breathing and his white, white face.

Since Sophie seemed not to find any words, Siobhan began praying aloud, "Hail Mary, full of grace, the Lord is with thee..."

Sophie soon joined her mother in prayer.

"I doubt he can hear you," the soldier said. "And anyway, I doubt a Kraut knows prayers."

Sophie whirled around. "Stop calling him a Kraut. He is a human being. His name is Hans. And I'm sure he does know all about prayers."

"Sophie!"

The girl turned back at her mother's startled cry. Siobhan pointed to the patient's face. Hans eyes flickered open and they searched, first for Siobhan's face, and then they found Sophie's.

"Hans! You're okay!"

He gave a wan smile.

Sophie turned to the soldier. "Please. Can I just squeeze his hand? Please?"

The soldier seemed to waver.

"Oh, what's the harm?" Siobhan said. "He's just a very sick boy. If one of ours was over there in some German hospital, wouldn't you want someone to give him a friendly touch, show that someone cared, give him a reason to get better?"

Sophie reached her hand out and took Hans's in her own. Tears leaked from the boy's eyes and then he seemed to sink back into a deep sleep. His hand relaxed and slowly slid out from under Sophie's.

Sophie fought back tears.

"You two will have to leave now. The doctor said, 'only a few minutes.'" The soldier stepped forward as if to lead the women out of the room.

"No, Mom," Sophie pleaded.

Siobhan put her arm around her daughter's trembling shoulders. "We can't push our luck. Hans knows you were here. You gave him courage. We can come again."

As they stepped out into the hallway, the soldier said, "No, Ma'am. I'm afraid you can't come again. No matter what the condition of the prisoner, they are going to transfer him tomorrow to the base at Fort Devens. In the eastern part of the state."

At the look of shock and dismay on Sophie's face, the guard seemed to soften. "Don't worry, Miss. He'll get very good care there."

Since Sophie seemed unconvinced, he added with surprising sympathy, "and I'm sure your visit will help him. It gave him a will to fight."

It was a long trip home. Sophie kept crying silent tears. She rested her head on her mother's shoulder.

They lost track of Hans, and Siobhan wondered if she would ever get her daughter back. She even missed their constant bickering. It felt like her heart would break when Seamus would quietly go over and hug his sister.

Then one morning John Callahan showed up.

His hands were wrapped around a bouquet of daisies.

The boy stood just inside the screen door, his eyes searching for a place to rest that wouldn't land him in enemy territory. His feet shifted from one side to another. Sophie bit her lip to keep from smiling.

Siobhan put the dish towel on the counter and prepared to leave the kitchen. "I'll give you two some time."

Sophie reached out a hand to her mother's arm. "No, Mom. Stay. Whatever it is he has to say, he can say it in front of both of us."

Just then Seamus came bounding up the steps to the porch, Francie chasing after him. "John! John! Wait till you see how many tricks Francie can do!"

The boy stepped away from the door as Seamus and Francie came onto the porch. Then there was silence. John Callahan looked down at the floor; Siobhan and Sophie stared expectantly at the visitor. They hadn't planned it, and if Sophie had realized they were doing it, she would have immediately dropped her arms, but mother and daughter were both standing erect, arms crossed across their chests, heads tilted to the left, waiting for the miscreant John Callahan to give an account of himself.

Seamus stared from his mother to his sister to John Callahan. "What's wrong?" There was a tremor of fear in his voice. Siobhan extended her arms towards her son and Seamus ran to take cover there. Francie whined. Then Seamus turned to face John Callahan and all three Norowoskis stood demanding the lad give account of himself.

"Well, are you just going to stand there like the dope that you are?" Sophie demanded.

John Callahan raised his face to look at Sophie square in the eye. "I was wrong. I was out of line. I was thinking about me and not about that poor prisoner and his pain. I'm sorry." He held the bouquet out in front of him.

"And?" Sophie demanded.

John Callahan shifted his feet. "Well, I know things can't go back to where we were before all this started, but I miss you, Sophie. I just want to be your friend." He took a step towards her and lifted the bouquet up. It practically covered his face.

Sophie chuckled. "Well, aren't you the blooming idiot."

The air seemed to rush back onto the porch and all shoulders seemed to relax. Siobhan stepped out from behind Seamus and went to take the flowers. "They're lovely. Thank you, John."

"My mom picked them. From her garden."

Sophie stiffened. "Oh, so they're from your mother? Not from you?"

John Callahan blinked, realizing his blunder. "Well, uh, I was talking to my mother about the situation. About you. And well, I didn't know how to fix things, and she--"

"Oh! So, this whole idea is your mother's? You're not really sorry about the way you acted? So childish and thoughtless and actually, where Hans is concerned, very selfish and cruel?"

The girl's words seemed to give the lad some backbone. "Okay, Sophie, I was childish and thoughtless and selfish--"

"And cruel."

"Okay, yes, and I was mean to Hans. But I just didn't know how--"

"How to say you're sorry?"

"Yes, okay. I'm sorry, but you--"

Siobhan put a hand on John Callahan's shoulder. "Come in, John. You were right to talk to your mother." She gave Sophie a stern glance. "Boys, even men sometimes, get themselves into a pickle, and it's up to us, the women, to help them out of it."

The lad's shoulders relaxed once again. "Thank you, Ma'am. Don't mind if I do." He stomped his feet to shake off the dust from the fields, and he stooped to pat Francie's head. "And maybe later, we can see about those tricks." The dog whipped the air back and forth as she wagged her tail.

Sophie headed to the refrigerator. "We have some lemonade." She brought the pitcher over and sat it on the table. It thunked decisively, like a period, against the wood. "This doesn't mean I totally forgive you. And it certainly doesn't mean I'm your girlfriend."

"Oh, I know. I know. My mom pointed out that it's important to have friends who are girls as well as guys."

Sophie grimaced. "Again with your mother."

Siobhan interrupted. "She seems like a very wise woman."

John Callahan bobbed his head up and down vigorously. "Oh, she is, she is. I talk to her all the time. For advice and stuff." He turned to face Sophie. "But my Mom didn't tell me this, Sophie. You are a really good person and I want you for a friend. I've missed my friend."

Sophie turned, faking a need to go to the kitchen sink for something, and hiding the grin of satisfaction on her face. "Well," she said, over the running of water into the sink, "that's going to take some time. You need to earn friendship, you know, by being an actual friend."

Sophie went back to the table and sat down. There was an awkward moment of silence as all alternated stares at one another. Seamus broke the mood. "Is this mean we can all be friends again?"

Siobhan gave a light laugh. "Yes, Sweetheart, it means we can all work at being friends again."

Chapter Nineteen

Siobhan reached over and brushed her son's damp hair from his forehead. It was a hot August night, the air heavy with humidity. To make matters worse, the house was steamy from a day of canning beans. If only it would rain. How could the air feel so wet and yet not even a hint of rain? Tony was worried about the corn crop. Siobhan sighed. Farming. There was always something to worry about. It was exhausting.

Seamus's cheeks were flushed with the heat. No sooner had his head fallen back down on the pillow did his eyes flutter, fighting sleep. Siobhan made as if to stand up and slip out of the boy's room. "No, Momma," he mumbled. Tell me another story about Daddy." His eyelids lifted briefly.

Siobhan sighed. Sophie had relinquished her bedtime story-telling after Hans's accident. Once the pain of his absence began to subside, and once John Callahan's friendship had helped soothe her aching heart, Sophie took advantage of the long summer nights without school and homework to spend time with her friends. When she finished the supper dishes, she'd bend over her mother and plant a rushed kiss on Siobhan's forehead. "Bye, Mom. Off to Millie's. Yes, I know, back by 10:30."

And then she'd be gone in a rush, the tiredness from working in the fields splashed away by the water from the pump and erased by the prospect of another night out with friends. Siobhan was sure her daughter was not spending evenings at Millie's, but embarrassment still reddened her cheeks whenever she remembered the time she had decided to check up on Sophie. That evening, she had given into her doubts and called over to the Baranowskis', only to have her doubts flung back in her face when, moments later, Sophie came to the phone, breathless. "What's wrong, Mom? Is Seamus okay? Why are you calling?"

Trapped, Siobhan mumbled something stupid. "I just wanted to remind you you're picking beans tomorrow in the field out by the barn."

Siobhan heard that heavy exasperated sigh her daughter had developed the day after her sixteenth birthday, the sigh Siobhan had missed after Hans's accident, and the very one she had begun to welcome back. "I know, Mom, you told me at supper."

"Oh, yes," Siobhan had stammered. "I'm sorry, Sophie. I just forgot. You've been working in the Meadows so much..." Siobhan had let her voice trail off. "Well, apologize to Millie's parents for me, please."

So no, even though Siobhan was fairly sure her daughter was out in the fields somewhere or down by the river with John Callahan, she had resolved never to call over to Millie's again to check on her daughter.

Siobhan pulled the sheet up over her son. "No, Momma," he fussed, pushing back at the sheet. "It's too hot. Tell me another story about Daddy."

"How about the time he was in the barn and a wasp stung him on his nose?"

"No, Momma. Sophie already told me that story."

"Well, then, how about you tell me?"

Seamus stared up at his mother. She could see he was tempted. Then he sat up. "Okay. Well, Daddy's nose got as big as a baseball." Seamus raised both arms and shaped his arms around an imaginary baseball. Siobhan grinned. It was more like the size of a basketball. "And, Daddy's nose got big and bigger and bigger." The boy's hands stretched out farther and farther, away from each other. "And he couldn't hardly even breathe. He had to breathe through his mouth like this." Seamus panted vigorously through his open mouth. Siobhan smiled, imagining Sophie telling her son the story. "And Daddy looked really, really funny. Not even like his Daddy self."

"You told that story very well, Seamus."

The boy smiled proudly and let his head fall back onto the pillow. "Yeah, I'm a good storyteller."

Lately, Siobhan was having trouble telling the stories her son begged for so he'd have memories of his soldiering father who had died when he was only five. She had thought they would help her in her grief, and she did want her son to know his father. But the stories had only made her sadder, lonelier. And the sadness scared her. It threatened to pull her away from the present and paralyze her in the past. She was determined to fight against that sadness. Her children needed her. She couldn't just abandon life, much as she wanted to. Especially on nights like this, hot nights when it was hard to sleep. Hot nights that pressed like irons against the body, against the soul. Hot nights that made it hard to care about life.

Seamus turned over in his bed and surrendered to sleep. Francie got up from the floor and put her muzzle against the boy's face. She licked the boy's cheek, and then found her spot on the rug again, circled twice, and, just before lying down, looked over at Siobhan.

"Okay." She patted the dog on top of her head. "I'm going. You're on duty now."

Siobhan's foot ached from constantly pressing on the pedal of the sewing machine. That was one plus of Sophie's escapes from the house each evening. The house was quiet after Seamus went to bed. Siobhan could work on the dress she was making for her daughter as a surprise. But pretty soon she'd have to do a fitting. It was hard to guess about Sophie's maturing bust line and slim waist when all her daughter wore were the baggy old undershirts that she had appropriated out of her father's dresser drawer. When Siobhan commented how thin and worn they were getting, Sophie flew into a rage. "Don't you dare, Mom! These were Dad's. I feel like I'm close to him when I wear them. Besides, it's sooo hot out in the fields. You have no idea how hot it gets! At least the white reflects the sun."

Siobhan smiled now, recalling the conversation as she took the thin handkerchief and blotted the sweat from her forehead and cheeks. Then she took the handkerchief and unfolded it from all its crumplings. Sophie may have the undershirts, but she had the handkerchiefs. Mother and daughter each treasured their relics. Siobhan pressed the worn linen flat with the iron of her fingertips, reverently lingering over the initials embroidered in one corner. SAN. Stanislaus Anastasius Norowoski. Someone had embroidered them for Stan's confirmation. Siobhan wondered idly which of his many aunts had done so. It was just another thing she hadn't found out in time, before her husband died. Now there was no one to ask.

Well, Tony, yes, but for some reason she held back from asking him things like that. Siobhan couldn't explain it even to herself. There were just things about her husband that she wanted to hug all to herself, like invaluable treasures that she didn't want anyone else touching. Anyway, she shrugged, as if settling the conversation she was carrying on with herself, it wasn't likely that Tony would know about initials embroidered on a linen handkerchief.

Siobhan gentled the blue cotton out from under the needle of the sewing machine and tenderly folded up the dress. She lifted the mending out of the basket on the floor, set the dress inside, and then stacked the older clothes on top, careful to cover over any hint of the dress below. It was a wasted effort as Sophie steadfastly refused to come anywhere near the sewing machine. "No way, Mom," she'd said. "No way *I'll* be stuck at home, mending, cooking, cleaning. Like a servant. *I'm* gonna have a career." Siobhan noticed, however, that her daughter had set one of her father's undershirts on the top of the mending stack. The neckline was unraveling.

As she headed down the hallway to the kitchen, Siobhan had that spooky sensation, again, that she was the intruder. On those hot summer nights when the crickets made a din outside, when Seamus was worlds away in sleep up above and Sophie out again with her friends, the house seemed to shrink away from Siobhan as if once again she were judged and found shunned as an outsider. Outsider? Not so much, anymore. There was that ever-increasing pile of used children's clothes that threatened to overtake the front parlor. Clothes waiting for her to sort, clean, mend, and ready for her exchange store. Women would come and hand them over to Siobhan, lovingly folded, often caressing the pants or skirts one last time, saying goodbye to the memories of their small children. The women would look up at Siobhan, face to face, as they gave her their treasures. They had begun to accept her. Just that morning, Helen Wojtowicz glanced down at Seamus and smiled. Then she looked up at Siobhan--it seemed that Siobhan was the tallest woman in Hadley--and Helen had smiled. She reached a bony hand to caress Siobhan's cheek and said, "Well, you know, they grow too fast."

So, yes, Siobhan would have to get to that pile soon. It would be September in less than two weeks. Parents would begin thinking about school and about how to dress the lanky limbs of their growing children. "Soon," Siobhan promised. She wouldn't admit to herself that she didn't know exactly how to go about getting permission to use the Town Hall as a distribution point. Maybe she should just ask one of the older Polish women, the ones for whom she wrote letters to their sons and grandsons, if they could pave the way for her.

So yes, things had improved greatly with the townsfolk but, in the empty hours of the late evening, she would find herself shuddering in loneliness and wondering if she would ever belong. But belong she did and Siobhan stepped firmly against the wide-hewn floorboards of the hallway. "This is *my* house," she reminded it.

In the kitchen, moonlight slanted through the window above the sink. The quart jars of canned beans cooling in a line on the counter were caught in the moonlight. They made symmetrical elongated shadows on the kitchen floor. Soon she would have enough to get them through the winter. That was her goal. Enough beans, enough corn, enough tomatoes, enough squash, to last through the cold days of winter. And this year they'd have strawberry jam. She had swapped some of her asparagus for the right to pick strawberries at the Czajkowski farm. Maybe she could swap some corn for peaches at the orchard on Bay Road.

Siobhan settled down at the table to wait for Sophie. She didn't always wait up for Sophie but she missed her daughter. There was that closeness after the accident with Hans, and then they fell back into the familiar patterns of mother and rebellious teenage daughter. Siobhan didn't bother to turn on a light. It would only set the mosquitoes and other night raiders to bang against the screen door. Before long, she heard the light steps of her daughter as Sophie skipped up the steps and across the porch floor.

Siobhan watched as her daughter slipped off her sandals and rubbed the soles of her bare feet across the mat in front of the door.

"Sophie?"

The girl whirled around, her eyes searching for her mother's face in the shadows beyond the moonlight. "Jesus, Mom! What are you doing lurking in the dark? You scared me half to death." Sophie flicked on the light switch at the sink and the spotlight blinked on. Then, as if she had just thought of it, Sophie spun around. "Seamus? He's--?"

"He's sleeping." Siobhan was always touched by her daughter's protective love of her little brother.

"Well, Mom, what are you doing up? You must be exhausted."

The words tumbled out before Siobhan remembered that she and her daughter were back in antagonistic mode lately. "I miss you."

Sophie stared at her mother. "Oh." Buying time, she went over to the icebox and poured herself a glass of water. "You?" she nodded towards her mother.

"I'm fine, thanks."

"Well, Mom," Sophie began. Siobhan smiled. Sophie was taking it on herself more and more to lecture her mother.

"Sit." Siobhan pointed to the place across the table from her.

Sophie hesitated.

"Oh, come on. Just sit a few minutes. I never see you anymore."

"Well, whose fault is that, Mom? You have me out in the fields all day long and--"

"Hmmm. I think it was you who coaxed Tony into giving you more field work. Something about earning money for college."

"Okay, okay." Sophie sat down opposite her mother. "What are you doing sitting here in the dark? You're not getting funny in the head, are you?"

Siobhan smiled. "No, I just finished some mending and decided to wait for you. We never talk anymore."

"That's because you turn everything into an argument, Mom."

"*I* do? Okay, okay." Siobhan waved her hand. "I don't want to fight. It's just you never seem to be here anymore. Always rushing to get out the door, to get away."

To Siobhan's surprise, her daughter suddenly seemed overcome with emotion. She started to say something, then gulped several times.

"Sophie, what is it?"

"Mom, this just isn't a happy place. You're always so tired. Always so sad. It depresses me. I know you miss Dad. I do, too. And I miss Hans." She shook her head vigorously. "But I don't want to be sad all the time. Being with my friends helps. And actually, I don't know how to help you."

She reached across and cupped a hand over her mother's. "I know you're lonely. But I don't know what to do about that, Mom."

Siobhan flushed with shame. It was not her daughter's job to worry about her mother. It should be the other way around. Mothers worried after their children. But Siobhan had let her home slip into sadness. No wonder the house resented her presence.

Her mouth began to talk. Siobhan was stunned. She wondered where the words were coming from. "Well, let's change that."

"What? How?"

"Let's have a dinner party."

"A what?"

"A dinner party. You know, where we have a nice dinner, put on a tablecloth and napkins. Get dressed up. Use the good china from Ireland."

Sophie started laughing. "Mom, this is Hadley. They don't do dinner parties here. We're down-to-earth Polish folk."

"Well, they have dinner parties in Ireland. Leastwise that's what your grandfather told me. Where you get out the nice Irish linens and set a fine table. So let's have a dinner party. You *are* part Irish, you know."

"Okay." Sophie sat back in her chair and grinned at her mother. "So tell me about this dinner party. Who's coming? Your letter writing club?"

Siobhan's face went blank for a moment. Then it lit up. "We'll invite Uncle Tony. We'll make the dinner in his honor. To thank him for all his help."

"Hmmm, I dunno know, Mom. I can't see Tony at a fancy dinner party."

"Yes, we'll tell him he needs to dress up special. Wear that nice suit he wore at his father's funeral. Give it some use."

In spite of herself, Sophie felt her mother's enthusiasm catch. "Well, who else would we invite? Does a fancy dinner party only have one guest?"

"I have an idea about that."

"Mom! What are you up to?"

"Well, you remember that pretty young organist at Dziadziu's funeral?"

"That new lady?"

"Yes. We'll invite her."

Sophie's eyes lit up with delight. "Mom! You're going to play matchmaker? With Uncle Tony? He'll kill you!"

"We won't tell him."

"I gotta see this! Ambushing Unk!"

"And," Siobhan drew out the "and." "You can invite that Callahan boy."

Sophie's cheeks flushed red. "Oh, well, I don't know, maybe he, well, okay, sure if you want to. It's up to you. If you think he'd like to come."

"Oh, I'm sure he'd like to come."

"What about Seamus?"

"What do you mean?"

"Who can he invite?"

"Hmmm. I'll have him invite those boys that used to call him names. Iggy and Leon. They've gotten to be very kind to Seamus. I'll tell them they have to wear church clothes. And behave."

"Okay. And you, Mom, who will you invite?"

Siobhan smiled. "With you and Seamus here, I have everyone I want in the whole world."

"Oh, geez, Mom. Don't go getting all mushy."

Mother and daughter sat smiling at each other across the table. "This is nice, Mom."

Chapter Twenty

The day didn't start all that well.

When Siobhan chose the day for the dinner party, in her mind she had planned for it to be dry, not so much humidity, and one of those early evenings when the sun seemed to be resting low in the sky, the hot work over for the day. Clouds of course would be arranged in white fluffy pillows scattered here and there against a bedspread of royal blue. That morning, however, dawned gray and so thick with humidity that it was like breathing in steam. Siobhan could feel the cinch of a headache tightening its pinch across her forehead, the low-pressure system headache she always got when a storm was on the way.

"Maybe you should cancel," Sophie said. "Nobody's going to feel like dressing up and sweating in their fine clothes."

It was tempting. "No, it'll be okay. Too many arrangements have been made. Everything is in place. And we can bring down the fans from our bedrooms to circulate the air. Actually, why don't you go up and bring them down now?"

"Mom! I'm already late for the fields. Besides, I'm going to need the fans upstairs when I take a bath after working. We can bring them down later."

That's when the phone rang and it was Maria Rytuba, the new organist at Holy Rosary. "I'm sorry, Mrs. Norowoski, but--"

Siobhan's spirits plummeted. "Call me Siobhan, please."

"Oh, okay," she said, stammering something that sounded like "Shove-on." "I'm afraid I have a problem about tonight."

Siobhan walked over to the table already set with the Irish linen her father had said belonged to her mother. It had made the trip from Ireland in a steamer truck and had a musty smell from all the years it had lain folded up in tissue paper. Siobhan had aired it out on the clothesline in the back yard the day before, then wound up having to wash and press it anyway late that evening, because an afternoon wind had come up--a hot one, not a cooling one--and it blew dust from the powder dry fields onto the tablecloth.

And now another part of the plan was under threat. Siobhan sank down heavily onto one of the chairs, the very ones she had Seamus crawl around the night before to dust the rungs. The phone cord stretched tight. "Oh," was all Siobhan could manage.

"Yes, I don't know if you knew Chet Borowski," Maria paused.

"Not well. My brother-in-law knows the Borowskis. I understand Chet has been ill."

"Yes, well, he passed last night and the funeral is tomorrow. "

Siobhan felt defeated. She could hardly protest Maria's wanting to attend the wake. "Oh, well, I understand. "

"But Mrs. Norowoski, I mean Shove-on, I was really looking forward to it. I was wondering, well, I mean, I can pay my respects to the family this afternoon, but then Dan, Chet's uncle, wants to sing at the funeral and asked if he could practice with me tonight after he gets in from the fields."

Siobhan couldn't suppress a sigh of disappointment. "Oh, well, that comes first."

"I told Dan to come to the church as soon as he can tonight. I told him I had another commitment so if possible could he come straight to the church after he got off the fields." Maria laughed. "I even told him not to bother with a bath first. So, I was wondering if I could still come, even if I'm a little late."

Siobhan stood, her spirits instantly lighter. "Of course. I can hold dinner until you get here. I was planning on us perhaps having a glass of wine first. Not the boys, of course, I have lemonade for them, and maybe a little cheese."

Maria sounded delighted. "Oh great! I don't think Dan will need a lot of practice. He's singing the Ave Maria at the offertory and then the verses of Serdezna Mahtko at the end of the Mass. It's traditional, that hymn. He's done it before. I'll get to your place as soon as I can. I think I can get Dan to drop me off. Are you sure I can't bring anything?"

"No, no, you're the guest. We want to welcome you to Hadley."

"Well, okay then. I'll see you tonight. I've got to go now. The little Simkovicz girl is here for her piano lesson."

Siobhan clapped her hands together after she hung up the receiver. "Crisis averted." She went back to the counter to knead the bread for its second rising. She took the towel off the bowl and was dismayed to see that the yeast, despite the heat, had risen the dough just a little over half of what it usually rose. She made a fist and punched the dough. It felt heavy and stuck to her fingers as she kneaded it for the second rising. "Damn this humidity," she muttered. "Might end up being a cracker instead of bread."

"Are you making crackers, Momma?"

Siobhan looked down at Seamus. His cheeks were flushed and his hair was matted against his head. Siobhan brushed her hands against a towel and reached down to press a palm against her son's forehead. 'Please don't be sick,' she prayed.

"No, Momma." Seamus dodged his mother's hand. "I'm just hot because me and Francie were practicing her tricks." Seamus had the idea that after dinner, he and the dog would put on a show of Francie's tricks.

Siobhan glanced over at the dog who was pawing at her pile of old rags in front of the door to the shed. As if looking for Siobhan's sympathy, the dog glanced over at her, stretched out long and straight on her side, and panted, her sides heaving up and down. "I think both you and Francie should relax and stay inside. It's too hot."

"Uncle Tony says it's gonna rain. Uncle Tony says we need rain."

"Rain," Siobhan muttered. "That's all I need."

"Yes, Momma, we need rain. Uncle Tony says--"

"Yes, yes, I know what Uncle Tony says. Go sit at the table. At your regular place. I have the tablecloth folded back so you don't get it dirty. I'll make you a sandwich then maybe you should take a nap--"

"But Momma, I'm too big for a nap!"

"Yes, I know, but you are tired from working with Francie. Look! She's taking a nap. Besides you want to be able to stay up past your bedtime, don't you? Be rested up for doing Francie's tricks and all."

Seamus tilted his head to the right, a familiar posture when the boy was thinking things through. Then he brightened. "Yes, okay, Momma. I'll just rest my eyes a little bit after lunch."

After lunch--Seamus only ate about a third of his sandwich saying it was too hot to eat--the boy went upstairs to "rest his eyes" and Siobhan set about making a chocolate cake for dessert that evening. Then she set the table with her formal dishware; she polished two silver candlesticks, which also had made the trip from Ireland, put two beeswax candles in them, and set them on the table. She stood back to admire everything and smiled. Sophie was right. It had been a long time since they had celebrated anything, a long time since they had decorated the table and had a fine dinner. She tilted her head, wondering how long ago it had actually been, and she realized that that was the reason her son tilted his head when thinking anything through. He was mimicking his mother. Siobhan felt a wince of pain when she realized they hadn't really celebrated anything since Stan had gone off to the war. Even the past Christmas had been a sad and lonely affair for the family.

Siobhan looked up and out, past the screen door, past the porch to the ominous gray of the sky outside. Then suddenly there was a bolt of lightning so bright and so close that Siobhan felt the air crackle with electricity. The hair on her arms stood on end. Almost immediately there was a clap of thunder so loud and so close that Francie jumped up from her bed of rags and started howling. Siobhan heard Seamus scream and turned to run upstairs to her son's bedroom. She got to the door just as Seamus leapt out of bed and ran to her arms. "Momma! What was that!"

Just then there was another zig-zag of bright light so close it seemed right outside the boy's window and almost immediately another boom of thunder that seemed to shake the floor they were standing on. "Hold me tight, Momma!"

'Sophie!' The thought screamed through Siobhan's mind as she gripped her son tightly. Surely, Tony would get her out of the fields. The lightning was too close, too dangerously close.

Mother and son became aware of the howling down below. "Francie!" Seamus shouted, his own fear suddenly gone as he wrenched himself free from his mother's arms and tumbled down the steps to the kitchen. Moments later Siobhan rushed into the kitchen to see her son kneeling next to Francie, and petting her, whispering to her in a soothing voice. "It's okay, Francie. You're okay. Nothing bad is going to happen."

Siobhan hoped that that was true. 'Nothing bad is going to happen,' she whispered reassuringly to herself. Another flash of lightning lit up the back yard and the fields behind the barn, but the clap of thunder afterward told her the lightning had moved some seconds away from the house. Then the winds picked up and the stalks of corn out back beyond the barn bent over nearly to the ground. Seconds later, the wind sent rain to lash against the side of the house. "Seamus! Go back upstairs and close the windows!" Siobhan shouted as she ran to close the door to the side porch and then over to the kitchen sink to close that window. Seamus was just ahead of her in the hallway as she sped down to the front room to slam down the two windows open there.

Mother, son, and trembling dog stood inside the kitchen watching the rain pelt the driveway just beyond the porch. "Do you think Sophie is out in the rain, Momma?"

"I sure hope not."

"No," Seamus decided. "She's not out in the rain. She's in Uncle Tony's truck. She's safe, Momma."

Siobhan smiled down at her son. "I'll bet you're right."

Seamus looked up at his mother, suddenly worried. "Are we still having the dinner party, Momma?"

"Oh, goodness! My cake!" Siobhan turned and ran over to the stove. She glanced at the clock. "Oh no! The power went off!" She hesitated, debating. If she opened the oven, any remaining heat would escape and the cake would flop for sure.

"I hear Uncle Tony's truck, Momma!" Francie began to bark and pawed eagerly at the screen door.

"Sophie!" Siobhan turned and ran to the door flinging it open. Her worry changed to relief and she couldn't help laughing at her bedraggled daughter. Stan's tee shirt was so soaking wet it was transparent against the girl's body, hugging the curves of her emerging figure. Sophie's hair was plastered against her head, and her face and arms sported alternating streaks of mud and clean where the rain had lashed against her.

"Oh, nice, Mom! Laugh at me! I could have been killed by lightning!"

Siobhan reached to hug her daughter who ducked past her to stand in the kitchen, water and mud dripping off her onto the floor Siobhan that had gotten up early that morning to wash and wax.

"I'm sorry, Sweetheart! I was just so worried about you being caught out in the fields when it started lightning, and then when I saw you, and you were okay, I was so relieved that--"

"So relieved you thought you'd laugh at me!? Nice, Mom, really nice."

"She *was* worried," Seamus protested. "I heard her worrying. And her face was all like this." The boy scrunched up his forehead and turned his lips into an upside-down smile. Sophie laughed. "So don't be mad at Momma, Sophie. Don't be mad at her."

Sophie studied her little brother and her mother. Francie barked. Then Sophie laughed again. "Well, it was pretty scary! We were just talking about how hot it was, John and me, and could it please, please, please just rain and all of a sudden there was a white-hot line of lightning at the end of the corn row we were working on. And thunder so loud it made my ears hurt!" She cocked her head and banged against her ear with her right hand. Then she switched sides and hands and banged again. "The thunder is still ringing inside my ears."

Seamus's eyes were huge with wonder. "Did you get hit by lightning, Sophie?"

"No, but almost. John and I dropped our hoes right there in the middle of the corn and ran like crazy back to Uncle Tony's truck." Sophie danced about the kitchen acting out her words. "Then pretty soon we heard Uncle Tony come hopping down the path towards the truck, shouting a lot of Polish swears, and he flung the driver's side door open." Sophie gave a dramatic sweep of her right arm and drops of water splashed down onto the kitchen floor. "John and me were already in the truck. Uncle Tony threw his cane up at me." Sophie swiped her hand through the kitchen air and snatched the imaginary cane. Seamus's eyes bulged with wonder. "Unk grabbed onto the door handle, and hopped up into the truck next to us. Then we drove around and picked up the prisoners. They had to get in the back of the truck because there wasn't any room up front with us so they got rained on good." Sophie looked down at her sopping wet shirt; her shorts clung to her wet legs. "Worse 'n me! Their shoes must be filled with water and mud." She pranced around the kitchen leaving mud tracks on the freshly waxed floor. "They sounded like this: Squish, squeak, squish, squeak." Seamus let out a squeal of delight at Sophie's antics. "Anyway, Unk dropped them off at his barn and then brought me over before taking John home." And at that, Sophie took an elaborate bow. "Thank you, thank you, my good people." Siobhan joined her son in applause. Francie barked.

Siobhan turned to thank her brother-in-law but all she heard was the truck as he backed out of the driveway.

"Some night you picked for a party, Mom!"

"Look, Momma!" Seamus shouted. "There's a rainbow."

"Where?"

All three of them ran out to the porch. The rain was already abating and, sure enough, a rainbow arched over their barn. They watched enthralled.

"I didn't never saw a rainbow so pretty."

"'Didn't ever,'" Sophie said.

"Hey! Feel the air, Momma!" Seamus waved his hands about. "It's really nice air! Not sticky air!"

Sophie spun around, drops of rainwater spinning off her onto her mother and brother. She had her mouth open, gulping. "Taste it, Mom! This is delicious air!"

Siobhan smiled. Even as she headed over to get the mop, she knew that everything was going to be okay. "All right, you guys. Get upstairs and wash up and get dressed up nice for dinner. There's a surprise for you, Sophie on your bed."

Siobhan had finished Sophie's dress the day before. She had guessed at her daughter's growing shape and crossed her fingers that the dress would fit. She stole a look at her daughter's thin body, thin despite her feminine shape. Sophie's figure was outlined by the soaking wet tee shirt and Siobhan wondered if the dress wasn't too big through the waist. No matter, she could pin it for that night if need be.

Siobhan listened as brother and sister giggled and raced up the stairs, Francie joining in with jubilant barks. She went to get the mop and then wiped up Sophie's muddy drippings which had pooled on the kitchen floor and then marked her path down the hallway to the stairs. Siobhan opened the oven door and stared at the cake which had only begun to rise before the power went out. She closed the oven, hoping the remaining heat would help it along. "Maybe I can turn it into a sort of pudding," she mumbled.

But the chicken, she would definitely need power to cook the chicken. And then she remembered! Their old stove, the wood burning one, was still out in the barn. If she had to, she could feed it some of the logs left over from the past winter and she could cook the chicken out there if it came to that. And the potatoes too.

She grinned. "Nothing can stop me," she announced. And for the first time since before Stan left for the war, Siobhan felt like her old self was rushing back.

Siobhan smiled to see Iggy and Leon race up the stone path to the porch. Their otherwise unruly hair was slicked back off their foreheads and gelled flat into place. They both sported ties awkwardly anchored around their necks. "Walk, don't run, gentlemen!" barked Tony behind them and the boys immediately pulled up short and walked stiff legged up the steps. Francie barked eagerly upon seeing the boys and jumped up on their legs. "Down!" ordered Seamus, then, "Sit!" The dog reluctantly obeyed, whining. "Wow! That dog is really smart!" Leon said, as Iggy leaned down to pet Francie.

"Where's your manners?" Tony thundered.

Iggy and Leon immediately straightened and addressed Siobhan. "Good evening, Ma'am," they chorused.

"Thank you for inviting us," Leon said, pulling out a bunch of daisies from behind his back and extending them towards Siobhan.

"Why thank you, boys! These are lovely! I'll put them right on the table." Siobhan turned and ducked into the storage room off the kitchen. She came back with a vase in hand and headed to the sink to fill it with water.

"Get the wine!" Tony ordered, and the boys flew back out across the porch to the truck.

Siobhan heard the boys arguing. "I'm bringing it! I got here first!"

"No you're not! I'm older 'n you. I'm bringing it."

"Older don't mean nothing. Let go of me!"

"Give me that!"

And then there was the sound of glass breaking.

"Uh-oh!"

"Now see what you did!"

"Tony is gonna kill us!"

"You got that right!" Tony roared, whacking his crutch against the porch floor in anger and frustration.

Siobhan stifled her laughter as she reached up to her brother-in-law's shoulder. "It's okay, Tony. I have wine, but I so appreciate the gesture."

Tony's face was flushed a murderous red. "Those boys will never be gentlemen. You miscreants will clean up every bit of that broken glass! I don't need my tires getting a flat because of your stupidity!"

Francie barked.

"And I don't want to hear that the dog got a sliver of glass caught in her paw. Every bit of glass, you hear?"

"I'll get the broom and a dustpan." Siobhan turned her back to her guests to hide her grin.

"I'll help." Seamus grabbed the dustpan and broom from his mother and darted across the porch.

Siobhan called out after him, "Be careful! Don't get cut. And don't get dirty!"

"Too late for my miscreants." Tony pointed to the two boys who stood in shame-faced guilt. Wine splashes had darkened the fronts of their Sunday shirts and pants.

"Miscreants?" Siobhan teased.

"Don't you start with me, Siobhan."

She stifled the laughter bubbling to get out and turned to call out at her son again. "Seamus, show them where the trash is out by the barn. Then when you boys are finished, come on in and let's see if we can't get some of those stains off your clothes." She beckoned to her brother-in-law. "Come, Tony. The boys will take care of it."

"I oughta whip those boys. That was an expensive bottle of wine!"

Siobhan reached over and kissed Tony on the cheek. "I really appreciate the thought. But let it go; accidents happen."

Tony's face reddened at the unexpected gesture of affection from Siobhan. He collapsed onto the chair closest to the door and surveyed the table set with the fine Irish linen, china, and goblets. "My! This is very nice, Siobhan. Very nice, indeed."

Siobhan blushed with pride. "Well, it's time we celebrate some things in life. Life should be more than work and sadness."

Tony nodded. "Amen."

The boys tumbled up the steps, across the porch, and bounded into the kitchen. Siobhan wet a rag and set about blotting the wine stains from the boys' pant legs.

"Sorry about the wine, Ma'am," Iggy mumbled.

"What!?" Tony roared. "Speak up like a man!"

Iggy shouted, "We're sorry about the wine, Ma'am. And thank you for inviting us to dinner."

"Everything's okay, Momma. We cleaned it all up," Seamus was quick to reassure his mother. "They didn't mean to do nothing wrong."

"My little peace-maker," Siobhan said.

"Stop that, Francie!" Seamus giggled. The dog was licking at the wine drops on Leon's pant legs. "I think she likes it, Momma."

Tony laughed. "She has good taste, that dog."

There was a moment of awkward silence as Seamus pulled the dog away from Leon and Siobhan finished wiping off the boys' pant legs. Then using the fingers of her hand, she combed their hair back into place. "Good as new," she said.

"Mom! It's so beautiful!"

They all turned to stare at Sophie who stood in the doorway from the hall. She had on the blue dress that Siobhan had stayed up late the night before to finish. Sophie looked stunning, a far cry from the wet bedraggled and bemudded girl who had dashed in from the rain only a couple of hours earlier. She had brushed her dark hair till it shone and it hung in a beautiful cascade over her shoulders and down her back. The dress hugged her curves accenting her young womanhood. She twirled around once and the skirt of the dress danced over her bare feet.

No one said anything until Seamus ran over to hug his sister. "Sophie, you look so beautiful! You look like a real lady!"

Everyone laughed at that, including Sophie whose eyes were shiny. Siobhan felt her own eyes flood with tears as she stared at the vision of loveliness that was her daughter.

Even Tony seemed caught in his niece's spell. His voice was thick and hoarse. "Your father would have been so proud."

Embarrassed, Sophie laughed nervously. "Okay, okay. It's the same old me. Relax." She turned to her mother. "Thank you so much, Mom. I absolutely love it! When did you ever do this? You are always so busy taking care of us. The farm, the house. I just don't know when you could have done this."

She hugged her mother.

"You're forgetting those long nights when you are out and about."

Sophie blushed. "Oh, yeah."

"Wow!"

They all turned to see a spiffed up and gentlemanly John Callahan standing in the doorway, a bottle of wine in his hand.

"Oh good," Iggy said. "Now we'll have wine." He went to take the wine from John when suddenly Tony's crutch flew up to bar his access.

"You leave that bottle alone, miscreant. John, hand that to Mrs. Norowoski."

"Here, Mrs. Norowoski. Thank you so much for inviting me." He handed over the wine and spoke without ever taking his eyes off Sophie. "You look beautiful." He suddenly faced Siobhan. "I mean you, Mrs. Norowoski, I mean--"

Sophie laughed. "Suave, John, real suave."

"Well," Siobhan took charge of the situation. "Let's all go into the front parlor and we'll have some hors d'oeuvres."

Seamus looked up to his mother and wrinkled his face in puzzlement. "Hors--?"

"Snacks, Sweetheart."

Sophie's face went blank. "But Mom--"

Siobhan shook her head as if to say, "Not to worry."

As they entered the front parlor, Siobhan bringing up the rear with a tray of cheeses and crackers, Sophie's eyes widened in surprise. "Where--?"

"It's all in my bedroom."

"Oh," Sophie nodded, realizing that her mother had moved all the donations for the clothes swap.

After they settled into chairs, Leon and Iggy on the floor in front of Tony, Siobhan announced, "Seamus and Francie have a little show to put on for all of us."

Francie delighted in the oohs and aahs she got as she performed her tricks for her young master. Her tongue hung out and her face seemed broad with doggy smile. There was lots of clapping and in the end, both dog and master took a bow. Francie was rewarded with a treat from Seamus's pocket.

Iggy and Leon argued over who would get to sit next to Francie when Seamus, ever the peacemaker, suggested they sit one on each side of the dog. "I get to sit next to her all the time," he said, diplomatically. Francie relished the attention as the boys fed her bits of their crackers.

Then Francie bounded up all of a sudden and headed down the hallway. Seconds later, they heard someone call out, "Hello? Anybody here?"

"Oh," Siobhan stood. "That would be our last guest."

Moments later, Siobhan led Maria down the hallway and into the parlor. She glanced over at Tony to catch his reaction as she introduced the latest arrival. "This is Maria Rytuba, the new organist at the Polish church."

Siobhan was thrilled to see Tony blush and sit up straight in his chair. She was right. She knew there was an attraction there. Siobhan felt a smug satisfaction. Her plan was working. John Callahan and Sophie immediately stood to greet the latest guest. Tony struggled to his feet. After they got a tap on the back of their heads with Tony's crutch, Leon and Iggy also stood, muttering a polite, "How do you do?" Introductions were given all around.

"I'm sorry I'm late." Maria explained how she had to rehearse the soloist for tomorrow's funeral service. "Which was a little silly because, as you know the power is out, so we couldn't practice with the organ, but we did the best we could."

Nothing seemed to fluster the pretty woman who made a fuss over the handsome young Seamus as he extended the tray of snacks towards Maria.

"So you are new to Hadley, Maria?" Siobhan asked.

"Well, sort of. I actually didn't know I had a cousin here. I was studying music in France when Hitler marched into Poland. My parents were still there, back in my home in Poland, I mean, and my little sister, but, you know, after Kristallnacht, well--"

They all stared as the seemingly unflappable Maria was suddenly overcome with emotion. She swallowed hard as if it were the cracker she was eating that caused her to hesitate. "I'm sorry. But, well, after that, my family in Poland just seemed to disappear."

"What's Kristall--or whatever you said, what's that?" John Callahan asked.

"Oh, Kristallnacht. It means Crystal Night. It was a pogrom, an attack, against the Jews in Germany and Austria."

Sophie looked shocked. "How awful!"

Seamus, puzzled, insisted, "But why is called Crystal Night?"

"That means the Night of Broken Glass. Hitler's soldiers came into the homes of Jewish families and smashed everything. They broke the windows of all the Jewish families and stores, even the synagogues. So that's why it's called Kristallnacht."

Seamus shuddered and wrapped his arms around his chest, hugging tight. "That's scary. Hitler is a really, really, really bad man."

"So you are Jewish?" Siobhan asked. "But I thought you were a member of our church."

Maria glanced down at the floor, buying time to compose herself. She took a sip of wine. Then she looked up at Siobhan, struggling to put on a brave face. "No, I'm Catholic. My father was a doctor and he was good friends with a Jewish doctor, well, our whole family was. Dr. Daniel, as we used to called him, and my father, well they grew up as friends when they were little boys. They used to talk about becoming doctors and curing sick people when they were kids and they actually did live out that dream. They stayed friends all their lives and we kids grew up with Dr. Daniel and Miss Rebecca's three boys. My father and Dr. Daniel always used to talk over their medical cases together and they helped each other."

Siobhan thought about the way people used to taunt her and her father when they came to the open-air market in Boston. They would shop there, all the while looking down their noses at the ignorant Irish immigrants. The women were the worst. They were just maids working in fancy houses, but they thought that that made them better than the Irish people waiting on them, people just like the maids, all struggling to make a living.

And then there was the loneliness and isolation when she was rejected again by the Polish community in Hadley. Siobhan nodded. "That's the way it should be. That friendship crosses all those artificial borders."

Seamus looked up at Maria. "What happened next?"

"Well, when Hitler's soldiers went into Poland, my family took in the Turowicz family and hid them. My father was going to try and help them escape from Poland, but before he could, Hitler's men found out what my father had done. At least that's what I've been able to find out from a neighbor, Anelie. She got a letter smuggled out of the country to me in France. She said she saw the Germans go into our house and drag everybody out, including my mother and father and little sister as well as Dr. Daniel's family. The Germans took them away. They just disappeared. Nobody knew where they went. Anelie said that a few days later, the German soldiers came back and they took over my parents' house and made it a military post."

"That's really scary," Seamus said. Siobhan reached for him and he went to sit on her lap. He curled his head against her shoulder and stared out solemnly at Maria. Siobhan wasn't so sure that her young son should be listening to Maria's story, but the war and talk of the war was everywhere. Seamus had lost his father. She couldn't protect him from that terror and perhaps it was better that he listen to such stories in her presence, when she could be there to calm his fears and hold him tight.

Maria traced the rim of the wine glass with her finger. "I couldn't find out anything about my parents. I wanted to go back to Poland, but the cousin I was staying with persuaded me that that would be very foolish. That my parents would want me to stay away. And that they would want me to save myself."

Siobhan glanced at Tony who was staring at Maria, his face stricken. She was surprised to hear John Callahan speak up. "Your cousin was very wise."

"Yes, yes, she was. You see, I was lucky to be studying piano and organ in France. My family was very wealthy. Before the war, I mean." Maria stopped, overcome with emotion. Siobhan reached over her son and squeezed Maria's hand. Maria looked up at her gratefully, then her gaze swept the room.

"I'm sorry. I've told this story so many times, you'd think I would be used to it. But being with all of you, in this beautiful family that you have, Shove-on, well, it just seems to make me very emotional."

Siobhan was startled to hear the thick emotion in Tony's voice. "How did you end up in Hadley?"

Maria seemed to relax with the question. "Well, that's a good question! My cousin in France thought we should leave that country. Even though our French friends thought it would be impossible that Hitler would dare invade France, we felt that it was just a matter of time before the German soldiers would be marching in. So we pooled together all the money we had, my cousin and I, and bought passage to sail to Boston. I really didn't want to leave. It felt like I was abandoning my family, my country. Going further and further away from my homeland. But my cousin, she was much older than I, actually more like a grandmother to me, she said that things were only going to get worse and that it was her responsibility to protect me."

Siobhan could see that her daughter was thinking of her own father. Sophie spoke up. "She was right. Hitler is a monster. Look at this terrible war that he started. All the lives lost."

Maria looked over at her, her face soft with compassion. "Yes, I know of your family's loss as well."

It was Seamus who broke the uncomfortable silence that followed. "Did your boat come all the way to Hadley?"

They all laughed, all but Iggy and Leon, who looked at each other, and then joined in the laughter so as not to be left out. It was clear that they didn't understand what the laughing was all about.

Seamus's face turned red. "I mean, did your ship come down the river?"

Siobhan set her son down on the floor. "No, Sweetheart. The ships that come from France are too big to come down the Connecticut River."

"Oh." Seamus looked over to Maria. "My Daddy died in France. That's why I named my dog Francie."

The dog lifted her head and whined, acknowledging the importance of her name.

"She's a good dog, aren't you, Francie?" Seamus reached over to pet the dog's head and Francie responded by thumping her tail against the rumps of Iggy and Leon.

Again, everyone was startled to hear Tony's strained voice. It wasn't the voice of the usually confident and cocky Uncle Tony they all knew. "How did you get to Hadley?"

"Oh, well, my cousin and I landed in Boston and we rented a room. We gave piano lessons and that's how we made some money for the rent and for food. My cousin got very sick. We couldn't afford a doctor so we didn't really know what the matter was. I made her go to an old retired Polish doctor who lived in our neighborhood and he said she would have to go to a hospital and get a lot of tests. He said it seemed like her heart was failing."

"How awful for you," Siobhan said. "It must have been very scary."

"Yes, yes, it was. I made her go to the hospital. We waited a whole day before someone finally came to look at her. The doctor agreed that it was her heart and that she needed a very serious operation which she might not survive. I wanted her to have the operation. I would have given my life's earnings for the rest of my life to pay for it, but she just looked at me. I'll never forget what she said. She said, 'We don't have the money. And I'm old, I've had a good life. It's okay. I can go when it's time.'"

"What a brave woman," Sophie said, reaching for John Callahan's hand.

"Yes, yes she was. So we went back to our little room. My cousin, Nellie was her name, my cousin said that she thought we had more relatives in America, so she started asking where Polish people had settled, and by asking and asking, she discovered other cousins of ours in Hadley, the Zalots. She wrote to them and they invited us both to come and live with them. But before we could, my dear cousin Nellie died."

No one said anything for several minute. "Oh, look, now, what I've done. I've made you all sad. And this is a wonderful, happy occasion. I'm sorry, Shove-on."

Siobhan leaned forward to protest but Maria continued. "In the end, mine is a happy story, really. The Zalots are wonderful people. Kind, generous. They took me in and right from the start I was one of the family. Everyone in Hadley has been so kind. They needed an organist at the church and now I am giving music lessons, too, so I can help this wonderful family."

John Callahan spoke up. "The Zalots? Is Frank in that family? We heard an incredible story about his rescue at sea."

"Yes, yes. He's back at sea and we haven't heard from him in a long time. He's fighting the Japanese. We pray every night for his safety and that of all the sailors. But still, we worry."

Maria was conscious of everyone looking at her, sympathy in their eyes. Siobhan noticed the compassion and admiration on Tony's face. He had not taken his attention away from Maria.

"So really, when you think about it, mine actually is a happy story. I'm so blessed, so lucky when I think about what has happened to my family and others back in Poland. We are so fortunate to be in this wonderful country."

"Yes," Tony nodded, clasping his hands back and forth as if he didn't know what to do with them.

"I'm hungry," Seamus said.

"We are too," added the boys sitting on the floor near Tony.

"Oh, my yes!" Siobhan got to her feet. She excused herself, saying she had to finish up the preparations for dinner. She was more than a little pleased when her daughter stood also. "I need to help Mom." The two headed out to warm up the potatoes, the chicken and the beans on the stove out in the barn. When the food was ready, Sophie went to get John Callahan to help them bring everything back into the kitchen.

The power still had not come back on after the late afternoon storm so they dined by candlelight. Tony tapped Iggy on the back of his head saying, "Leave some for the rest of us," when the lad was dipping back into the bowl of mashed potatoes for a second helping, even though his plate was already overflowing.

"However did you manage a cooked dinner with no power?" Maria gushed. "Everything is delicious!"

They were eating dessert, a sort of modified pudding made from the half-baked cake and topped with fresh raspberries when the siren went off. Sophie's face went white as she stared at her mother. "That's the third one this week!"

Iggy shouted, "That means the Germans are coming to bomb us!"

Siobhan put down her napkin and stood, glancing at Maria. The young woman held her fork above her dessert dish. Her hand was shaking as if she had a palsy.

"No, sir!" Seamus's tone was matter-of-fact as he slid off of his chair. "It's just a practice. And even 'ifn it wasn't, we make everything black so the German planes can't see us up in the sky and they can't find a place to drop the bombs."

"Yes, my sweetheart, you're right. Run upstairs and put the flaps down across the windows. Sophie, you'll get the windows in the front parlor. John, can you douse the candles?"

"No!" Leon insisted, with exaggerated terror. "It means the Germans are going to attack us." He made his arms shake as if he were in throes of epilepsy.

"No, it doesn't!" Tony thundered. "Stop kidding around." He cuffed the boy lightly on the back of his head. "Miscreants!" He turned to Maria. "I happen to know that last Saturday, when the Air Raid siren when off, a sentry found a house in North Hadley with its lights still on. So they're punishing us with these extra drills."

Siobhan rushed over to the sink where she pulled the dark cloth across the window. The kitchen fell into blackness. Siobhan listened to their breathing as everyone wondered, "What next?" They heard Sophie's footsteps as she made her way back down the stairs. And then a bump in the hallway. "Hey, Pip Squeak, watch where you're going!"

"Silly! How can I watch where I'm going when everything is black?"

At that, everyone laughed. Siobhan and her children groped their way back to the table and sat down.

There was silence as everyone wondered what to do. Suddenly there was a blast of music coming from the radio which Siobhan kept plugged in on the counter near the stove. Laughter bubbled up inside Siobhan and she bent her head over the table, trying to catch her breath. "Oh, *now* the power comes back on!"

They all heard the surprise in Seamus's voice. "Momma! You can laugh? Really laugh?"

Siobhan was momentarily stunned. Yes, it had been a long time since she had laughed like that. It was a good feeling, the way her insides shook all over. She promised herself then and there that there would be much more laughter.

The "miscreants" began singing along with the radio: "'Happy Days are Here Again!'" They were waving their heads back and forth in rhythm with the tune and using their forks and knives as drumsticks against the tabletop. Tony's hand flew over to grip Leon's hand. "Stop that banging! You boys have no table manners!"

"No, no!" Sophie covered her ears with her hands. "I like FDR but I hate that song!"

"FDR! He's my favorite president!" Seamus began an imitation: "'We are an arnesal of democracy!'"

"'Arsenal,'" Sophie corrected her brother. "And, so far, he's the *only* president you've known in your short life, Pip--" she broke off, remembering she'd promised her brother not to call him Pip Squeak in front of Leon and Iggy.

Siobhan made her way over to the counter and her hand groped around in the dark until she found the knob to turn off the radio. At that moment, a cloud moved on and light poured into the kitchen from the screened in porch. Joy lit up Siobhan's face. "Oh, good! Moonlight!" The eerie milk-white light wrapped around the six shadowy forms at the table

"Now what, Momma?" Seamus asked as his mother returned to sit at the table.

"I know!" Leon said. "Let's tell ghost stories!"

"Yeah!" Iggy echoed.

"Good idea," Tony said. "I'll start. Did you ever hear about the Creaky Barn door and the Hairy Arm?"

Siobhan could feel her son tense with excitement.

And so the next half hour was spent with loud laughter and shrieks as Tony entertained the dinner guests with spine-shaking tales of Hairy Arm, the ax-murderer who lived in an old broken down barn with wild coyotes.

The all-clear sounded and, as Siobhan slid her chair back from the table, Seamus and the boys voiced their disappointment. "No more stories!?"

The party broke up soon afterward, Maria saying she didn't know when she had had so much fun. John Callahan volunteered to stay behind with Sophie and clean up the dinner dishes insisting that Siobhan "go rest after all your hard work, Ma'am." Siobhan watched as Tony fumbled around for the words to invite Maria to ride home with him in the truck. When she asked if there would be room, Tony said, "The miscreants can ride in the bed of the truck, right, boys?"

"Yes, Tony." They scrambled towards the porch door arguing over who was going to be first to climb into the truck.

Tony thumped his crutch against the kitchen floor. "Don't you boys have something to say?"

As one they stopped in their tracks, straightened their bodies, and addressed Siobhan. "Thank you so much for the delicious supper."

Siobhan hid her grin. "You're entirely welcome."

They all waved goodbye as Tony, Maria, and the "miscreants" headed out the driveway.

Siobhan turned and began to clear the table. Sophie put a hand on her mother's arm. "We got this, Mom."

She looked over to John Callahan who nodded. "This was a really fun time, Mrs. Norowoski. I'll help Sophie clean up."

Siobhan shrugged, poured more wine into her glass, and headed down the hallway to sit in the peace and quiet of her front room.

"You look really beautiful, tonight, Sophie," she heard John Callahan say.

"My mom made this dress."

"Really? It looks like a fancy store-bought dress. It's beautiful. Like you."

Siobhan smiled to herself. "Store-bought indeed."

Epilogue

"Uncle Tony is so nervous!" Seamus said. Siobhan stared at her young son. He was growing up way too fast. Eight, he was eight already, with a successful second grade under his belt. The pant legs on his new suit, a suit she had shopped for among the donations in her now quite successful clothing exchange, fit the month before but were already brushing the tops of his socks. It seemed like he was growing an inch a month.

"He's nervous?" Siobhan looked towards the front of the church where Tony was standing, waiting for his bride-to-be, the lovely Maria Rytuba, to walk down the aisle towards him. He did indeed look uncomfortable. He kept running a finger under the stiffness of his collar and his face was flushed. Siobhan looked down at her son. "Aren't you supposed to standing up there with him?"

"Yes, Momma. But I need the ring."

"Oh, right." Siobhan reached into the little lace purse that was hung on a silk satin string around her neck, the very purse she had worn at her own wedding a lifetime ago. Stan. Her thoughts had been filled with Stan as she got ready for Tony's wedding that morning. "Here. Now don't run. Just walk up and stand next to Tony."

Despite the excitement of the wedding, Siobhan was tired. She'd been cooking, for days it seemed, for the celebration at her farm after the ceremony. Why August, she wondered? Why did they choose such a hot month? But she knew why. It was the anniversary of when they had met at Siobhan's, the night of the dinner party nearly two years ago, the night she herself decided to take her life back and live again.

A lot had happened since then. They had wept as they huddled around the radio, listening to the news that Roosevelt had died. And they had cheered when it was reported that Hitler

216

had died, taking the coward's way out by committing suicide. But Siobhan had made her children pray for his soul. "It's the Christian thing to do. Jesus told us to love our enemies." She herself marveled that the hard spot of hatred was gone from her own heart.

The war was over. There had been a lot of shouting at the news. Bands blaring. Dancing in the streets even. Then horror as the discoveries of the barbaric terrors of the concentration camps made their way into American newspapers. Even the German prisoners were shocked, disbelieving at first, saying that it was propaganda. The American people seemed to turn on the prisoners, then, as if they personally had been responsible; the government couldn't ship them off the land of the free quick enough. But the people of Hadley felt sad at their leaving. The prisoners had become partners tilling the soil alongside the few remaining Polish men who hadn't been called to service. Their lands could not have been farmed without them. Even Siobhan's heart ached as she saw the boys who had come as prisoners return now as men, sad and spirits broken, to uncertain futures in a homeland which had been destroyed. Siobhan was secretly relieved that Hans had left them sooner. She couldn't imagine the heart-tearing sadness if Sophie had continued a relationship with the prisoner, continued to let her feelings grow, imagining a life of bliss with him. Such feelings were hopelessly doomed, yet another tragic fallout of the war.

At the declarations of peace, there had been lights of hope in the hearts of the Polish women of Hadley who looked forward to the return of their men. But the men didn't come back, at least not right away. There were the peacekeeping missions in Europe and Japan; their husbands and sons were needed there. So it was tough times for the farmers again, fields to plow, crops to plant, and very few hands to do the labor. And shortages. In many ways it felt as if the war were still being waged, only then it was against hunger and want and need. And loss: some beloved sons of Hadley never returned.

But this, this was a good thing, Tony and Maria's wedding. A cause for joy and dancing and for forgetting sadness and loss. Siobhan was determined to make it so. When Sophie, covered in dust and tiredness, sat at the kitchen table just a few weeks ago and asked her mother, "What's life for anyway? If it's just about work, work, work and always being so tired. If people you love just get ripped away anyway. Like Dad, and..." Her voice drifted off but Siobhan knew she was thinking of Hans. Siobhan had gone to the table, sat beside her daughter and caressed her daughter's sweat-matted hair. Remarkably, Sophie had not pulled away. Instead she blinked fast to keep tears from falling. Siobhan told her then, what life was for. "It's true. Life is short. And often very hard. But we work at it. We work to make beauty happen. To make love happen. And that's worth all the struggle."

Siobhan felt a light tap on her shoulder and turned to face her daughter. She was again struck by the beauty Sophie had become. She was wearing the dress Siobhan had made for her daughter two years ago. Siobhan had had to take it in a bit more at the waist and let the bust out a bit more.

"The organist, that lady from St. Mary's in Northampton, she just flashed me the sign. She's getting ready to play the march and we're supposed to process down the aisle. Come on, Mom. You're first."

"I don't know why I can't just wait in front with Tony and Seamus." Siobhan stared down at her own dress self-consciously. She knew she wasn't old, but that morning she felt old. She had modified her wedding dress for the event and dyed it blue to match Sophie's.

"Mom, you look beautiful. I don't know what you're worried about."

"Soph, they're ready." Siobhan turned to stare again at Barney Mokrzecki. He was so handsome in his army uniform. "What about John Callahan?" Siobhan had asked when Sophie told her that when Barney was home on leave, and she was going to ask him to accompany her down the aisle for Tony's wedding.

Sophie had made a face. "Oh, he's history. Again. I couldn't stand his jealousy. When I told him I wanted Barney to be my escort at the wedding, to honor him for his service, John had a fit. Sooo," Sophie gave her mother a flirtatious smile, "he's history. For now."

"Oh, Sophie, look at Maria!"

The bride had appeared at last escorted by her cousin, Frank Zalot. She was radiant in a long white wedding gown embellished with lace at the bodice and at the wrists of the sleeves.

Siobhan smiled at Maria who smiled back at her, completely at ease. Maria never seemed nervous about anything. Siobhan turned to look at Tony standing up at the altar. He, on the other hand, looked as if he were about to come undone at any minute.

The organ began to play and quickly Siobhan and her daughter fell into place to begin the procession down the aisle ahead of the bride.

Acknowledgments

Siobhan's story would not have been possible without the help of the following residents of Hadley and Hatfield, Massachusetts who, for the most part, were children or teenagers during that era and who willingly gave me hours of interview time sharing their memories. Many thanks to:

Theresa and Barney Banas
Patricia Dubiel
John and Ann Mish
Ken and Phyllis Parsons
Chester "Chet" Szawlowski
Margaret "Peggy" Tudryn
Frank Zalot
and
Joseph Zgrodnik

Frank Zalot's story recounts an actual historical event in which he participated as described in Chapter Fourteen. It's a story which hadn't been told until 2012 due to the secrecy imposed at the time by the armed services. Japan was not to know of the Navy's maneuvers in the South Pacific.

Thanks also to my husband Ray Brown and the friends who read drafts of the novel and made valuable suggestions: Sue Broderick, Christina Fantini, Marilyn Francis, Funwriters (especially Ian, Ed, Linda and Don), Karin H. O'Neil, and Cynthia Rivendell.

Bibliography

Buck, Anita Albrecht. Behind Barbed War: German Prisoners of War in Minnesota During World War II. North Star Press of St. Cloud, Inc., 1998.

Carlson, Lewis H. We Were Each Other's Prisoners. Basic Books: A member of the Perseus Books Group, 1997.

Greene, Bette. Summer of My German Soldier. Puffin Modern Classics, 2006.

Koop, Allen V. Stark Decency: German Prisoners of War in a New England Village. University Press of New England, 1988.

Krammer, Arnold. Nazi Prisoners of War in America. Scarborough House Publishers, 1979, 1991, 1996.

Thompson, Antonio. Men in German Uniform: POWs in America during World War II. Legacies of War, G. Kurt Piehler, series editor, Knoxville: The University of Tennessee Press, 2010.

Trosclair, Carroll Paul. America's Last *Real* Home Front. CreateSpace Independent Publishing Platform, 2011.

Waters, Michael R. Lone Star Stalag: German Prisoners of War at Camp Hearne. College Station: Texas A&M University Press, 2004.

White, Michael C. A Brother's Blood. Cliff Street Books (An imprint of Harper Perennial), 1996.

Photos

Front cover, clockwise from top left:
Three unidentified boys at Middle Street School in Hadley MA, 1953.
Courtesy of Hadley Historical Society, Hadley MA

St. John's Roman Catholic Church, Hadley MA. Courtesy of Hadley
Historical Society, Hadley MA

Prisoners of war in in Windsor Locks CT. Courtesy of Hartford
History Center, Hartford Public Library, Hartford CT

Hopkins Academy Cheerleaders, 1941 (Wanda Podolak, Adeline Baj,
Helen Zawacki). Reprinted from *Hopkins Academy: 1664-1964.*
Courtesy of Hadley Historical Society, Hadley MA

Back cover:
Top: Spearing tobacco in Hadley MA in the 1940's. Courtesy of
Raymond Brown, Hadley MA

Bottom: Candid of Cathleen Robinson, Courtesy of Raymond Brown,
Hadley MA

Proofreader's note:

After working with Cathleen Robinson for almost 20 years at
The Williston Northampton School and then continuing my
friendship with Cathleen following her retirement, I was delighted
when her husband Raymond Brown mentioned that he was hoping
to publish the novel that Cathleen worked on for at least a decade. I
volunteered to do the picky proofreading (a skill Cathleen had taught
me) and copyediting and then to prepare the manuscript to be
printed by Collective Copies in Florence MA. Any remaining errors
are mine. My thanks to Alan Weinberg of the Hadley Historical
Society for his help with photographs. Claire Frierson